P9-DJV-692

THE COYOTES OF CARTHAGE

THE COYOTES OF CARTHAGE

A NOVEL

STEVEN WRIGHT

*An Imprint of HarperCollins*Publishers

This is a work of fiction. Names, characters, places, and incidents are products of the author's imagination or are used fictitiously and are not to be construed as real. Any resemblance to actual events, locales, organizations, or persons, living or dead, is entirely coincidental.

HarperCollins books may be purchased for educational, business, or sales promotional use. For information, please email the Special Markets Department at SPsales@harpercollins.com.

FIRST EDITION

Designed by Paula Russell Szafranski

Library of Congress Cataloging-in-Publication Data
Names: Wright, Steven, 1979-author.
Title: The Coyotes of Carthage: a novel / Steven Wright.
Description: New York: Ecco, [2020]
Identifiers: LCCN 2019019750| ISBN 9780062951663 (hardcover) | ISBN 9780062951687 (pbk.)
Subjects: LCSH: Political fiction.
Classification: LCC PS3623.R5649 C69 2020 | DDC 813/.6—dc23 LC record available at https://lccn.loc.gov/2019019750

ISBN 978-0-06-295166-3

20 21 22 23 24 LSC 10 9 8 7 6 5 4 3 2 1

For Brandi and Alleah

The [First] Amendment is written in terms of "speech," not speakers. Its text offers no foothold for excluding any category of speaker, from single individuals to partnerships of individuals, to unincorporated associations of individuals, to incorporated associations of individuals . . .

—Justice Antonin Scalia, concurring, Citizens United v. FEC *(2010)*

Corporations have no consciences, no beliefs, no feelings, no thoughts, no desires. Corporations help structure and facilitate the activities of human beings, to be sure, and their "personhood" often serves as a useful legal fiction. But they are not themselves members of "We the People" by whom and for whom our Constitution was established.

—Justice John Paul Stevens, dissenting, Citizens United v. FEC *(2010)*

Now what you gon' do with a crew that got money much longer than yours, and a team much stronger than yours . . .

—The Notorious B.I.G. featuring Puff Daddy, "Mo Money Mo Problems"

THE COYOTES OF CARTHAGE

PART I

THE STRAW MAN

CHAPTER ONE

Andre marvels, watching a kid, a stranger of maybe sixteen, pinch another wallet. This lift makes the kid's fifth, at least that Andre's seen this morning—two on the train, two on the underground platform, and now this one on the jam-packed escalator that climbs toward the surface. The kid's got skills, mad skills. He makes his lift and keeps on moving. There. Right there. The kid picks up another, his sixth, with the practiced grace of a ballerino, this time the mark, some corporate chump, probably a lobbyist, with slicked-back hair and a shit-eating grin. No one suspects a thing, and why should they? This kid blends in, looks like a prep-school student—and, who knows, perhaps he is—his aesthetic complete with a bookbag, khakis, and a dog-eared copy of de Tocqueville tucked beneath his arm. The kid reminds Andre of himself at that age—lean, hungry, steel eyes with smooth skin—but Andre concedes that he never possessed this kid's talent.

Aboveground the kid disappears into the big-city bustle, and Andre thinks, Good for you, li'l man. Go in peace. For sure, the kid has plenty of places to hide. Northwest this morning is a mess: snowy, busy, noisy, the perfect urban jungle in which to flee. Andre works around the corner, and a lifetime ago, his family made a home inside a boarded-up rathole six blocks over. Andre has, in fact, lived in the District his entire life, thirty-five years save a stint across the river, two years in juvie for a grift gone bad on a nearby street. Seventeen years ago, when he left kiddie correctional, he never imagined he'd work on K Street, or that he'd own a walk-in closet full of three-piece suits, and the sudden realization, that he might lose it all, cuts like shards of glass crushed into the lining of his stomach.

He trudges a path through wet snow. Last night's blizzard has caused panic in DC; the streets, slick with black ice, prove too difficult for all but yellow cabs. He wishes he'd taken a different route, perhaps down L Street, where hobos toss dice and the high-rises don't funnel the cold. He's tired of freezing winters. Tired of cold that blisters his fingertips. Tired of crowds and congestion and construction. If he loses his job today, and he's pretty sure he will, he'll move across the country, someplace with palm trees, someplace where no one bothers to vote.

On the corner, a homeless man sits atop a grate, his fists punching a peg leg that peeks from beneath his blanket. The man howls, frustrated that no one will help a white veteran. Most folks ignore him. Some folks laugh. A doe-eyed blonde, maybe nineteen or twenty, drops coins into his tin cup. The man sifts the change, sorting nickels from pennies, then pitches the gift back into the blonde's face. "Bitch, what the fuck am I supposed to do with eighteen cents?"

The blonde, stunned and shamed, looks toward Andre, her wide eyes asking: *What did I do wrong?* Andre wants to shrug, to say the guy's an asshole, but he has a point. Three nickels, three pennies: that won't even buy you ramen noodles. Instead Andre furrows his brow and, in his most apologetic tone, the voice he knows comforts young white women, says, "My God, are you okay? He has no right to treat you that way. Should I call the cops?"

He knows the blonde will say no, and when she does, her humiliation vanishing, she smiles with the confidence of a fool assured by a complete stranger. Andre pops his suit's collar, breathes warmth into his fists, takes pride that he hasn't lost his touch.

The homeless man shouts, trembling with rage, his sunburned face and filthy beard giving the appearance of a downtrodden Santa. Andre suspects this guy's newly homeless. If this bum had lived on the streets for long, he'd know that the archdiocese opens hypothermia shelters when the weather gets this cold. He'd also know that today, near Dupont, the Methodists distribute leather-bound Bibles and burlap sacks brimming with groceries. Louder and louder the homeless man screams, claims he's a veteran of Kandahar, an assertion Andre doubts. The VA, for all its faults, can do a lot better than a peg leg, a wooden cone that looks like part of a preschooler's pirate costume. Andre suppresses the urge to snatch the man's blanket, to expose his working limbs, to prove that the peg leg is nothing more than a prop. Everyone else in Washington has a scam; why shouldn't this guy?

Andre pushes forward, passing chain bakeries and trendy cafés, remembers when white folks feared walking down these streets. This morning, the tourists have flocked here, defying the cold, crowding the sidewalks, in search of apple-spice muffins, pumpkin lattes, and silly trinkets like bobbleheads that double as proof of patriotism.

Two more blocks, his woolen socks now soaked, Andre reaches his office building. A dozen women huddle fifteen feet from the entrance, shivering, cigarettes in hand. He recognizes each of them—analysts he's led in the field—and his stomach sinks when each avoids meeting his eyes.

He enters the building through brass revolving doors, finds custodians mopping footprints from the marble floor. He crosses the lobby, access card in hand, and rushes the turnstiles that separate him from the elevators. This is the test, he knows. If the turnstile fails to read his card, he's finished. So when the security light flashes green, allowing Andre to pass, he feels a moment's relief. He strolls toward the elevator, head held high, shoulders pinned back, the smoothest brother he could possibly be. Behind the front desk, the guard, a barrel-chested ex-marine, stands and clears his throat.

"Excuse me, Mr. Ross," Sabatino whispers. It's not his fault. Sab's just doing his job. Still, Andre remembers getting Sabatino's smart-ass nephew an internship on the Hill.

"Sorry to bother you, Mr. Ross. Mrs. Fitzpatrick, she called down, said to call ahead when you got in." Sabatino looks both ways, then leans close. "But say I didn't see you? That'll give you time, five, six minutes. Get you a good head start?"

Andre chuckles. Never doubt the loyalty of a U.S. Marine. He claps Sabatino's shoulder, smiles to show his gratitude, says, "Thanks, I'm good. Go ahead. Call her. I'm heading up now."

"Yes, sir," Sabatino says. "Is there anything else I can do for you?"

"A small favor. There's a homeless guy by the Metro stop."

"The lying fuck who says he's a vet?"

"Contact city hall. Tell them to send a van. Use the firm's name. Someone needs to get that asshole off the streets. Otherwise he'll freeze to death."

Sabatino agrees, then calls the elevator. The brass doors open, inviting Andre inside, where, over a hidden speaker, plays Coltrane's "My Favorite Things."

"Good luck, Mr. Ross," Sab says. "Let me know if you need backup."

Andre presses his access card against the control panel, and the doors shut. The panel beeps twice, and the elevator whisks him skyward, past six stories of analysts and researchers: the well-paid statisticians, pollsters, accountants, media trackers, copywriters, and investigators, many of whom will be happy to see him gone. Their glee isn't personal. They simply want his job. A senior associate falls, one of them rises. Office politics, plain and simple.

The elevator doors open. The lights of the eighth-floor lobby flicker, and Andre knows this may be the last time he steps into the nerve center of Martin, Fitzpatrick & DeVille. He sidesteps the receptionist, pursues the hall that leads toward his office. The path is a straight shot between the offices of the other senior associates, with their Ivy League degrees and inherited vacation homes. Halfway down the busy hall, he passes a glass-enclosed conference room and casts a sideways glance inside. He recognizes a face, no, two faces, no, three, four, five, six, seven. Shit. Then he spots a poster-board map of Indianapolis, and a heavy weight shifts inside his chest. He knows he'll be fired by the end of the day, but now he's pissed. For Christ's sake, he's worked Indianapolis for six months, made media contacts, registered his political action committee, presented an electoral strategy that pleased the finicky billionaire client. He feels his anger spike but resolves to play it cool, left hand slipped inside his pocket, a dash of swagger in his step. He knows they're watching him, judging him, sizing him up, and he will never—never—let these white people see him sweat.

In his office waits Fiona Fitzpatrick, the sole female founding partner. He appreciates that she's come in person to announce his fate. For nearly seventeen years she's been good to him, a second mother, the trusted mentor who shepherded his career. He has few regrets about his most recent campaign—his assignment was to form a political action committee that would get a governor elected, and that's precisely what he did. But he understands that his tactics may have brought shame upon the firm and, quite possibly, embarrassed the woman who has shown him nothing but kindness. The notion that he's complicated Mrs. Fitz's life, that he has somehow tarnished her reputation, that he may have betrayed her faith in him—these accusations burn the blood around his heart. He takes a deep breath, struggles to cool his rage. It is the same rage he felt at the peg-legged man, at his gleeful colleagues, at her decision to reassign Indianapolis, but, if he's being honest, it's mostly the rage he feels toward himself.

Mrs. Fitz, seventy-something years old, her pantsuit the shade of red wine, wastes no time. "Our internal polling had your candidate ahead by twelve points. Twelve points. You could have won in a landslide. And, bright boyo that you are, you decide to do what? You decide to run up the score. To go after the opponent's family. For the love of God, what could've possibly possessed you?" When Mrs. Fitz gets angry, she prefers to ask and answer her own questions. Andre adores this about her. "I'll tell you what possessed you. Your pride. You wanted bragging rights. Wanted to come back here a hero, to strut around this office like—"

"Excuse me, ma'am. My ego is not that fragile."

"Don't interrupt me again," she says. "And your ego is precisely that fragile."

"Yes, ma'am."

"I know you want to make junior partner," she says. "I want that too. But when you make reckless mistakes like this, you don't make it easy. I mean really, Dre. Really. Thoughtless.

Lighting a fire that you couldn't extinguish. Did you not think of that? No."

She throws up her hands, plops into the chair beside his desk. He worries about the strain that creases her face. When he's her age, he'll have the good sense to retire. She's accomplished so much, a trailblazing career: aide to Bobby Kennedy, counsel to Teddy, deputy White House chief of staff—then there are the six sons she's raised and the two husbands she's buried. She should be living in Miami, angry at squirrels that invade her bird feeder. Instead she runs a political consulting firm that bears her name, trying her best to get the right people elected, she says, comfortable with the reality that she'll get the wrong people elected along the way.

He says, "I'll clear out of here in an hour."

She dismisses his resignation with a wave.

"I don't want to cause you any more trouble."

"If you didn't want to cause me trouble, you wouldn't have hashed it up in the first place."

"Ma'am, I know. I—"

"Stop trying to be noble," she says. "It's tacky."

Andre reads her expression, and, for the first time, he clearly sees the predicament. He suspects she's already called around town, trying to find solid ground, a comfortable place for her protégé to land. But finding him another job, he now recognizes, presents challenges even beyond her influence. To begin with, she has few friends among the Republicans who control both the White House and each chamber of Congress. But even if she could find a quiet, out-of-the-way post—a press secretary to a friendly senator, an advisor to a politically ambitious NGO—she still would have to convince the firm's two other founding partners not to invoke the ironclad noncompete, the clauses of which would prohibit Andre, for one federal election cycle, from lobbying, campaigning, or pursuing any paid political activity, a nebulous phrase whose meaning could be decided only by an arbitrator of the firm's choosing. And if, by some miracle, she overcame the arbitration obstacle, a herculean task at which others have tried and failed, he'd still be a thirty-five-year-old black man with a criminal record, four felonies the court long ago sealed but that still appear each time he Googles his own full name. *Toussaint Andre Ross.* He sits behind his desk, changes his socks. "So what do we do?"

She points toward a manila envelope on his desk: *Carthage County.*

He skims the executive summary: $250,000 in dark money to pass a ballot initiative in the boondocks of South Carolina. Secret corporate-financed campaigns keep this firm afloat, but everything about this specific assignment is offensive: the puny budget, the insignificant location, the utter lack of prestige. Worst of all, no bonus if he wins. And though he knows this assignment is beneath him, Andre will not be ungrateful. He realizes that to save his career, his patron has had to horse-trade, sacrificing something she valued to soothe the angst of others. So, for her, he will not whine; he will not complain; he will not act like a homeless man too good for eighteen cents.

"It's rubbish," she says. "But the assignment is short, thirteen weeks. You're close enough if an emergency arises with your brother."

"Probably best I lie low," he says. "What did you have to give them?"

"It is what it is." She takes a tin from her pocket, plucks a mint from inside, then tosses him the tin. "Didn't I buy you gloves for Christmas?"

Andre eats a mint, which is bitter and tart. Who eats these things as treats? Maybe, if he does find a new job, he'll summon the courage to finally tell her that, while he loves her, she has terrible taste in sweets.

She says, "You leave tonight."

"Thirteen weeks in South Carolina?" he says. "I can do that."

"Good." She rises, straightens her suit. "It's not like you have a choice."

One hour later, Andre raps on the door of a two-story rowhouse. He doesn't like this Northeast neighborhood: icy sidewalks, pulsing music, teenage boys who loiter on stoops. Two weeks ago, while Andre was away, rival gangs sprayed bullets across this street, the sole casualty a seeing-eye dog that seemed to know every command except for *duck*.

"Dre? Honey." Vera opens the door, hugs him and invites him inside, where he's overwhelmed by a stench that he guesses is sour milk. Yet the smell is only the beginning. Dirty clothes litter the living room carpet, and oyster pails lie spread across the table. He tries to resist the urge to judge but can't help himself. Damn, Vera. You don't have a job; the least you could do is tidy your home.

"I'm so glad to see you." She points toward a sofa that he must clear to sit. The couch, lumpy, sticky, faces a bare wall, where, a year ago, a flat-screen TV hung. The television was a gift, something Andre bought to comfort his brother. Vera swears a burglar snatched it. She even filed a police report. Andre suspects she hocked the television and pocketed the cash, insurance against the possibility that, if Hector dies, she might again be cast onto the streets. Andre doesn't hold that against her—he remembers sleeping in alleyways, remembers the compulsion to squirrel away cash—but he'll never again buy this house nice things.

"Excuse the mess," she says. "Handsome, baby, c'mon in here."

Handsome, a square-headed eight-year-old, stomps into the room wearing only plaid boxers. Andre cannot see himself in his nephew. Nor, for that matter, can he see Hector. But Vera and Hector have a complicated relationship, forged first as junkies, then maintained through sobriety. If Hector doesn't question the boy's paternity, then Andre's happy to ignore the obvious.

"How you doing, little man?" Andre refuses to call the kid by name. The boy is, at best, odd looking: widespread forehead, crooked teeth, small ears. "Shouldn't you be at school?"

"Say hello, Handsome," Vera says, and the boy tilts his head and squints. Andre thinks the boy should be tested. He never speaks. But Vera doesn't trust school psychologists. The school system, she likes to preach, has incentive to diagnose your child as broken.

"Oh, ain't that cute?" she says. "He's shy around his big-shot uncle. Handsome, baby, why don't you go take the roast out the oven? Mama will fix your plate in a minute."

She gives her son a kiss before he runs away. Andre doubts there's a roast in the oven. In fact, he's certain that Vera doesn't know how to cook. She's nearly fifty and wants people to think that she's respectable, the perfect wife and mother. She's ashamed that she's spent most of her life in shelters; that, long before she met Hector, a court declared her unfit to care for her three daughters; that her criminal history includes prostitution, possession, petty theft, and extortion. Andre doesn't care about her past—hell, he has a past—so he plays along. Sure, Vera, you're a great mother. But some might question why your mute, funny-looking son is standing half-naked in a pigsty on a school day.

"He's getting so big" is the nice thing that Andre chooses to say.

"Oh, and he's smart. All the teachers say so. But that school he going to ain't worth shit. And the principal, don't get me started." She rubs her palms together. "I used to be down there all the time. Volunteering. Nowadays, things have changed. I'm talking to a lawyer. The lawyer says we got a case. A great case. We might get paid. But how are you? How's Cassie?"

"We broke up."

"The engagement too?" She gasps. "Oh, Dre. Baby, I'm sorry. She was a good one. You still workin' for that white lady?"

"I work for a firm. I'm a senior associate. I'll make junior partner next year." He thinks, but does not say, Or so I hope.

"But the same white lady?" she says. "When you gonna start your own business? Be like those folks on TV. The ones talkin' politics. I watch the news. I think, 'Dre could do that.' Bet they get paid millions."

Andre dislikes many things about his brother's wife, but right now, he dislikes her assumption that she understands the world in which he lives.

"I should go check on him." He rises, but she takes his hand.

"One minute," she says. "Actually, I'm glad you came."

He sits. He waits. He knows what's next.

Vera closes her eyes, and when she opens them, tears fall. "I was running errands, getting Hector's meds; you know how I like to stay busy. Then I slipped on ice. I filed for disability, and you know the government, they don't want to hand out that money."

Andre pays the rent on this Section 8 house, pays for her cell phone so she can reach him in case of an emergency, pays the van service that ferries her and Hector wherever they want to go. He hesitates to volunteer another dime, especially now, while his fate at the firm feels precarious. Yet, for all her faults, Vera provides excellent care for his brother. She asks questions of therapists, manages prescriptions, keeps the notebooks that log the information that the neurologists require. He knows all this because he checks her cell phone records, and calls the clinics from the road, and pays the medical bills online. To Andre, nothing else matters. Besides, who else could take such good care of Hector? Andre travels fifty weeks a year; their mother is a bipolar schizophrenic with whom neither brother has spoken in eight years and who lives, last they heard, on the West Coast. He says, "How much do you need?"

"I wasn't asking for money. I was letting you know our situation."

"Please, I want to help."

She thinks hard, smirking, eyes rolled back in her head, a child ready to present Santa her list.

"Maybe twelve hundred. Fourteen hundred if you can spare it. Enough until my disability goes through. I'll pay you back." He agrees, would have given her far more. Vera kisses his hand and says, "I knew I could count on you. You always good to family."

He takes his hand away, heads toward Hector's room, where his brother trembles in a wheelchair. The room is spotless. A laptop plays a colorized episode of *The Three Stooges*, and a jasmine aromatherapy candle sweetens the air. Andre lowers his eyes, regrets thinking that Vera doesn't know how to keep a home.

For a moment, Andre pauses inside the doorway, stunned, as though awaiting an invitation to pass. He doesn't quite recognize his older brother, a man who, years ago, could outrun every Metro cop. For most of their lives, people confused the brothers: schoolteachers, police detectives, social workers, and neighbors. Hector's a mere two years older; only their mother could tell them apart. Now look at Hector. No one will ever confuse them again.

His last visit, two months ago, Hector hadn't seemed this

frail. In fact, his brother spoke—not good words, but close approximations of words that Andre mostly understood. But ALS has since stolen Hector's speech, as well as the use of both legs and his neck, which refuses to support his head.

Andre glances around the room packed with catheters and pill bottles, with moist towelettes and diapers. Andre feels like a schoolboy, wondering whether he needs permission to sit on the bed, which is perfectly made, sheet and blankets taut, the way inmates learn in prison. In the corner is a walker with medical tape around the handle. A local ALS charity loaned them the walker, which Hector can use until he no longer has a need, a time that Andre realizes has come.

"Go ahead, have a seat." Vera sneaks up behind him. "You'd like that, Hector, wouldn't you?" She wipes the spittle from Hector's mouth. "Andre, talk to him. He understands everything."

Andre feels shame as he wonders how the hell anyone could ever know.

Hector is well groomed—shaven, hair combed—and thin. For most of his life, Andre has steeled himself for his brother's death. It seemed inevitable that Andre would receive a midnight call, the news that Hector had perished by the hand of an angry mark, or the bullet of a rival, or the baton of an aggressive cop. But ALS. How the fuck could he have prepared for that?

Andre takes Hector's hand, which is soft and fleshy. He knows that Hector isn't near death, that Hector has another couple years. But the doctors have warned that ALS is unpredictable, that Hector's decline will break his heart. For Andre and Vera, the experts have also recommended therapists and support groups. Vera goes each week; Andre hasn't gone once.

Somewhere forty thousand feet over Appalachia, a pudgy girl, no younger than six, though old enough to know better, races along the business-class aisle. The flight attendant has twice asked the girl's parents to restrain the child, but her father naps, her mother reads. The girl disturbs each passenger, singing, laughing, but what can anyone do? The flight lasts about ninety minutes, and the plane, already behind schedule, has cruised across the halfway mark. So the attendant folds her arms, perhaps hoping they'll hit a patch of rough air. The pudgy girl, wearing a tricorn hat, bumps Andre's elbow, causes his scotch to spill onto the open pages of his dossier.

The attendant brings a napkin. *Yes*, her eyes say, *I pray that turbulence will bounce this brat against the hull. Now you and I have a secret.* Andre gives a flirtatious nod—*I hope your prayer comes true; I will cherish our secret forever*—then returns to work.

The firm's briefing memo, now blotchy and wet, is succinct. South Carolina nears the end of a modern-day gold rush, and PISA, an international precious metals conglomerate, has discovered traces of gold in the mountains of Carthage. The gold sits deep below publicly owned land, one thousand acres of Appalachian rain forest that the county refuses to sell. Thus, PISA will sidestep the five-member county council and solicit the land directly from The People.

In fairness, Andre can't blame the county for refusing to sell. The county's struggling economy depends upon fishing and hunting. Tourism is, by far, the largest source of revenue. Gold mining, the memo notes, puts all that at risk. To extract the gold, PISA won't dispatch a wagon train of gray-bearded, pick-wielding prospectors. No. Mining in the twenty-first century is a nasty business, requires pumping millions of gallons of cyanide deep into the earth to leach gold from solid rock. The state has tentatively blessed the mining operation. So have the feds. Imagine how much PISA had to fork over to make that happen, quickly and with little fanfare.

Andre predicts he'll supervise a small team: a social media expert, a volunteer coordinator, a private investigator to conduct opposition research. He hasn't led a team this small in years, not since Mercedes County, his first assignment as a team leader. He made his bones working that referendum. The client, an online retailer, hoped to build a shipping center in Mercedes, but county officials refused, an ill-conceived protest in the name of some righteous cause he can no longer remember. Was it the environment? Union jobs? Free trade? Municipal governments are full of big-principled fanatics with little practical experience. But Andre made Mercedes see reason, made them understand that if he lost this time, he'd be back the next year. Printing ballots, hiring poll workers, mailing registration cards. Each special election would cost the county a quarter mil. A quarter million dollars each year until he won. Mercedes buckled.

An announcement from the cockpit: "Please take your seats. We're approaching our destination." To Andre's surprise, the girl, her tricorn hat in hand, stops and stares overhead, slack-jawed, as though bearing witness to the voice of God. She climbs into her seat, fastens her belt. Now she's ready to land.

Thirty minutes later, the crew opens the concourse door, and the girl bursts through the gate. The clock stands at half past ten, and the airport has bedded down for the night. Merchants have shuttered their shops. A kiosk hums behind an accordion gate. A prune-faced janitor waters a fern, and a hickory scent taunts the travelers, as though to say: *If you'd arrived only minutes earlier, you could've appreciated our fine restaurants, but please, instead, enjoy your choice of stale vending-machine snacks.*

The hickory reminds Andre that he hasn't eaten, yet his belly is drowning in airline scotch. He's not drunk—not by a long shot—though he welcomes the feeling of freedom that the liquor brings. He carries his pack over his shoulder, follows the sleepy crowd through the concourse, burdened by the feeling that he's been here before. A heartbeat later, the memory comes to him. The tiled carpet, the drab walls. This place feels like a visitors' lounge in juvie.

He ducks inside the men's room, settles before a mirror, surprised by the nervousness that beats like a second heart inside his chest. He needs to make a positive first impression. His team will be reporting back to Washington, their biased early dispatches supporting the caricature that, even for politics, this temperamental black asshole is reckless and unprofessional. But Andre knows he can win over his team. He's a good-looking guy, never been accused of lacking charm. He changes into a fresh cotton shirt, rinses the taste of scotch from his mouth. If he were a religious man, he might say a prayer. But he's not, so he stares at himself in the mirror, vows that he will not fail.

Back in the concourse, a practiced assuredness in his step, he passes a checkpoint where a guard takes a nap. In the airport terminal, the overhead speaker plays bluegrass. A sailor in his dress uniform kisses a redheaded girl, which reminds Andre: Call home, let your fiancée know you've arrived in South Carolina. But Cassie isn't his girl anymore, now, is she? Last he heard, she'd found a new beau, a player for the Redskins, an over-the-hill placekicker who hasn't seen a second of playing time. But this new fella doesn't know what Andre knows: that Cassie likes to change her mind.

As the terminal empties, he takes the escalator to baggage claim. The fluorescent lights flicker. The air ducts rattle. The wall-mounted, backlit advertisements promote opportunities to earn online degrees, increased incomes, frequent-flyer miles, and eternal salvation. The pudgy girl, with boundless energy, circles square columns, arms outstretched, tricorn hat bouncing atop her head. She zips between passengers, then twirls beside a handsome young man, who flashes Andre a smile. The young man, in his early twenties, tightens his grip around a whiteboard, *Toussaint Andre Ross* written in marker.

"Mr. Ross?" His hemp necklace and sun-bleached hair suggest California. "Mr. Toussaint Andre Ross?"

"Please. Call me Andre."

The young man tucks the whiteboard beneath his arm. "Pleasure to meet you, sir. I'm Brendan. Your assistant."

Andre offers a polite smile, wonders whether the two have met before. Maybe. Human Resources prefers to hire the same kind of pretty boy, fine-featured college grads whom Madison Avenue might hire to sell toothpaste. And yet, isn't this kid a little more beautiful than the rest? Side-swept bangs, flawless skin, the pink cheeks of a cherub. This kid could make a fortune running cons on the street.

A horn, a siren, the carousel comes to life. Smaller airports have few advantages but among them are shorter waits for luggage. Brendan rents a baggage cart and awaits Andre's instruction. Andre remembers his own early months at the firm, the eighteen-hour days, the pressure to impress the senior staff. He wishes he'd known he needn't have worked so hard, that the firm ultimately sought employees with a flexible moral code, political mercenaries happy to manipulate entire communities to earn a buck. This kid looks awfully soft, in his heavy olive coat and thick corduroy pants, and Andre wonders whether this delicate boy possesses the inner toughness their vocation requires.

"Welcome to Greenville-Spartanburg International Airport," the overhead speaker blares. The girl in the tricorn hat races the length of the baggage claim, parroting, "Welcome to Greenville-Spartanburg International Airport."

Andre asks, "The rest of the team meeting us in Carthage?"

"Excuse me?" his new assistant says.

"The advance team. Have they already arrived?"

His assistant blinks.

"Please tell me it's not just you." Andre hears the defeat in his own voice. "It's just you, isn't it?"

Andre pinches the bone between his eyes, understands what has happened. This lone intern is the best Mrs. Fitz can do. No one else at the firm will work with him. He's toxic, his career imperiled, his reputation tarnished. He can't blame his colleagues. In their shoes, he would have done the same. Political consultants in Washington come and go. A prize one day, poison the next.

"And Brendan." Andre stresses each syllable. "How many campaigns have you worked?"

"Including this assignment? One."

He takes a good look at the kid, doubts he'll last all thirteen weeks.

The girl wearing the tricorn hat circles Andre and Brendan. She blows raspberries, a poor imitation of a sputtering plane. Andre spots his garment bag rolling along the conveyor belt, and as he approaches, arm extended, the girl races between him and the carousel, blocks his path. Andre snaps back off balance, watches his bag sail away.

"Sir, I know I'm young," Brendan says. "You should know I have a master's in econometrics."

"No one's questioning your academic qualifications."

"I've also been through the firm's twelve-week analytic training."

"I'm sure you're qualified, Brendan."

"You seem a little upset."

"I'm not."

"You sure?" Brendan studies his face. "'Cause you look pissed."

The girl with the tricorn hat circles yet again, zooming, and Andre wants to smack her. Or, at least, smack her parents. He clears his throat, hoping to catch their eye, but both mother and father are too busy reading their phones. He's ready to approach, to say, *Damn it, control your brat*, when Brendan tugs his sleeve. As the girl makes yet another pass, Brendan inches his foot forward, just enough for the girl to take a tumble, crashing hard against the black-and-white tiles, her tricorn hat thrown through the air and landing yards away. The girl rises quickly, shamefaced and near tears, eyes shifting from Brendan to Andre and back to Brendan.

"Brendan, did you tell me your last name?"

The kid says, "Fitzpatrick."

"And Mrs. Fitzpatrick is—"

"My nana."

CHAPTER TWO

Comfortable in his passenger seat, Andre counts another cross. The past mile, he's spotted six, not including those that grace bumper stickers, cemeteries, or billboards predicting the apocalypse. He could've counted any roadside attraction—election signs, dead deer, strips of tread torn from tires—but instead, for reasons he can't articulate, his mind has settled on the cross.

Their Jeep hits a stretch of broken pavement, and for the first time, Andre wonders exactly to where he's been exiled. The past hour, since leaving the airport, he's passed through miles of old-growth forest, deep into tall pine trees broken by an occasional lonesome town. He knows little about South Carolina, and what he thinks he knows, he dislikes. He associates this state with slavery and segregation, with Sumter and secession, with firebombed churches and bus boycotts and the bodies of dead black babies. Fifty, sixty years ago, this very road must have terrified blacks traveling at night. A siren in the rearview mirror would portend a gruesome death. For all he knows, it still could.

Andre's not the least bit comforted by assurances that the

South has changed. The New South, he's been told, appreciates diversity. The New South elects black activists to Congress and sends the children of Indian immigrants to governors' mansions. The New South, they say, has achieved Dr. King's dream. And yet, as white teenagers in a faded pickup whiz past, horn honking, music blaring, Confederate flag cloaking the rear window, Andre suspects that the New South looks an awful lot like the Old.

"You think the same person puts up all these crosses?" Brendan says. "Some guy who heard the voice of God and now drives around the state in his pickup with a bunch of two-by-fours. You know, like the guy who planted all those apple trees, you know, what's-his-face? Johnny Appleseed? You think Johnny Appleseed was real? You think that was his real name?"

"Brendan, do you say everything that pops into your head?"

"I'm Irish. Chattiness is part of our charm."

Andre likes his new assistant, really he does, though, yes, the kid talks too much. The past hour, the kid's shared his whole life story. Graduated high school at sixteen. Earned his bachelor's three years later. He spent last year studying in Dublin on a Fulbright, an experience that inspired the kid, who's now twenty-two, to reclaim his Irish roots. The boy wonder started doctoral studies last fall, applied mathematics, but something interrupted those studies, compelled the kid to assume a voluntary one-year leave of absence. The kid gets sheepish talking about his leave, acts like an ex-con trying not to share the details of his crime. Andre doubts the obvious: cheating. Kid's far too bright, too straitlaced for that. Maybe the kid mouthed off to the wrong professor; perhaps he seduced the department chair's wife.

Brendan reaches behind his seat, retrieves a monogrammed cigarette case. The silver case, once opened, is empty except for a few flakes of tobacco. "You wouldn't happen to have a cigarette, would you?"

"I don't." Andre discreetly sniffs the air, detects a hint of smoke. "Listen, I don't care if you smoke, but I'm guessing the rental agreement forbids smoking inside the Jeep. Companies take that shit seriously."

The two cruise across the next few miles in silence, the faint stench of smoke, now found, impossible to ignore.

The Carthage TravelMart, bright beneath stadium lights, is an island of roadside commerce, two paved acres surrounded by a sea of trees. At the island's center sits a plaza, a tripartite complex that houses a gas station, pancake house, and liquor store. In front, a checkered lawn provides a retreat for travelers with children, a modest park with picnic tables, swing sets, and a fenced-in yard complete with a fire hydrant for the family dog.

"We've got another twenty miles." Brendan steers the Jeep beside a pump. "The county's pretty spread out."

Andre decides to stretch his legs, and as he steps out of the Jeep, the cuffs of his pants dip into an iridescent puddle. The air here, thick yet cool, makes his suit stick against his chest, and he hopes that the final miles quickly pass. A day like this, without a moment's rest, he needs a soft bed, perhaps a nightcap. What he wouldn't give for the touch of a woman. The week he's had, he thinks he deserves all three.

"Another pack of cowboy killers?" Andre says. Brendan reaches for his wallet, but Andre shakes his head. "I got it. You're old enough to smoke, though, right?"

"You gonna quit making fun of my age?"

"Not till I find a better reason to mock you."

Andre heads toward the plaza, passes a community bulletin board on which pastel flyers in bold fonts advertise guided fishing trips, evening Bible studies, spare bedrooms, and opportunities for army enlistment. One flyer, black italics on blue paper, promises fifty dollars for information about a missing, yet adorable, old woman, and Andre wonders whether this woman's family is poor, cheap, or indifferent to her actual return.

Inside the liquor store, music plays over the loudspeakers, a boy band trying to cover Motown, the soul gone, replaced by a rockabilly beat. The shop is a warehouse of booze, pallet upon pallet of beer, wine, spirits: all prices, all brands, for all tastes. He wants to buy a bottle—maybe he'll buy two—but decides against it. Their first day together, he doesn't need Brendan wondering whether the boss is a lush.

The doughy cashier meets Andre's eye and blanches. She drops her face, slips her hand beneath the counter. He knows what she's thinking—This black man's here to rob us—and Andre knows exactly how to handle this. Indeed, every brother in America knows how to handle this. Flash a warm smile, show your empty hands, and pray this terrified white girl isn't gripping a Glock.

"My friend, the blond guy out there, he's buying gas." He uses his least threatening tone, gestures softly toward Brendan. "It's okay to use your restroom?" The cashier glances over her shoulder and relaxes.

"Oh sure. Go on ahead, mister." She sets her hands atop the cork countertop and smiles as though nothing has passed between them. "Help yourself. Y'all don't have to buy nothing, but the diner starts sellin' day-old donuts soon. The maple frosted, I promise you, mister, they're a little piece of wonderful."

"I like maple frosted." He doesn't, but if favoring syrupy treats prevents this white girl from shooting him full of holes, then he's pleased to change his taste. "Bathroom's in the back?"

"Next to the audiobooks."

The bathroom is, in fact, a locker room: benches, toilets,

showers. In one shower stall, a tall man sings. In another, a short man whistles. The bank of sinks, well lit and immaculate, smells like aftershave, and a raven placard above the fogged mirror warns, in big bone-white text: LEWD CONDUCT IS A FELONY PUNISHABLE BY JAIL, FINES, AND PUBLIC RIDICULE.

Andre splashes cloudy water on his face, notices a dispenser that sells temporary tattoos. The tattoos, two for a quarter, cost far less than he remembers. But he hasn't worn a temporary tattoo in years, not since he ferried bindles across Southeast. The bindles, aluminum packets the size of his thumbnail, fitted easily inside the tongues of his Velcro shoes. He had thought he was clever, a teardrop tattoo on his face, a Japanese symbol on his arms, distinctive physical characteristics that he could erase if anything went wrong. In those days, he thought he was so damn smart. Smarter than the cops. Smarter than the junkies. No way anyone could touch him. In hindsight, he regrets much about that life. Sure, he enjoyed the thrills of small-time dealing. Try to find a fifteen-year-old dropout who wouldn't. But now, washing his hands in the sink, he counts himself lucky that he's not rotting in some potter's field.

He leaves the men's room, follows a row of refrigerators that keep cool beer, wine, strawberry milk. He wants bottled water. Tomorrow, he fears, will bring a hangover. Maybe next time he shouldn't drink so much on the plane, but then again he thought that the last time he flew. In one refrigerator, on a shelf beneath jugs of water, white cartons of live bait, each labeled by hand, are stacked like bricks of snow. Nightcrawlers, crickets, maggots, and sand fleas. He closes the door, empty handed, repulsed by the proximity of beverage and bait.

At the checkout counter, a security camera records the cashier flirting with Brendan. She preens her hair, bats her eyes, covers her mouth to laugh. Brendan, a pack of cigarettes in one hand, a maple-frosted donut in the other, seems to enjoy the attention.

"Andre, buddy," Brendan says. "Try these donuts. They're a little piece of . . . what did you say?"

"Piece of wonderful." The cashier glows. "Where y'all from?"

"What makes you think we're not from here?" Brendan radiates a confidence and cheerfulness, both of which irritate Andre.

"Your friend here, his suit's too nice." She points toward Andre, then lets her eyes drift back to Brendan. "And you, you don't look like folks around here. I'd remember you."

"We're just passing through." Andre picks a postcard—*Carthage County, a Sportsman's Paradise.* "Do you have stamps?"

"My uncle owns a hunting lodge, if you're interested." She tugs her hair. "Five hundred acres. Private land. It's very luxurious. Very classy. Great price."

"Stamps?" Andre says.

"Sold out." She tears a napkin, finds a purple pen. "Here's my uncle's number. And here's mine too. Just in case."

She scribbles digits in sparkling ink, slips the napkin into Brendan's palm.

"We gotta go." Andre plunks down a dollar, catches Brendan's eye. "Now."

A mustached man, sporting fatigues and a safety vest, stands outside the entrance and holds open the door. Andre thanks the hunter, finds himself beside the man's idling pickup, a sleeping hound in its cab, a kill in its bed. Andre doesn't know the difference between a wolf and a coyote—one is larger, he assumes—but this creature, no matter its size, is impaled by two feathered arrows, one beneath the throat, the other between the ribs. In thirty-five years, Andre's never seen dead wildlife. Not really. Not up close. In Washington, he's seen his share of belly-up pigeons, feral cats stiffer than a prison cot. Once, in Northeast, he witnessed a paddy wagon flatten a corner girl's iguana. But here, inches away, this creature looks peaceful, silver fur soaking up its own black blood.

"Isn't that gorgeous?" Brendan says. "How big is she?"

A bolt of irritation strikes Andre. Is Brendan really starting yet another conversation with yet another stranger? Now? An hour past midnight?

"Twenty-eight pounds," the hunter says. "Took an hour to track her."

Andre wonders what the hunter means. Track her? Did an hour pass between the first arrow and the second, or did an hour pass between spotting and killing the prey? He wants to ask for how long this poor creature suffered, but he bites his tongue. Because even if it weren't the middle of the night, and even if Andre weren't trying to keep a low profile, and even if the airline scotch weren't wearing off, even then, this animal would still be dead, a fact that he's powerless to change.

"What kind of wolf is this?" Brendan asks.

"It's a coyote, actually." The hunter runs his hand along the spine of his prey. "We got a huge coyote problem here. Damn beasts almost ruined the turkey stock last year. If y'all are looking for guides . . ."

"We're just passing through." Andre tugs Brendan's sleeve. "We should be going."

Andre retraces his steps, passing the swings and picnic tables and fire hydrant. Fifteen minutes he's been in Carthage, and already he hates this place.

"Everyone here's so nice." Brendan starts the engine, glances at Andre. "Something wrong?"

"We're not candidates. We don't shake hands. We don't kiss babies. We work best when no one knows . . ." Andre realizes that he's tired, that he's had a terrible day. He doesn't want to whip the kid with his frustration. "Listen, this is a small community. Twenty-eight thousand people. You never know who's paying attention. For all we know, that guy, or the gal working the register—"

"I didn't tell them anything."

"Do you know who opposes the gold mines? Everyone. Hunters and hunting lodges will hate the idea of losing a thousand acres of public hunting land. The sport fishermen won't appreciate the runoff. That's to say nothing of terrified parents who fear millions of gallons of cyanide seeping into their children's drinking water." Andre takes a breath. "Soon enough, people might notice someone's running an anonymous campaign, and the first person they'll suspect—"

"The new guys asking a bunch of questions." A series of panicked expressions chase each other across Brendan's face. "I'm sorry."

"Keep your head down, your eyes open, your mouth shut," Andre says. "You're not here to make friends."

"Head down. Eyes open. Mouth shut." Brendan mumbles the phrase, once, twice, three times, as though each time the words are new. "I need to be more careful. I'll do better. Seriously, Mr. Ross, I'll do better. I will. I will. I will!"

Andre has an ongoing feud with Alenushka Romanov. Alenushka, a Russian naturalized citizen, works the desk at the firm's travel office, her duties including booking tickets, calculating per diems, and monitoring use of the company credit cards. When teams hit the road for lengthy, faraway campaigns, she scours the Internet for houses that the firm could lease, a cost-saving alternative to renting each employee an individual hotel suite. She has a reputation both as a thoughtful steward of the firm's finances and as a bureaucrat who plays favorites, bestowing upon her closest friends first-class accommodations. And because she possesses this power to grant comforts, staffers compete for her favor: flattery; gifts; inquiries about her son, Daniil, a high school swimming sensation. She enjoys sharing pictures, the pale, sinewy boy in swim caps and briefs, brags that one day Daniil will medal in the Olympics.

Once each year, she takes up a collection, donations to help finance her son's latest international competition. Toronto and Tokyo, Sochi and Rio. Daniil's traveled the globe, each trip financed through his mother's old-school strong-arm shakedown. Most people quietly complain, but everyone pays. Junior associates give one hundred dollars; senior associates give twice as much. Shit, even Mrs. Fitz antes up; last year she gave a solid grand. Andre knows the game, each year writing a check, but this year, he forgot; between work and Hector and the breakup with his girl, he failed to meet Alenushka's deadline, an oversight he didn't realize until she denied his request for reimbursement for a client dinner. He assumed he'd eat this one expense, that this cost would teach him his lesson, but now, standing on the veranda of a broken-down Victorian gothic, replete with gargoyles and turret, a house that surely should be condemned, Andre understands that Alenushka still holds a grudge. "We're staying at an abandoned funeral home?"

"Funeral home and taxidermist." Brendan fumbles the keys that unlock the front door's three dead bolts. The porch, bowed planks beneath their feet, smells of rot. The only light is from the full moon and the glow of a bug zapper. Andre can't see much, but he can make out shapes, filled garbage bags against the rail, and beside the front step, a water heater inside a clawfoot tub. Brendan says, "This used to be the whites-only funeral home. You know, back in the segregated days. African Americans weren't allowed inside."

"And who says Jim Crow was all bad?" Andre feels a gnat fly into his mouth and, without thinking, swallows. He spits, though it's too late for that, swats the swarm circling his face. "Did these gnats follow us from the Jeep?"

"I think we've been walking through one continuous swarm."

Andre glances over his shoulder, catches a shadow, perhaps a rabbit or raccoon, scurrying across the lawn. He estimates fifty-five feet between the porch and the pebbled drive. A continuous swarm of gnats? Well played, Alenushka. He steels himself for whatever's inside. No matter what he sees, he knows he's survived far worse. For most of his childhood, his family moved around. By his twelfth birthday, Andre and Hector and their mother must have lived in a dozen different homes, the most luxurious of which could have generously been described as a slum. More than once, they had no home at all. His social worker in juvie called his life peripatetic, a word he did not know and assumed was fancy white-people speak for pathetic. He cursed his social worker out, threatened to beat her ass, a threat that got him thirty days in seg, which, he now thinks, may have been better accommodations than this Victorian shithole.

"The house has four levels." Brendan opens the door. "The embalming room is downstairs in the basement. That's mostly storage now. Then, there's this floor. The living quarters are upstairs on the second floor, and the attic's above that. I haven't been in the attic yet."

"Don't bother." Andre grips his luggage. "It's where they keep the ghosts."

Brendan flicks a switch, and the vestibule comes into view. Dangling from a live wire, a single bulb flickers above a stack of soiled mattresses. At once, Andre recognizes, swept into a corner, the mark of junkies: broken vials, used Band-Aids, ash-tipped matches in dove-shaped ashtrays. He's surprised by the absence of rusty syringes, but maybe Brendan's cleared away the best evidence. He wonders what caused the junkies to leave, then wonders whether they plan to return. This house seems too perfect to simply abandon: hidden deep behind a stand of black willows, far from the country road, not a neighbor for three miles.

"I started cleaning yesterday, when I got here," Brendan says, seemingly not in search of praise, but as an excuse to say, *I can do better given more time.* "I concentrated on the apartment upstairs. And, you know, getting rid of the smell."

Brendan pushes forward, passing beneath an archway, and flicks another switch. The viewing room is small and square, with walls stained by graffiti and shotgun spray. A lone dusty pew faces a felt-topped altar, and an exposed overhead pipe drips into a champagne chiller. Andre doesn't have much experience with funerals; in his entire life, he's attended only two. Last year, a senior associate drove his Ford Fusion into the Potomac after failing to make junior partner. Six years ago, Mrs. Fitz's second husband died of colorectal cancer. He didn't know either man particularly well, and he realizes that one day he will attend his brother's. A soft sigh escapes his lips. He imagines standing in the shadow of Hector's casket, imagines the loneliness of losing his only kin. He knows that few mourners will attend. The brothers didn't keep many friends, and the ones they did are now missing, imprisoned, or dead. Maybe Mrs. Fitz and their mother will pay their respects. Maybe Cassie will too. Every person Andre's ever loved fitting in half a pew.

"Our hardware is supposed to arrive tomorrow afternoon." Brendan opens a side door that leads to a tomblike hall. "I was thinking we might set up shop on this level. Lots of room for monitors and maps. Plenty of workspace."

"That's thirty grand worth of equipment, and this floor doesn't look secure. Or dry. Maybe the attic. Higher floors might give us better access to the satellites." Andre spins around. "She really put us in an abandoned funeral home?"

Brendan leads the way down the hall. A wolf. A bear. A mountain-lion cub. Mounted heads decorate the walls. Andre expects at least one face to show surprise, but instead, each shows aggression, curled lips revealing hind teeth as though each beast expected to win this one last fight.

The hall ends beside a curved staircase missing a rail. To Andre, the bottom stair feels infirm, and for the first time, he questions his own safety. In thirty-five years, he's survived one manipulative, mentally ill mother; two years' imprisonment; and three Democratic national conventions. Wouldn't it be a shame to die here, neck broken after falling through a flimsy floor? So he ascends the staircase quickly, a step behind Brendan, avoids placing too much weight on any one step, until, at last, they reach a platform that also threatens collapse.

"I did my best." Brendan slides open a door to reveal a parlor and kitchen. The combined space is far from perfect—why is the air so muggy in here?—but Brendan has cleaned and made improvements, furnishing cheaply, playfully, with futons, beanbag chairs, basketball hoops above each door. The space has a sterile, almost toxic smell: ammonia, bleach, a hint of lye. He suspects the chemical cleaners might bond to form a carcinogen, but cancer's a small price to pay for thirteen weeks of inoffensive air.

"Everything's up here. The kitchen, bathroom, both bedrooms," Brendan says. "All the electrical outlets work, as does the plumbing. Though I don't recommend we drink the water. Your room's over here."

Andre expects bunk beds, lofts made of two-by-fours, pan-

African posters of Bob Marley. Instead, the bedroom, small and square, contains one twin bed, a plywood desk, a banker's lamp, and a wooden armchair. The built-in shelves slant slightly, pointing toward the glue traps that line the wall, and a draft sways wire hangers hooked to a rod that runs the length of the room. Brendan says, "I hope you like it."

"You did all this?" Andre appreciates the gesture, appreciates Brendan's willingness to prioritize his comfort. This kid must have spent the past thirty-six hours scrubbing floors and washing walls. "Listen, Brendan, I can put you up at a hotel. I'll cover the cost myself. You might have to choose a motel in a neighboring county, so you'll have to commute back and forth each—"

"You don't like it?"

"Oh. You've done great. Honestly. I'm grateful," Andre says. "It's just not fair to ask you to stay here."

"And where will you stay?"

Andre won't give Alenushka the satisfaction. "I'll stay here."

"Then I'll stay too." Brendan nods. The subject is closed.

Maybe his new assistant isn't all bad. The kid's already proven himself hardworking and well mannered. Mrs. Fitz should be proud. She's got an all-American boy. Andre hopes the kid isn't a mental case—the kind too often attracted to politics—who's clean and sunny outside yet dark as a mine inside. Last year, one of the firm's senior associates, a petite blonde with a penchant for puns and limericks, got caught fighting pit bulls along the Eastern Shore. She took photos of herself, laughing, winking, as she drowned muzzled dogs, her kitchen-gloved hands clasping their collars, submerged deep in a hot tub brimming with bloody water. She got herself a good lawyer, a plea deal with two years stayed and suspended, promising the judge that she'd dedicate her life to public good. She still works at the firm. Just made junior partner.

Shit. Crazy bitch wins elections. Plus, she bakes a mean-ass strawberry scone. Who cares about anything else?

"I think I should get some sleep. I'll cook something special for breakfast." Brendan rolls his head around. "And, again, I'm sorry about the gas station."

"Already forgotten."

"You gonna tell my grandmother?"

"In the field, teams live by rules. Road rule number one: what happens on the road stays on the road."

"Do people actually follow the rules?"

"I do."

The answer seems to please Brendan. Perhaps because now the two share a secret. Now they are brothers keeping mischief from their nana. Brendan makes his exit, closes the door.

Andre sits, exhausted, on the bed's edge, hopes he can fall asleep. He's been working all day, on full alert, shuffling from place to place, but now, alone in this strange dank room, he feels the sudden evaporation of adrenaline, a sensation not unlike drowning that leaves him off balance and hollow. The end of each day, he knows, makes every traveler feel a little lost, a little lonesome, a little homesick. Travel, by its nature, disorients. And yet, the barrenness he feels isn't just about loneliness or fatigue. He also feels a hint of dissatisfaction, about himself, about his life. He's worked hard, achieved much, his professional life the envy of others. But the truth is, even if he weren't on the road, even if he were lying beneath the blankets of his own bed, Andre would still spend this night alone, restless, a drink in one hand, the remote in the other, a vain attempt to distract himself from the cold reality that he needs something more than this disappointing, peripatetic life.

CHAPTER THREE

Andre sleeps maybe four hours in restless shifts that never exceed fifteen minutes. He usually sleeps better on the road, but then again, he usually enjoys accommodations where the mice don't skitter so noisily inside the walls. His sleeplessness, however, has provided the opportunity to plan this campaign, and now, he concludes, he doesn't need a larger team. Sure, a private investigator might be nice, and yes, a volunteer coordinator would help. But Brendan's qualified to analyze their data, and Andre's mastered the skills required to win with less.

He's studying recent election results when a smoke detector sounds in the next room. Andre hurries into the kitchen to find Brendan standing atop a stool, arms flailing, the alarm beyond his grasp. The high-pitched beep grates on Andre, who grabs a broom, sweeps the ceiling, knocking the alarm to the ground, where it breaks into pieces.

"The sensor must be sensitive," Brendan says. "I wake you?"

Andre helps Brendan down, notices his assistant's buzz cut. The haircut brings into focus Brendan's new look: a face now textured by thin, uneven patches of blond stubble, contact lenses that turn blue eyes gray. Did he bring those with him? For sure, Brendan appears older, slightly more masculine, but apparently no mask can hide his baby face.

"I thought about what you said," Brendan says. "Our job is to blend in."

Brendan returns to his makeshift kitchen, where a pine door atop cinder blocks serves as a counter for a hot plate, toaster oven, microwave, and electric grill. From seven feet away, Andre can feel the appliances' heat, worries that Brendan might set the house afire. In a skillet, eggs sizzle in butter. In the toaster oven, a yellow casserole browns. The sweet smoke makes Andre dizzy with hunger, and he can't remember the last time he enjoyed a home-cooked meal.

"I'm making a breakfast bake." Brendan points toward a card table set for two. "Don't worry. I didn't speak to anyone when I went out. I blended in."

"Good. I may need to blend in too." Andre sets his napkin in his lap. "I'm thinking three-piece suits aren't popular in Carthage. I'll find something casual when we head into town today."

"I bought everything I needed this morning. And I got a call from the moving guys, they'll be here soon." Brendan slides the fried egg atop the casserole, brings breakfast to the table. "You want the Jeep? Carthage's pretty easy to navigate."

Andre eats his first forkful of breakfast bake: ham, tomatoes, eggs, shredded potatoes, and so much butter that he imagines, somewhere in this fire hazard, Brendan's hidden an Amish maid and churn.

"I fixed plenty. Help yourself." Brendan bows his head, makes the sign of the cross, and starts to say grace softly beneath his breath. Andre sets down his fork, waits for the prayer to end. Brendan says, "Amen."

Brendan starts to eat, flexing his left biceps, on which appears a tattoo: a green shield enclosing a soccer ball and the word *Ireland*. The tattoo, Andre thinks, is solid work: strong lines, perfect symmetry, well shaded. In juvie, bored kids found expression through tattoos. A contraband lighter, a toothbrush, and a busted Bic could memorialize the name of the sixteen-year-old girl who swore she'd wait for the rest of her life—the same girl who, three months later, wrote you a letter saying she'd been reborn courtesy of a new man. Sometimes the juvie art was beautiful, but often the tats were blotchy, crooked, accompanied by bleeding, infection, or second-degree burns.

A pickup whips past, and Andre tightens his grip around the steering wheel. He has a license, though three years have passed since he last drove. For most of his life, he's had no need to drive. In fact, he lied on his application to join the firm, claimed to possess a valid driver's license issued by the District of Columbia. On that same job application, he also claimed to speak Arabic and to adore crossword puzzles, tidbits that he thought would enhance his résumé. For a while, he got away with these lies, dropping the occasional *as-salaam alaikum*, until ten years ago, during that presidential primary so nasty that both parties forever changed their rules. In New Hampshire in December, the road fat with snow, Mrs. Fitz asked him to drive her around to the day's meetings. Behind the wheel, bewildered by the controls, he felt shame that he lacked a skill mastered by most sixteen-year-olds.

"Have you ever driven in snow?" asked Mrs. Fitz.

"Well, technically, no." He hoped to engage the windshield wipers yet succeeded only in flashing the high beams. "Actually, fuck it, truthfully, ma'am, I don't know how to drive. At all."

"How old are you?"

"When would I have learned? Juvie?"

"People learn all types of useful things in prison." She popped a mint into her mouth. "You really don't know how to drive? During all your youth—the street scams, the drug walking—during all those delinquencies, you're telling me that you never stole a car?"

"I broke into plenty. Stole tires and rims. But no, I never stole a whole car," he said. "You sound disappointed."

"How was I to know that you lacked ambition?"

That evening, Mrs. Fitz pounded on his hotel room door, there, he assumed, to send him home. Instead, she slapped the car keys into his palm, saying, "You might as well learn to be useful." For the next two months, after each end-of-day briefing, in a vacant lot deep inside a Manchester park, she mixed driving instruction with political wisdom. *Ease off the gas. Straighten the wheel. New England Republicans claiming to be libertarians are like gay men claiming to be bisexual; who are they fooling?*

The stoplight ahead turns red, and Andre panics, pumping the brakes, the Jeep stopping hard seven feet behind the nearest car. On campaign trips an intern usually chauffeurs him around, and he realizes that he's out of practice. Crashing, dying: neither really worries him, but he's unsettled by the physics of cruising down this boulevard: a two-ton Jeep propelled at forty miles per hour down a four-lane road, past a hock shop named the Gospel of Pawn, past a payday lender with a neon sign that blinks: GET FAST CASH TODAY, BECAUSE YOU COULD DIE TOMORROW. He's surprised by the glut of storefronts with out-of-business signs, by abandoned service stations stripped of color. Andre searches for a bank, a broker, an insurer. Instead, he spots a law office whose shingle claims expertise in personal injury, paternity testing, Social Security disability, and bankruptcy protection. The stoplight turns green, and Andre gently feeds the Jeep gas.

A billboard displays an acne-scarred white man, a physically unattractive—no, downright ugly—school board candidate. His slogan, written in gold biblical font, is "One Nation Under God. Teaching Tradition." Andre assumes billboards around here are cheap, because most small-town candidates can't afford a full billboard. Small-town candidates might run their entire campaign on less than one thousand dollars. Two years of saving a few bucks from each paycheck.

One block later, beside a dollar store, a pictureless billboard displays the name ARETHA MERRIWEATHER, her slogan "Making schools work for *our* children." At once, Andre draws two conclusions. First, Aretha Merriweather is black. Second, thirteen weeks from now, when the polls close, Aretha will lose in a landslide. She's wise to withhold her picture. White voters in racially polarized communities will take one look at her skin and immediately support her opponent. If Andre managed her campaign, the billboard would feature a stock photo of a young white mother, arms wrapped around an adorable blond-haired, blue-eyed boy. But where Aretha Merriweather has erred is in using her real name. Has anyone ever met a white woman named Aretha? Andre taps his thumb to each fingertip, counting the number of Arethas he's ever known: three in sum, all black, not including Her Majesty, the Queen of Soul. But just as fatal as using her real name, her slogan, with the italicized *our,* invokes the type of racial pandering detested by most whites. Such slogans may play well in Baltimore or Detroit, communities where a majority-black electorate will always support the black candidate. But African Americans make up 6 percent of Carthage County's total population, 3 percent of registered voters. So, Aretha Merriweather: go on ahead, sister, make these racial appeals, but be sure to have a concession speech ready on election night.

The next block, he pulls beside a strip mall anchored by a hardware store. A dozen men, each dressed in tattered jeans and a dirty T-shirt, sit astride the curb awaiting work. He steers the Jeep toward an empty corner, a tree-shaded space beside a newspaper box. Today's headline: SCHOOL WON'T LET BIG GIRL SWING. The front-page picture, above the fold, features a fifteen-year-old girl, maybe three hundred pounds, in her ill-fitting marching-band uniform, trombone in hand, sour expression across her face. Apparently, the school board has affirmed the principal's decision to expel the girl from the marching band. *Some parents complained that her shape set a bad example*, says the pull quote. *It was increasingly difficult to meet her special needs.*

Andre has one hour to buy clothes, but first, he visits the liquor store, which has the air of an interrogation room, one hundred square feet divided by glass two inches thick. Behind the spotty glass, on full display, sit rows of cheap high-proof spirits. Andre waits behind four wrinkled women, each with a violet bob and uneven bangs. The first lady in line, clutching a sheet of stationery, reads aloud a set of six numbers, then stops to watch the cashier transform digits into one lottery ticket. The process repeats, slowly, number by number, ticket by ticket, with no end in sight.

A decent rail gin. That's all he wants. Something to help him sleep. Can't he cut ahead in line? His mother, cursed too by insomnia, enjoyed White Russians to help her sleep, and Andre still fondly remembers those late nights when mother and son would watch British wildlife documentaries till sunup. Hector, who once slept through a hurricane, claims those nights are fiction. If anyone ever asked Hector, he'd say their mother was a selfish woman, a narcissistic eccentric who spent each night away from her sons: naked in her latest lover's bed, stoned with her bohemian friends in some ratty underground club, or, more likely than not, in jail, prison, or the DC psychiatric hospital.

In the attic, set atop an easel, rests a poster-sized sample ballot with small portraits stapled beside each candidate's name. Andre, exhausted, spacey, floats his gaze across the room toward a photo of Aretha Merriweather, candidate for school board trustee, who is, as he suspected, black, though, to his surprise, the lone female candidate on a ballot crowded with white men. Thirteen weeks from today, Carthage County voters will choose from among these ten candidates to fill four municipal seats: coroner, sheriff, probate judge, and at-large school board trustee. This ballot, he fears, is bland and uninspired, like Chinese food in Iowa, dull enough to keep the famished at bay. He won't know until the firm conducts a poll whether he'll benefit from low turnout, but for now, he assumes not, considers adding a second initiative, something spicy, something hearty, some social issue that will inspire the masses to stampede the polls. Perhaps a measure that grants landlords the right to evict transgender tenants; or, perhaps, financial penalties for daycares that tend to the children of undocumented workers; or, maybe, prohibit municipal courts from considering sharia law. In his experience, Americans enjoy nothing more than denying their neighbors happiness.

Brendan, grumbling to himself, swipes his forefinger across his tablet's screen. The kid has spent the morning transforming the attic into their headquarters, an admirable effort, though cobwebs still hover overhead and cardboard boxes, soggy and freckled with mold, fill the sunlit space with a spongy scent. The movers have come and gone, delivered a mobile command center: high-speed modems and personal global cell tower, server and wireless routers, two sleek flat-screens now mounted against the wall. Fine equipment, but none of which right now works.

"I don't know what the trouble is." Brendan plugs a surge protector into the wall, and the tech remains black.

Andre knows the problem. As a precaution against theft, a technician in Washington must remotely activate the equipment. All Brendan must do is make a call, a fact that Andre has denied his apprentice, a jackass move, he concedes, but necessary to postpone a presentation that Brendan promises will run two and a half hours.

"The sockets must not provide enough juice." Brendan unplugs the laptop. "I'd use my own laptop, but it doesn't have the software to show the database I put together."

"I've seen an index of voters before."

"Not like this. We bought the state's voter registration list. That gave us each voter's name, phone number, race, address, political affiliation, participation in past elections. We bought a mailing list from the post office. We also have court records, FEC filings, census data at the block level, precinct-level results, magazine subscription data, the white pages . . ."

Andre wants to say, *Yes, yes, I have seen that index too, every election consultant in America has seen that exact index*, but sharing this observation will lengthen his stay in this purgatory. Andre, breathing through his mouth, says, "I'm gonna take a nap."

"Five more minutes, Mr. Ross. Please. Five more minutes." Brendan tries to buy time. "Does our super PAC have a name?"

"We're not a PAC. Super or otherwise," Andre says. "We're just two citizens who want to share our message. You've got four minutes."

Andre closes his eyes, resists the call of sleep. He can't fathom how Brendan's presentation could take two and a half hours. This morning, in fifteen minutes, Andre studied past election results and two county maps broken down to the census-block level. Carthage County is overwhelmingly poor and white—a fact any novice could've guessed. For the past sixty-five years, county residents, by a margin of four to one, have cast their ballots for the Republican nominee for president and the Republican nominee for governor, and the Republican nominees for lieutenant governor, secretary of state, and attorney general. If Carthage residents ever had to elect a dog catcher, odds are he would be a white, free-market-loving, scripture-quoting, federal-government-mistrusting Republican. The remaining voters aren't Democrats. The rest are self-avowed independents, mostly former Republicans, die-hard conservatives who think that the party's gone soft.

"Mr. Ross." Andre feels a gentle hand on his shoulder. "Excuse me, Andre?"

Andre opens his eyes, checks his watch. Fifteen minutes have passed.

"We can start now." Brendan holds a laser pointer, faces a flat-screen on which appears: *The History of Carthage County. From 1790 to Today.* "I called the tech guys. Apparently, we had to remotely activate the equipment."

Andre wipes his eyes, says, "That must be new."

A little past midnight, Andre, gin in hand, sits at his desk, alone in the dark, face brightened by his laptop's glow. He's wide awake, refreshed by a late-afternoon nap, and now awaits an update to his ex-fiancée's Instagram account. Tonight, so says the site, Cassie's serenading a charity ball, a two-hundred-dollar-a-plate gala organized by a student-run nonprofit that teaches senior citizens how to practice safe sex. He guesses the gig will net Cassie a solid grand. Maybe more. About time his girl earned what she's worth. At twenty-nine, she's a working vocalist, days spent teaching tone-deaf housewives to broaden their range, nights spent performing sets for drunks who lack any appreciation of soul.

She's recently become the darling of local college students, particularly the well-to-do hipsters who pride themselves on knowing the lyrics to "Strange Fruit." So tonight, he knows, Cassie will indulge their fantasies, perform a set that ends with "Solitude," a gardenia blossom tucked behind her ear. He pities the students, because tonight Cassie will break their hearts. Standing beneath the spotlight, she will be hopelessly beautiful, her lilt soulful and vulnerable, with a woundedness that'll cause each man to believe that he, and he alone, can free her from a lifetime of sorrow.

The charity ball should've ended an hour ago, and he expects an Instagram update at any moment. She lives two miles from the event—far from the Mass Avenue condo they once shared—but before leaving the venue, she'll accept the students' plea to share a drink. *Please, Cassie, we're your biggest fans.* She'll have one drink—two and college kids get the wrong idea—and for thirty minutes, not a second longer, she'll pretend these privileged kids are as interesting as they aspire to be.

Andre drinks his gin, ice clinking against his glass, and the photos appear. There's Cassie between twin metrosexuals, both wearing bow ties and fur coats. Cassie singing beneath a spotlight, snapping her fingers, gardenia blossom behind her ear. Cassie leaning over a round banquet table, laughing, a glass of watery ice in hand. He wonders who took these pictures. Her fans? Her friends? Her new man? Right now, he doesn't care. Because these pictures affirm what he knows to be true: that nobody knows his girl like he knows his girl.

He drains his drink, craves another with clean ice.

In the kitchen, standing before the portable freezer, he hears Brendan cheer. The outburst lasts but a second, followed by a hysterical, if not maniacal, laugh. Andre indulges his own curiosity, knocking at the kid's door, then cautiously turning the knob.

The kid's bedroom is simple and tidy, cracked plaster walls on which hang the Irish flag, a poster of Joyce, and a wood-and-stucco sign that reads HELP WANTED: IRISH NEED NOT APPLY. Bookshelves are packed with ornaments of a curious mind: economic philosophy, political theory, the *Baltimore Catechism*, and a history of Northern Ireland.

Brendan sits in his boxer shorts, cross-legged on the floor, back against his bed, heavy-lidded eyes like sea glass. He's facing his flat-screen TV, a video game controller in hand. A small picnic lies spread before him, and, on his bed, within arm's reach, a stack of *National Geographic*s and a baggie of purple gummies.

"You having a little party?" Andre says.

"No. No. No. Well. Maybe. It's not a party. So, I take it all back. No. What was the question?" Brendan breaks into giggles, lifts the bag of gummies. "Edible?"

Andre can only laugh. Brendan's kind to share, but Andre hasn't gotten stoned in years. He doesn't have a moral objection to weed. He simply has too much to lose if ever he's caught. A second criminal conviction, no matter how minor, would ruin his career.

"So." Brendan takes a labored breath, face now grave and stern. "Is this covered by, you know? Road rules? Roads of the rules. It sounds funny when I say it out loud. Road. Rules."

Andre likes the kid a little more. He wants to assure Brendan that weed is tame by firm standards, to say that staffers find all sorts of ways to alleviate a career that vacillates between stressful and mundane. Most consultants spend their days saddled by tight deadlines and demanding clients, then spend their nights decompressing alone in a motel far from home. Gambling. Coke. Prostitutes. Imagine all the ways lonely men can cure boredom with anonymity and access to petty cash. He knows junior partners who volunteer for road trips, fathers and grandfathers who approach travel assignments like frat boys throwing a bachelor party during spring break in Acapulco one day before the end of the world. Last year, an intern returned from New Orleans with a Percocet problem and a drug-resistant strain of gonorrhea.

"Yes. What happens on the road stays on the road." Andre sits on the floor, takes the spare game controller. "Mind if I join?"

"Sure, please, mate. Yeah. It's football. I mean soccer. I mean . . . You play? Cheers, mate. Cheers."

"When this game came out, years ago? My brother and I played for cash."

Andre doesn't share that Hector bought a boosted console, that the game disc just happened to be inside, which, of course, is one of the many risks of buying anything from the corner junkie. Sure, the price is always right, but you never really know exactly what you've purchased. Hector's lucky that inside the console there wasn't a severed toe. Nonetheless Andre remembers those days with fondness, good days for them both, Hector newly sober, Andre building his career, days that promised a bright and stable future.

"I don't have a brother. Three sisters, I'm the youngest," Brendan says. "I always wanted a big brother. When I was little, my sisters, they'd put me in dresses. Practice their makeup on me. You don't know, man, but life is hard."

"We don't have to share. In fact, it's probably best we don't speak."

"This is awesome, Dre," Brendan says. "Are there any other road rules I should know about?"

"Pace yourself, kid. For now, one rule is as much as you can handle."

CHAPTER FOUR

Andre receives an e-mail from Mrs. Fitz. The client, PISA, wishes the team to meet a local contact. Corporate clients often instruct teams to consult local officials, but this specific request strikes Andre as odd. For starters, Duke Boshears holds no elective office. In fact, four times the voters have denied Boshears the honor of serving. In the most recent contest, the Republican primary for state agricultural commissioner, Duke Boshears finished seventh, dead last, two places behind a fraternity's write-in: Hugh G. Rection.

The Boshears meeting, however, may be an opportunity. The campaign needs a straw man: a local face lacking any real control, a figurehead to help collect signatures and submit those signatures to the county manager. The position is thankless: a lot of work, little influence, terms only a fool would abide.

"I still don't understand." Brendan yawns as a freight train, with stock cars of horses and cattle, crosses the road. The kid shows every sign of the lateness of their night. "Who's this guy?"

"Duke Boshears is one of the wealthiest men in Carthage,"

Andre says. "Once PISA buys the land, Boshears has a contract to clear away the trees."

"So he's a logger? A lumberjack?" Brendan leans back, ponders. "What's the difference between a logger and a lumberjack?"

"Who the fuck am I, Paul Bunyan?"

Brendan chuckles—they understand each other perfectly this morning—says, "So how will this meeting go?"

Andre sinks into his seat, ashamed to admit his poor track record of predicting these meetings' success. Just last year, in a hard-fought campaign to unseat Virginia's attorney general, Andre scoured the state for weeks in search of potential challengers and thought, at long last, he'd found the perfect candidate: a small-town judge, mother of three, twenty-three years' legal experience, thirty years married to a Gulf War vet. Her in-person interview, Andre assumed, would be a formality. And yet, two minutes into his visit, the judge began to rant against water fluoridation, spreading across her desk photos of deformed babies, proof, she claimed, that fluoride was no better than cyanide. Mass medication, she called it. Evil's poison of choice. *Did you know that Hitler put fluoride in the water at Auschwitz?* He counts that meeting as among his worst, an interview that left him both in need of a new candidate and forever mistrustful of water from the tap.

Brendan pounds the door of the one-story concrete building. "This the right address?"

Andre checks his e-mail—right place, right time—then casts a glance over his shoulder. Across the street is a shuttered hospital that occupies a whole city block. The four-story building is crumbling, as though a construction crew in a hurry took a wrecking ball to the place, removed the roof, exposed the studs. Car-sized rubble is everywhere. The county's encircled the block with a chain-link fence topped with barbed wire, and beside the gate appears a faded construction billboard, PARDON OUR PROGRESS, that promises a new hospital opening on this spot six years ago.

"You must be Andre Ross." A man, maybe five foot five, opens the front door, offers his hand to Brendan, who points toward Andre. Duke scratches his head, studying Andre, says, "I see. Come in."

A dozen desks face front, and a space heater broils the room. On the walls hang topographical maps and black-and-white photos of muddy lumberjacks and bone-thin mules pulling sleds loaded with felled pine.

"I gave my staff an extended lunch break. I know y'all like to keep your work confidential." Duke Boshears is a handsome sixty-year-old man with a silver-streaked pompadour. If he were two inches taller, he might have won a local election. If he were four inches taller, he could've been governor. "PISA mentioned only an Andre Ross."

Andre says, "This is my trusted associate. Brendan Fitzpatrick."

"Fitzpatrick, eh? Scottish?"

Brendan narrows his eyes. "Irish."

"There's a battlefield a mile up yonder. Terrible battle. Not a large battle, but an important one. Thousands slaughtered. Both rebs and Yanks. There was an Irish battalion. The South Carolina Third, sharpshooters. I'm a bit of a history buff. The battalion was led by an Irish colonel, what was his name . . ." Duke snaps his fingers as though conjuring a spell. "Tavish McKenzie, from Edinburgh."

Brendan sets his jaw.

Andre would like to see Brendan's wrath. A barrage of insults. A quick jab to Duke's nose. In Dublin, Brendan probably learned to dispense both. But, for now, the campaign needs

Duke Boshears, a master of history, though apparently not of geography. So, Andre takes his assistant's elbow and shakes his head as though to say: *Let a fool be a fool.*

"The county hosts a reenactment here every second year. Uses a lottery system to assign roles. Everyone wants to be a Confederate officer, everyone wants to ride a horse." Duke smacks gray gum. "We pull names out of the hat. Sometimes, though, if a fella's down on his luck in life, and he gets a good pull of the hat, then someone can buy the rank from him."

"Makes sense," Andre says. "Everybody wins."

"Exactly! I end up buying my rank every year. And every year, it gets more expensive. I bought a colonel ten years ago. Five hundred dollars. Last year, I bought a captain. Cost me two grand." Duke motions toward a back office. "I'm glad you understand."

In Duke's office, behind his desk is a mounted black bear, seven feet tall, on hind legs, paws raised. Against the wall leans evidence of a failed political campaign: buttons, bumper stickers, milk crates full of T-shirts and shot glasses and porcelain mugs. Duke must've spent a small fortune to lose that race. The primary passed a year ago; surely Duke must hate the constant reminder that 94 percent of fellow Republicans declined to check the box beside his name.

Andre takes a seat in a chair that is close to the ground; Duke sits behind his desk in a high-backed gilded chair, which gives him at least two inches over his guests.

Duke leans forward. "I want a progress report."

Andre scratches behind his ear. "We're still in the early stages."

"The early stages of what?"

"The early stages of planning." Andre forces a smile. "If you have suggestions, we welcome your thoughts."

"My thoughts?" Duke takes the gum out of his mouth, sticks the gray wad into yesterday's newspaper. "I want all your poll tests. Your financial records, the budget, any and all analytics you've got. Also, tomorrow, I want a list of ideas of how to collect signatures to get on the ballot. We got what? About three weeks? I want updates. Every day. Here's my cell. Don't call at six. That's when I take my supper."

Duke Boshears flings a business card across his desk. Andre lets the card sit there and casts a glance toward Brendan. The kid smirks, arches a brow: *Now it's your turn, Dre. Let a fool be a fool.*

"Christian radio's popular in this town." Duke opens a pack of nicotine gum, shoves two squares into his mouth. "I want you to buy airtime. In my last campaign, I hired a guy out of Charleston. It cost a pretty penny, but he penned a popular jingle."

"A jingle? I'm sorry. Were you running against Herbert Hoover?" Andre says.

"Should I be talking to you?" Duke points to Brendan. "What's your name?"

"Someone from PISA will be in touch." Andre stands, opens the office door to find a woman whose face seems unnatural, skin stretched taut against her skull, cat eyes that can't possibly close. And yet, despite her alien appearance, the violet in her eyes is striking and spectacular. Duke Boshears stands, pale and panicked. "Baby—"

"You told me this meeting was at our house," she says. "You told me this meeting was an hour from now. You knew I wanted to be here."

"Baby, there must've been a mix-up. But I got everything under control."

"I'm Victoria Boshears." She offers Andre her hand. "Y'all the consultants?"

"These fellas have to get going." Duke moves between

Victoria and Andre. “Thank you both. Get us those reports like I asked. My wife and I’ll be in touch.”

“If y’all can spare a moment, I have questions,” Victoria says. “It won’t take long, I promise. And I do very much appreciate hearing whatcha have to say.”

The right thing for Andre to do is to help Duke Boshears, to accept personal responsibility for any scheduling mishap, and to make a gracious exit before contacting Duke later in the day. But Duke Boshears does not seem like a man who appreciates a rescue. Duke Boshears seems like a petty aspiring politician who would brag about slipping a blade between his rescuer’s ribs.

“We’re happy to answer any questions you might have.” Andre accepts her hand. “We told your husband that we welcome your thoughts.”

Victoria pulls a chair beside Andre’s and sits. “Did my husband tell you that this company has been in my family for more than a century? That my great-great-grandfather started selling timber, and that for four generations, we were the most successful logging operation in both Carolinas?”

“Honey, I mixed up the times,” Duke pleads. “Was an honest mistake.”

“And all’s forgiven, sweetie. Accidents happen. I’ve moved on.” She invites Andre and Brendan to sit, which they do. “Did he tell you that my grandfather was the only logger in the region to hire African Americans, and that he paid these good men the same exact wages he paid his whites? Did he tell you that both my mother and father, rest their souls, that they marched on Washington, that, though my parents’ support for civil rights cost this company a great deal of business, my father never laid off a single employee?”

“Baby, please. Do we have to do this now?”

“And did Duke tell you that he himself has squandered my

family's fortune? That, in the fifteen years since Daddy died, he has gambled away my family's assets on silly ventures, ventures that I beseeched him not to pursue? Did he tell you that last year we had the first layoff in company history, that for the first time my family's company has more debt than assets, that he, without my knowledge, put our home up as collateral, that if this PISA contract falls through, then we will be thrown out of my family's house, the house in which I raised my babies—and that we would be forced to live in a cardboard box on the streets?"

"That will never happen." Duke rests his hand on her shoulder, and she jerks away. Duke says, "Vicki, I promise."

Victoria turns her back to her husband, her face red, eyes full of pain, slender frame casting a shadow over the bookshelf on which her pictures rest. These two have been together forever. Wedding photos. First-child photos. Looks like Duke and Victoria were prom king and queen. Now look at her. Disfigured. Destitute. Desperate. How many plastic surgeries has she undergone? Somewhere in Carthage, a sixty-year-old woman, still bitter over being prom queen runner-up, is having a hearty laugh.

Andre leans forward. Perhaps Victoria will be their straw man. "In order to appear on the ballot, county law requires a locally registered voter collect signatures and certify the authenticity of those signatures to the county manager. Brendan and I are obviously ineligible, but we can offer a substantial consulting fee to whomever you might recommend."

Duke comes alive. "How substantial a consulting fee?"

"No," Victoria says.

"I'm just asking."

"No," Victoria says. "Whoever submits those signatures is a lamb unto the slaughter. Mark my words, this ballot initiative, it's gonna get ugly. People here. A nest of vipers. You'll see."

Duke clears his throat. "Fine. How about Billy?"

"Billy? Billy who? Billy, your brother? Please." She rolls her eyes. "A meth-cooking womanizer missing a forefinger on both hands."

"How about Jed Dixon?" Duke says.

His wife replies, "Drunken wife-beater."

"Beau Carlyle."

"Got a fifteen-year-old pregnant."

"Bob Roers."

"Atheist. And stop naming your lodge buddies."

A burst of laughter breaks the conversation and echoes inside Duke's office.

"Damn it. I told you." Duke checks his watch, jumps to his feet. "Staff is back from lunch. You boys better get gone."

Duke slides open a side door, and Andre and Brendan follow Victoria beside the concrete building, past waist-high hedges and dog shit in dead grass. The three reach the Jeep, exchange pleasant goodbyes before Victoria takes Andre aside and whispers, "Please, Mr. Ross, tell me honestly. Will this ballot initiative pass?"

"We're optimistic," Andre says, not because he believes so, but because that's what he's been trained to say. If the first rule of campaign consulting is to never guarantee victory, then the second rule is to never admit the true likelihood of defeat.

Inside the Jeep, Brendan starts the engine, saying, "I got two questions."

Andre knows both questions and both answers. No, Victoria Boshears has never voted for her husband. And yes, Duke Boshears knows.

CHAPTER FIVE

Andre leaves the shower sweating, another frustration to which he's grown accustomed, a bathroom by turns icebox and sauna. He stretches beside the radiator, studies his form in the mirror, pokes the moist flesh above his hip, a spot he knows should be taut, not muscled, not marbled, but lean and firm, a torso of which he can be proud. Instead he taps a soft patch that ripples like a stone-splashed pond, and, at once, he blames five days of Irish breakfasts. Perhaps he should ask Brendan to cook a low-fat alternative, or, better yet, the two could skip breakfast altogether. Andre prefers to start his day light: black coffee; crisp toast; if he has a sweet tooth, a dab of raspberry jam. But Brendan enjoys fixing these elaborate feasts full of cream and butter and salted pork, and though each meal is a culinary delight, Andre sees the oily streaks that run across his bread-sopped plate, and he wonders how the life expectancy on the Emerald Isle could possibly be eighty-one. A social worker in juvie once said Andre shouldn't expect to live much past thirty. Now, at thirty-five, he worries each meal might bring him one day closer to that early grave.

Death is the least of his troubles. In two days, he has a scheduled call with Mrs. Fitz, a call in which she will expect a detailed progress report. And what detailed progress does her protégé have to share? Not a damn thing. Andre's interviewed six Carthage residents, each signing a confidentiality agreement, and thus far, he has yet to find a straw man to lead his corporate-backed dark-money grassroots campaign. Yesterday, he met a candidate recommended by PISA, an eccentric English teacher with elvish ears, a dilettante wealthy not by trade but by inheritance. She owns half a million dollars in PISA stock yet chooses to spend each day teaching fourteen-year-olds the tragedy of Hester Prynne, a worn-edged copy of which she kept splayed, facedown, atop her glass coffee table. In juvie, that book nearly caused a riot. A novel about a wife who cheats on her absent man. Hester Prynne got lucky, Andre's classmates claimed; for lesser sins, their fathers had beat their mothers black and blue. In some countries, the boys said, exotic faraway places where long-bearded men pray five times a day, a bitch who betrays her man might expect to get her face cut. A scarlet letter pinned against her breast? Shit, call that tragedy? Please. Motherfucker. Please. We're children in prison. Let's keep the real tragedy in perspective.

Andre, however, chose not to share that experience with the elf-eared teacher. Instead, he laid his game down flat, flirted a little, flattered a little, spoke with passion about PISA's commitment to the environment. But the schoolteacher refused to buy what Andre wanted to sell. Over cold cucumber sandwiches and butter cookies served on bone-china plates, she railed against corporate influence in politics, raised her voice an octave as she quoted the liberal truism that corporations are not—and never shall be—people.

So, where does this leave him? In a world of hurt. Without a straw man, he can't begin to collect the fifteen hundred signatures needed to appear on the ballot. But, more important, until he finds a straw man, Andre can't begin to sketch the contours of this small-time, humiliatingly simple campaign. These types of issue-centric initiatives, they have absolutely nothing to do with the actual issue. Voters have neither the time nor the expertise to weigh the costs and benefits of a complicated policy proposal. Instead, voters cast their ballot based upon instinct, based upon their gut. And that's why the straw man becomes essential, because a good straw man can make a voter believe that a ballot initiative, no matter how large or small, is a matter of life or death. Rename a city park. Tax a tin of tobacco. Change the day on which the city hauls away the trash. The best straw man, like midnight television commercials warning about the dire consequences of dull kitchen knives, can bring a fresh, sharp urgency to the most inconsequential issue.

Andre worries that he's wasted the past six days, and, crossing the hall to his bedroom, towel wrapped around his waist, he fears that he's exhausted his straw man options. He has one last candidate to meet: Tyler Lee, the latest recommendation from Duke Boshears. Tyler manages a local bikini bar popular with tourists and locals alike. Victoria Boshears swears that Tyler is the perfect choice, that Tyler is popular and reasonable, and for these reasons, she's set a meet, noon today at the Gray Wolf, the bikini bar where Tyler works. Andre has his doubts—no, more than doubts; about any nominee of Duke Boshears, Andre's mistrust is as solid as stone—but unless Andre finds a straw man, like in the next forty-eight hours, this campaign will surely be his last, and he's sickened by the thought that, for a second campaign in a row, he will have embarrassed both himself and his mentor.

Brendan calls, "Breakfast is ready," and Andre smells the orange zest of Brendan's fresh-baked soda bread. Andre falls naked against his bed. He'll need another moment before he's ready to face the day.

On the front door of the Gray Wolf is a poster of a plump, inebriated-looking toddler, winking, wearing a bowler and suspenders, who clutches a glass of wine. The poster reads: MUST BE 21 OR AWESOME TO ENTER. Inside, past the bat-wing doors, is a ballroom styled like a gunfighter saloon: muted murals of the Old West, whiskey barrels and chandeliers, spittoons and cacti set against the walls. An American flag hangs over a player piano. The rebel flag hangs, a tad higher, above the picture-frame stage, on which Andre imagines a string of can-can girls singing, kicking, arm in arm in a chorus line.

"We don't open till four," says a bespectacled lump behind the varnished-mahogany bar. He's practicing serving a standard shot, pouring from a nippled liquor bottle while spelling *Mississippi* aloud. "Come back later."

"Are you Tyler?"

"Tyler!" The bartender spills on the bar. "See what you made me do? Tyler!"

"Are they here?" A baritone echoes from an office behind the bar. "Shit. Give me one more minute. Get them a beer, on the house, and the good table."

The bartender's busy wiping his mess, so Andre and Brendan claim a table beside a dusty mural of pistol-wielding soldiers circling Indian braves. In the pastel background, near the horizon, a cavalry stampedes a tepee, while brown-skinned women in buckskins, babies clutched to their breasts, flee. White infantrymen—front and center, with bayonets and torches—appear strong, powerful, the braves scared, cowardly, defeated. Brendan runs his palm across his face, groaning, says, "Christ. I suppose it could be worse. It could be dogs playing poker."

Brendan unpacks his messenger bag, removes a fat folder of

forms, two dozen in all, including a confidentiality agreement, a liability waiver, and consent to investigate each detail of the signatory's life. From behind the bar appears Tyler Lee, a hulk with a mastiff's head. He's not fat nor obese, just huge, solid, like he should be chasing Jack down a beanstalk. Up close, he's recently shaved, a fact betrayed by his irritated nicked skin, fresh razor burn, and a sliver of prickles missed around his ear.

"Did he get y'all a beer?" Tyler studies the table. "Numb nuts, I said to . . . Never mind. What would you like? We got a couple imports on tap."

"We're fine," Andre says. "You have time to talk?"

"You're Mr. Ross? Mr. Fitzpatrick?" Tyler offers his sweaty paw, which Andre shakes quickly, as though he's slipped his hand inside the cage of a bear. Tyler says, "Nice to meet ya, brother. Real nice. Sure about that beer?"

Andre likes that the guy's trying, but he already worries that this colossus might not be up to the task. He's wearing a black clip-on tie beneath a crimson vest, an outfit that makes him look like a croupier. Is this Tyler Lee's idea of class, or is this the uniform he's required to wear to sling drinks in this white man's fantasy saloon?

"Punk's the owner's nephew." Tyler spins and straddles a chair that Andre fears might collapse. "But if he drops a bottle of champagne, guess whose paycheck suffers."

"We represent—"

"Miss Vicki, she clued me in," Tyler says. "Washington, DC. The land sale. Gold mining. The ballot thing. Referendum. Yeah, brother. It's wild. Real hush-hush. Like secret-agent stuff."

Andre doesn't mask his irritation. Yesterday, when he spoke on the phone with Victoria, he emphasized the need for discretion, said that he required anonymity for as long as possible. She swore she understood, promised, in her soft, honeyed tone, that she wouldn't share more than necessary. Andre says, "This meeting is just an initial introduction. We have other partners under consideration."

Brendan sends a look: *We do?*

"Cool, brother. I know the game." Tyler scratches the top of his head. "But I'll tell ya what, you won't find no one . . . you won't find no better partner that'll work harder for you. Brother, I'll tell you. Right now, I got like four jobs. I manage here. I haul pulp. I got my own landscaping business. I got all kinds of stoves in the fire."

Andre Ross does not consider himself prone to snap judgments—that, he believes, is the exclusive province of small-minded men and exceptionally beautiful women—but, sitting here, eyes fixed on Tyler Lee's nervous grin, Andre wonders whether holding four minimum-wage jobs is an accomplishment about which a forty-year-old man should boast. Andre strives not to be petty. Tyler Lee has the right attitude, and this interview, thus far, has gone better than all the others. But something about Tyler makes Andre uneasy.

"I'll level with you." Tyler leans close. "Miss Vicki, she says if I work with y'all, then her husband will hire me on his crew. Brother, that would be big for me and my kids. I've wanted to work for the Boshears, brother, I don't know, about my entire life."

Andre realizes why he dislikes Tyler. This giant, in his tight vest and cheap tie and black pants, looks like a juvie correctional officer. Put a brown baseball cap on his head, put a heavy Maglite in his hand, and Tyler Lee could easily pass for one of those illiterate brutes, lucky to have a union job, with a little power and a big grudge. Andre still has nightmares about those sinister fucks, assholes who got their jollies practicing cruelty, power-seeking yellow-eyed sadists who got a literal hard-on, watching, laughing, rejoicing, as young boys suffered.

"Thank you, Mr. Lee." Andre's on his feet. "We should go."

"What? Already?" Tyler Lee seems to sense his opportunity slipping away. "Did I say something? I mean, sometimes I say stuff. My wife says I shouldn't talk so much. I didn't mean to offend. I have a lot of respect for black people."

Andre and Brendan exchange a bemused stare.

"Wait, brother, I can be someone else. I can be anyone else. Just give me a chance. I have references. They'll tell you I work real hard, and I'm loyal, and I'm—" A clacking interrupts Tyler's plea. A busty redhead, probably not yet twenty, nears, wearing royal purple: panties, bra, and rhinestone heels. Her upper thigh bears a tattoo of an eagle clasping a serpent.

"Tyler, Sarah Beth's wearing purple again." She grips her breasts. "I told her fat ass to change, and she said that you said she could wear—"

"Amber Lynn," Tyler says.

"I have seniority. Purple is my color. You need to tell her—"

"Amber Lynn!" Tyler slams his fist against the table, with a force so strong that Brendan's papers fly through the air and scatter across the floor. "Can't you see I'm in the middle of business? I'll tend to your shit when I got time. Now go. Go! Now!"

Andre sneaks a glance at Brendan, whose slack-jawed face shines like that of a six-year-old boy who swears he saw a superhero fly across the sky. Andre wants to laugh, wants to pat Brendan's head and say, *Careful, kiddo. Girls like this, they're more trouble than they're worth. Their self-esteem is about as strong as their last compliment.*

"Please. Sit. Come on, brother. Just for a beer." Tyler falls on his knees, collects the papers, shouts at the bartender, "Two beers. The Guinness we put on tap this morning."

"Guinness?" Brendan says. Irish stout. Half-naked redheads. The kid may never leave. Brendan says, "On tap?"

"We're a bikini bar." Tyler puts the papers in a nice neat stack. "We're not licensed to show tits. But the customers start buying the girls shots and, well, the owner doesn't care. The sheriff, shit, that fat boy buys the first round. Every Friday and Saturday night, I have at least one drunk buck-naked Barbie either crying on my shoulder or puking on my boots. Brother, I've had this job for six years, and that shit got real old real quick."

Andre is amused. Drunk buck-naked Barbies crying on his shoulder or puking on his boots. That must be the chorus to a country-western song. But then again, isn't that the spirit of Motown and the blues?

"Listen." Tyler turns his body square with Andre. "I ain't the smartest guy in Carthage. I don't pretend to be. But I've lived here my whole life, and I got lots of good ideas. And I'm good with people. And I will work my ass off for you. I only need a chance."

In a perfect world, Andre would like a better straw man than Tyler, but Andre is not rich with options. So either he can hire this giant, or in two days' time, he can disappoint Mrs. Fitz. Because she will ask, *Why not this Tyler Lee?*, and he will answer, *Because he reminds me of a prison guard*, which is an answer that she will not accept.

Two hours later, Brendan drives west, deep into the temperate rain forest and up a steep Appalachian ridge. They're headed to the thousand acres that PISA hopes to own, which Andre wants to see. The mountainside is lush yet dank, an ecological anomaly where a sharp, rapid ascent transforms moist air into mist and rain. The Jeep crawls along this gravel road, weaves between a stand of shortleaf pines, and soccer plays on the radio.

They reach the highest point in Carthage, a frosted tableland marked by an obelisk, inscribed on its face: MOUNT KUKA, ELEVATION 3,552 FEET. Andre opens his door, steps into the thick, wet air, and, all at once, a sense of wonder touches his chest. He's not a man easily impressed by landscapes—you've seen one mountain, you've seen 'em all—but, staring down into the dell where PISA wants to mine for gold, he finds himself in awe. He imagines this place in the spring. Brambles, stone mounds, fields of crimson clover. Mother Nature must have spent centuries forming this valley, round as a bowl, blessed with rich black soil that nourishes groves of chestnut trees.

Brendan sniffles, clears away a tear.

"Sorry," Brendan says. "Reminds me of the midlands in Ireland."

Andre doesn't know what to say, so, back in the Jeep, he chooses silence. The next few minutes neither speaks as they bump along the dell's outer rim, a scenic route with cascading waterfalls and caves and trees older than any man. On the dell's opposite ridge, the road descends like a staircase, steep sudden slopes that ease into level plains. The Jeep cruises across each step, passing campsites and hunting lodges, and reaches the base of the mountain, which presents a fork in the road. The kid chooses the route that leads beneath an open arched gate, where a cobblestone path circles a straw cottage, behind which, set apart by a post-and-rail fence, tower two huge greenhouses that look extraterrestrial.

"This market got great reviews online." Brendan opens the door. "Think they sell rhubarb?"

"Hold up one second." Andre grabs for Brendan, missing by an inch, watches the kid hurry inside. Shit. Andre unfastens his seat belt and prepares for the inevitable. Brendan took one look at the valley and wept. What happens once he realizes the likely fate of this roadside shop? The mines. The cyanide.

The closure of this mom-and-pop operation is the best-case scenario. The worst case is both Mom and Pop getting a rare, mysterious cancer that kills slowly, the kind for which doctors always have a name but never a cure.

Outside the cottage, a sandwich board reads: *We're 100% Natural. No genetically modified seeds. No pesticides. No hormones.* Inside, the cottage is snug and quaint, the pine-plank walls bearing awards, plaques, framed certificates, and newspaper articles, each paying tribute to this modest organic market that offers a surprisingly vast selection. Front and center are potato-filled barrels, one of which bears a label: *Perfect for wild game stew. Trust us! These Red Bliss Potatoes are most a-peeling.* Andre cringes—what self-respecting black man doesn't loathe a pun?—but he imagines that upper-class tourists would love this place.

Brendan handles a rutabaga, says, "Tomorrow for breakfast. Leek-and-bacon pie or sausage-and-cheese strata?"

Andre thinks to answer, *Neither,* to explain that one more Irish breakfast may cause his heart to stop, but now is not the time or the place to discuss the excesses of Irish cuisine. "Whatever you want is fine. But hurry up."

"We found Tyler. Shouldn't we be celebrating?"

"There's still his background check, and we need to get the signatures."

The kid picks up a placard and, chuckling, reads in a whisper, "'Hakurei is great in a stir-fry, as a side dish, or in a salad. You'll be amazed how many new and exciting recipes will *turnip.*' Dre, these people are hilarious."

"Man, get your shit and let's get the fuck out of here."

Through a side door passes a handsome grandmother, wearing an apron, pearl earrings, and a cardigan with copper buttons. She welcomes her guests, arms open wide, and says in a soft tone, "Sorry, I didn't hear you come in. Can I help you?"

Andre crosses the market, a quick twelve paces, to intercept the shopkeeper before she catches Brendan's eye. "I see you sell hams."

"That's what we're known for." The woman strolls behind a deli counter, where, beneath glass, sitting on ice, are plucked chickens, skinned rabbits, and parts of pigs: feet, bellies, a whole hog's head. She stands atop an upturned crate, spreads butcher paper across the countertop. Clearly she wants to make a sale. But she doesn't sell ham by the slice. She sells whole hams, ten to twenty pounds each, the cheapest one costing more than the airfare that brought him to South Carolina. Andre Ross is no miser, but he refuses to spend that kind of cash on pork. He says, "My friend is about done."

"Take your time." She steps behind the register. "And just so you know. We host all types of weddings. *We're* very open. We do not judge. We don't discriminate. Everyone is welcome."

Andre looks up, confused, sees the shopkeeper's knowing smile. Then, he understands. He's considering correcting her assumption—*We're business associates and nothing more*—when Brendan sets a full basket atop the checkout counter.

"Dre, we're out of soap," Brendan says, then smiles at the shopkeeper. "Can we get a pound of bacon? You have an amazing market."

"Aren't you sweet?" She unrolls butcher paper. "Most of our business is out of county. We supply restaurants across the state. The artisan, locally grown crowd. We also run an agritourism program. Families learn about the farm, children pick their own vegetables. Go ahead. Take a brochure. There's one for weddings."

Brendan pockets two wedding brochures, says, "And a pound of your country sausage."

"My husband and I talk about making soap. But every time we sell anything new, we have to jump through bureaucratic hoops. See those pickles?" She points toward a shelf of jars. "The brine is vinegar based. Vinegar is acidic. So I have to register my recipe with the federal government. Plus, I gotta send samples to the university for testing. The state won't issue a pickle license without pickle testing."

Brendan selects two plucked chickens, and Andre questions whether the kid cares about the cost. For sure, Brendan comes from money: his father is chief of cardiology at some big-time hospital, his mother's the chief operating officer of a semiconductor manufacturer. But the firm grants interns only a modest per diem.

"It wouldn't be so bad if I only had to deal with one agency." She finds a pencil and receipt pad. "But to sell eggs, we need a license from the Department of Agriculture. To sell ham and bacon, we need permission from the Meat and Poultry division. To sell peanuts, the Department of Health and Environmental Control. That's just the state red tape. The feds have their rules. The county has its rules. The insurance company has its rules. I spend my entire weekend doing nothing but paperwork."

She tallies the bill, hands Brendan the sheet. The kid scans the figures and, to his credit, doesn't flinch. Brendan's reaching for his wallet, asking more about federal regulations that govern soap, when Andre realizes that, this week, Brendan's cooked and cleaned and hasn't asked Andre to kick in a dime. He worries that Brendan will think he's a mooch, that the kid will tell his grandmother that Andre's a mooch, that if he doesn't pay this bill, then he really is a mooch. And thus, Andre snatches the slip, smiles a fake smile, and reads the bottom line.

Appalling.

"I shouldn't complain," the woman says. "We're blessed, and no one wants to hear a successful person whine about the price of success. But I've talked to the county manager, Paula

Carrothers. She says there's nothing she can do. She just doesn't understand business. Bless her heart. Everyone says so."

Andre pays with a credit card. At least he'll earn some miles. He tries to mask his disgust, hopes, for this price, that these vegetables will extend his life, a sentiment that he brings back inside the Jeep, where Brendan says, "She seems nice. What? Did I talk too much?"

"You just can't help yourself, can you?" Andre says. "And, by the way, she thinks you and I are a couple."

"What are you talking about?"

"You've got two wedding brochures in your pocket."

"Me and you?" Brendan cringes. "Please, I can do better."

Brendan pulls the Jeep onto the road. Andre sits quietly, sulking, imagines all that he could have bought instead of overpriced organic produce. New Italian loafers. A good bottle of brandy. Maybe a house. The list is long and growing, and, with each additional item, his irritation rises. Then his anger finds use.

"The county manager. Paula Carrothers." Andre silences the radio. "Have we requested anything on her?"

CHAPTER SIX

Too early the next morning, at the Lee family dinner table, Andre recalls the details of his new straw man's background. Traditionally, the firm would interview neighbors, past employers, archenemies, and ex-lovers. People would be amazed at the things their postman knows about them and astonished by how cheaply he'll sell their secrets. But, for this assignment, the firm's investigators are not authorized to travel or to make calls. Too much risk. Too small a community. Too little time. Therefore, the background check is limited to online databases, the records, both intimate and impersonal, purchased for a modest sum.

"I don't see why we can't stick to the one issue." Chalene Lee sits in her husband's lap. Tyler's wife is a cheery, dimple-cheeked woman, twenty-two weeks pregnant with their seventh child. She's birthed five sons, adopted one more, says she loves them all the same. Her background check is pretty clean: secretary of her church's women's missionary society, part-time manager at a laundromat, part-time school bus driver for kids with disabilities. She's popular with parents and with her employers, has but one blemish on her record, an incident six years ago when, driving the bus, she seized the cane of a blind eight-year-old who kept smacking a quadriplegic girl. Chalene's applied for a third job two counties over, third shift at a factory, the nation's second-largest producer of Going Out of Business signs. With another child on the way, the Lees make no secret that they could use the extra cash. Their jobs, six between the two of them, and federal assistance aren't nearly enough. Even their eldest son, an eighteen-year-old high school senior, works part-time, scrapes a grill at a burger joint, shares his wages with Mom and Dad. Chalene says, "When my Tyler talked to Miss Vicki, she didn't say nothing about three initiatives."

Tyler's rubbing her thigh; she's caressing his nape. The past half hour, the two haven't kept their hands to themselves. Kissing. Caressing. Cuddling.

"These three ballot initiatives share a theme. Each says that the government has gotten too big, too out of control." Andre needs his straw man's wife to buy into the campaign, because if he can't convince her, then what hope should he have of convincing anyone else? "Remember, we're trying to rein in government. To take the power away from the bureaucrats and special interests. The local government, the state government, the feds in DC. Someone needs to remind them about American freedom. Someone needs to take a stand."

"Big Brothers at their worst." Tyler pets the small of Chalene's back. "Sweetheart. This is good for everyone. It's good for the county. It's good for us."

Tyler places both hands on his wife's round belly.

Andre shifts his eyes toward Brendan, who stares through a window at Tyler's twin sixteen-year-old sons. Each is the spitting image of their father, and they're wrestling on the front lawn.

Andre shifts his sight again, past another son asleep on the fold-out couch. Finally, Andre sets his gaze above a faux mantel, where hangs a pastel portrait of Jesus. Andre wonders whether Tyler and Chalene have any shame, pawing at each other like love-struck teenagers in front of their Lord and Savior.

"Instead of one ballot initiative, we'll have three. The first is symbolic," Andre says. "The county must post the Bill of Rights at the door of every government building. To remind those government bureaucrats that this country was founded on principles of freedom and liberty."

"Who can argue with that?" Tyler says. "Honey, remember that time the boys got a citation for burning lawn clippings in our own front yard? Private property. Boys weren't causing no harm. And the county comes and gives us a fine."

"And, did you know, the county government is the largest landowner in Carthage? The county owns . . ." Andre looks to Brendan, who's mesmerized by the twins' punching each other's arm. "Brendan? Brendan? Land ownership? The county owns how much land?"

"Oh. Seventy-six thousand, four hundred acres." Brendan calculates. "Which is about one hundred twenty square miles."

Tyler leans back, clicks his tongue, a child king passing judgment from his castle's throne. And look at this castle. Andre's never set foot inside a mobile home, and, truth be told, he's impressed. He supposes he envisioned a camper with spare tires and propane tanks and breakfast nooks that double as beds, but this three-bedroom home, with its starched white curtains and trimmed garden terrace, is larger than his own condo.

"One hundred twenty square miles," Andre says. "The island of Manhattan is only . . ."

Brendan sighs, waits a beat. "Twenty-three square miles."

"If that doesn't scream big government, I don't know what

does." Andre reads Chalene's face, wonders whether the logic has any traction. He likes the comparison: public landownership as a proxy for the size of government. Cut the county's landholding, cut the government's power. "Again, the second initiative is symbolic. One thousand acres. Put the land up for public auction. Anyone can bid. Let the people and free market decide. Lastly, the third initiative—"

Brendan groans, and Andre wishes the kid would keep his displeasure to himself.

"Sweetie, you okay?" Chalene leans toward Brendan. "You look a little pale."

"He always looks like that," Andre says. "Lastly, Paula Carrothers—"

Brendan releases a deep, sorrowful sigh, and, in a flash, Chalene's on her feet. She fills a glass with whole milk, stirs in canned seltzer and chocolate syrup. She claims to have invented this home remedy herself, that her concoction will clear up acne, alleviate joint pain, and settle any stomach. *You think, maybe, I might should get a patent?* She sets the glass atop a placemat, folds a linen napkin, opens a tin of sugar cookies. And then she's back in Tyler's lap.

"Lastly, Paula Carrothers, the county manager, makes ninety-five thousand dollars each year," Andre says. "That's more than three times this county's median family income. If we gathered three ordinary families in Carthage, each with two hardworking parents, she'd make more money than all three families combined."

"That's our tax money, and she's getting rich." A vein throbs in Tyler's throat. "She's not even married. Don't have no kids. She owns that big ol' house on the lake. Drives that fancy car. That ain't fair. I got four jobs."

Chalene's clearly skeptical, which Andre respects. She's

being asked to assume an enormous risk, to publicly challenge her government, to potentially alienate the county's business elite. If she and Tyler fail, they could fall further down the social ladder—which isn't a far fall, but a short one that would surely shatter their bones.

"Listen, Chalene, I understand your hesitancy," Andre says. "But I can't win without your husband. Victoria Boshears, she personally vouched for him. Trust me. I do this for a living, and I don't say this to everyone, really I don't, but I see that Tyler has the common sense and charisma and persona to be a great leader. This initiative is only the beginning. Mark my words, your new future could start right here at your kitchen table."

"You see that in my Tyler?" She blushes, and just like that, Andre knows he's won her support. She brushes her husband's cheek, says, "I see that too."

"Then we're set." Andre draws from his pocket a blank check. "Right now, between you two, you make, what? Six hundred dollars a week? Do I have that right?"

Tyler and Chalene stare at the check.

"Here's a signing bonus." He writes the check for five thousand dollars. "Tyler quits his other jobs and works full-time for the campaign. Chalene can keep her jobs, but the campaign will need her help too. Part-time. After work. Weekends. Especially early on, collecting signatures. I need a wife to stand by her man."

Andre slides the check across the table, watches their eyes widen, sees that all their problems are solved.

"I'll pay Tyler fifteen hundred dollars a week for the next twelve weeks. If we win, you'll get an additional victory bonus." Andre opens his bag, retrieves Chalene's confidentiality agreement. "I've also talked to PISA. If we win, they promise to take care of you. A cushy management position. Good pay. Good health benefits."

Tyler fails to fight back an imbecilic grin. Andre knows, to them, this trifle is a fortune, so he's not surprised when the two celebrate with a passionate kiss. Now Tyler can stop working those four jobs, especially the one at the saloon, which, Andre assumes, will also please Chalene. Andre's curious why a woman of faith would permit her husband to work at a place like that, but he knows the answer, the same reason that the girls work there. No one dreams of working at the Gray Wolf, but opportunities are few in Carthage, and sometimes, you just need the money.

They're stuck in traffic, and Brendan broods behind the wheel. He sulks because he abhors the third initiative, thinks that Paula Carrothers, a career civil servant, should be immune from political attack. Andre knows all this because the kid has said so, once this morning, twice last night.

"How's traffic so bad?" Brendan says. "There're like ten people in Carthage."

Andre rolls down his window, tries to see beyond the crowd and line of cars. "Maybe the circus is in town?"

Brendan lifts a finger, points toward a freckled tween wearing a black velvet suit. At first, Andre assumes the boy's dressed for a special occasion—a wedding, a birthday, maybe a casino-night fund-raiser—but then their Jeep fills with the chime of church bells, and, instantly, he realizes it's Sunday, nine A.M. He counts seven chapels on this block alone, not including the two-thousand-seat megachurch that sits in the sunshine atop a distant hill.

The Jeep crawls forward, reaches a busy intersection, where a hunchbacked senior citizen directs the flow of traffic. Andre doubts she's a cop, a suspicion confirmed by the stitching on her vest, bright glittery text that reads *Crossing Guard for Christ.*

"I want to go to Mass tonight," Brendan says. "There's a cathedral in Greenville. Far enough away. Big congregation. Lots of migrant workers. No one will notice me. Last-chance Mass is at six."

The crossing guard permits a crowd to pass, and as each pedestrian goes by, the old woman receives a warm salutation. Fathers shake her hand. Mothers kiss her cheek. Children hug her leg.

"Tell me, how are you cool with this plan?" Brendan erupts. "Tell me, how is it acceptable that South Carolina has no real campaign finance laws?"

"Fifty different states. Fifty different rules. The laboratories of democracy. Someone has to experiment with the Fisher-Price chemistry set," Andre says. "Listen, B. If you're uncomfortable with our work, that's not a bad thing. There's no shame if you decide to leave. This job isn't for everyone."

Brendan wouldn't be the first intern to walk away mid-campaign. The firm loses new staffers all the time, especially during the federal election season, when the stakes are high, the travel grueling, the tactics amoral. In his first year at the firm, Andre often considered pursuing a different career. In those days, the senior partners assigned him to every team where the black vote mattered, and, in pursuit of a client's agenda, Andre has bribed black pastors, labeled good white men bigots, and run smooth-talking brothers to split the black vote. He doesn't regret his conduct—a win is a win is a win—but he admits that for his people, he might have done more harm than good.

"I don't want to quit. I like the job. I like you." Brendan sinks into his seat. "It's just strange. Lawless. Like the Wild West."

"Are we the good guys? You my deputy?"

"Dre. It's not funny. Outsiders can run a quarter-million-dollar campaign—"

"Three hundred and fifty thousand dollars."

"I'm talking about our campaign."

"Yeah. Me too. I pitched the three-initiative strategy to PISA last night, and they liked it." Andre watches the kid turn red. "What? PISA thinks they could have persuaded the council, if not for the meddling of Paula Carrothers."

"They're willing to pay an extra one hundred thousand dollars just to enact their petty revenge upon a small-time county manager?"

"Don't be silly. They're a multibillion-dollar international corporation. To fuck over Paula Carrothers, they'd be willing to pay millions more."

"One hundred thousand dollars? Do you hear yourself?"

"I know. I should've asked for more. But let's not be greedy."

"All that money. Every single penny. It's corrupt."

"On the bright side, there's plenty of it," Andre says. "In order to win, our team needs to feel that someone else will lose. Elections are a zero-sum game. Winners and losers. This time, Paula Carrothers drew the short straw."

The crowd clears the intersection, and the old woman waves the Jeep across. In silence, Brendan and Andre cruise past the woman, and Andre suppresses his urge to give the bird the finger. They pass another two blocks before stopping, this time beside a chapel, where a sign advertises: TRADITIONAL SERVICE AT 9:00 A.M. CONTEMPORARY SERVICE AT 11:00.

Alone in the attic, Andre plans the next twelve weeks. He appreciates the extra cash that PISA's thrown his way, part of which he's set aside to buy airtime on Carthage's sole local radio station. That station offers twenty-four hours of evangelical talk, a fire-and-brimstone format obsessed with tales of evil and sin.

Right now, the station's broadcasting a lively call-in show, an interfaith panel that features four kinds of Baptists. This week's topiç is the demise of feminine grace.

Despite the views expressed, the show's chatter isn't half-bad. The panel has chemistry, timing, rhythm, and style, with each pastor, like an actor in a troupe, playing a role. There's the bookish one, the funny one, the charming one, the worldly one. Andre thinks to accept their invitation to call in and join the conversation. *Hello? Am I on the air? First-time caller, longtime listener. My boss, an older Irish lady, she uses profanity all the time. I mean all the time. She curses like a one-armed pirate caught in a typhoon. What the fuck's a good Christian to do?* The thought tickles Andre, but he saves the prank for another day.

Gin in hand, Andre studies Brendan's voter database. The kid's done a decent job, but the database is shallow. They'll need more precise and discriminating information about each voter. One Internet service provider has a monopoly in Carthage, and, for a price, the provider will sell intimate information about its clients. The provider will also install custom tracking cookies on its customers' computers, the same tech that empowers merchants to tailor online ads based on a person's web searches. For an additional fee, the provider, which bundles the Internet with cable and phone, offers a package that includes digital fingerprinting, spyware that supplies a buyer with precious data mined from each client's e-mail, texts, television, and cell phone. The personal information to which the campaign will have access is virtually limitless.

The panel takes a break for words from sponsors. A missionary appeals for donations to buy solar-powered audio Bibles for illiterate African orphans. A British financier claims that smart investors prefer silver. And a barbecue shack on Carthage's east side promises discounts for families who proclaim *Jesus saves* at the time of their order.

That night, Andre wakes, soaked and trembling, like a drowning man pulled from an icy sea. He can't remember the whole dream, only the final image: his head in Cassie's lap, her soft touch against his cheek. The image is a fraud, a scene born not of memory but of hope, and, as his senses sharpen, he realizes he's been tricked, made blissful one moment and heartbroken the next. He hopes that if he drifts back to sleep, then he'll slip back inside his dream. It's a fool's fantasy, but in this moment, the dream represents the only possible future that could ever bring him joy. He lies in bed, wide awake and frustrated. The image has faded, vanished from his mind, left in its wake the same abject loneliness he's known each night since Cassie left.

He spins his feet onto the floor, bathes his toes in a ray of chalky moonlight. One glass of gin and another. He picks up his phone. The time is two in the morning—Cassie's probably still up—and if he doesn't hear her voice, doesn't express how he feels, then he fears that his dream will never come true. They haven't talked since their breakup—and God, he misses her voice—but he knows a phone call now will do more harm than good. Besides, what if she's with her new man, a relationship he'll never understand? He gets she needs to rebound, needs to explore her options, needs not to sleep alone. He needs that too. But if he lives a thousand years, he'll never understand why she picked her new man. The Redskins experienced their worst season in five years, and her guy, a Canadian at that, couldn't get ten seconds on the field.

On the verge of a panic attack, which seems to happen more often these days, he paces his bedroom, notices that the house is dead silent. In the kitchen, in the attic, he can't find Brendan, and he wonders whether the kid returned from Mass. He doesn't worry that Brendan is bleeding in a ditch but fears that his young apprentice, disgusted by their campaign, has bought a ticket and flown back home. A quick search of the house and he finds Brendan on the porch, leaning against a square column, cigarette ablaze in his hand. Brendan brings his forefinger to his own lips, points toward a naked willow and an outcropping of shale. Andre narrows his gaze and, at first, feels a moment's frustration, blind to whatever his attention is being drawn to. But then he sees a flurry of movement, and three cottontail rabbits, blended into the overgrown garden, bounce into view. A sobering wind cuts his face, and Andre takes a seat atop the porch, arms folded against the cold. He watches a snowflake float onto his lap, and he's grateful that tonight Brendan is here.

PART II

THE CANVASS

CHAPTER SEVEN

Seven seconds left, and Brazil has the ball. The score, 2–1, favors Ireland, but Brazil's bone-thin striker storms the field, propels the ball between a pair of sluggish defenders. For a moment, it feels inevitable that the score will tie, but this ball is not fated to pass Ireland's goalie, who flies through the air, arms spread wide, and smashes his forehead against the ball. The video game resets, and Brendan breaks into dance, a few choice moves he's choreographed for this very event. The performance is a sort of hip-hop-infused *Riverdance*, looks like an epileptic rat stuck in a glue trap. Proof that while Brendan Fitzpatrick possesses an array of talents, dance is not among them.

"Switch controllers," Andre says. "Mine is broken."

"How much do you owe me? Five losses in a row. Let me get my calculator." Brendan checks his phone. "Oi, Dre. It's nearly four thirty. We're supposed to meet Tyler in five minutes."

"Again?" Andre looks outside. The sun won't rise for three hours. "Shit."

"I'll load up the Jeep." Brendan grabs a sweater. "Meet downstairs in ten?"

Half an hour later, the Jeep races into the darkness, passes two hunters in orange vests who march along the road. Some twenty miles to Tyler's home, time enough for Andre to assemble four signature-collection kits. Grunt work that, in any other campaign, an intern would do, bundling glossy pamphlets that explain the nexus between small government and American freedom. These he binds with star-spangled ribbon, then slips the set inside one of four denim bags, made in Ecuador, that bear a banner that crosses the American and rebel flags.

He removes the plastic that seals four fresh ledgers, confirms that each page features the text of all three initiatives. Andre pats his breast pocket, checks beneath his seat. Brendan says, "Glove box."

There, Andre finds his pen with erasable ink. He scans each ledger's first page, scribbles inside one dozen fake names. In his experience, a voter is far more likely to sign a petition if the voter believes that the initiative already enjoys popular support. No one likes to sign a petition first, or second, or eleventh for that matter, but every red-blooded American dreams of joining a noble political cause. He'll erase these fake names later.

The laser-jet printer, powered by a cigarette-lighter socket and secure as a baby in a car seat, spits out lists of names, addresses, and corresponding bar codes. These names are today's targets, the fifty registered voters whose signatures each canvasser must collect. Brendan has combined polling data with his index of voters, creating an algorithm that assigns each of Carthage's sixteen thousand voters an individualized score between 1 and 100. The score predicts the likelihood that the voter will support the liberty initiatives. Three weeks into the canvass, the algorithm is a success. In the first four days, canvassers solicited each registrant assigned a score between 90 and 100, with a 96 percent success rate. The following days, the team approached voters assigned scores between 80 and 90, and then 70 and 80, and then 60 and 70. If only life were that simple: friends, lovers, strangers on the street, each with their own compatibility score.

Brendan says, "Door hangers."

"Door hangers!" Andre reaches beneath his seat, retrieves a box of door hangers embossed with the details of the campaign's website and social media. Each door hanger features a quote from a founding father, hawkish lines that summarize an essential principle of American liberty. *Rebellion to Tyrants is Obedience to God. —Benjamin Franklin.* Andre's favorite door hanger includes: *Only kings and fools will live for tyranny, and only the brave and righteous will die for freedom.* Wise words from the Honorable Thomas Peyton Whitford, a fictitious founding father entirely of Andre's creation.

"I feel like we're forgetting something," Andre says. "Didn't we make a checklist?"

"We left it back at the house," Brendan says. "Maybe we should make a second checklist to remind us about the first."

They pull onto a utility road that runs between forested hills and feels like an entryway into nowhere. Lonesome rusted trailers sit atop concrete slabs, and an occasional flat, small house is abandoned, with uncut grass, a foreclosure sign, and boarded-up windows.

Two more miles and Brendan parks across from the Lee home, a modest lot with no neighbors for miles. Tyler, scowling, sits in an idling truck whose grille is ready for battle: stainless-steel guard, mounted floodlight, winch spooled with cable. Tyler wears his campaign sweatshirt, navy, snug, the logo atop white cursive script: *Carthage County, Proud and Free.* Brendan says, "Cell phones."

"What?"

"You forgot the cell phones."

Andre removes four custom phones from the shoebox at his feet. Each is loaded with an app that allows a canvasser to scan a bar code assigned to each individual target. To Andre, this app is a godsend, allows him to analyze real-time signature-collection data, to confirm who's bringing in names and who's not.

"Ready?" Brendan dons his parka, a pair of thick thermal gloves. One thing about the kid: he fears the cold. The slightest chill and he mews like a kitten caught in a storm. "We rush the street on three?"

"Why is that asshole in his truck?" Andre gestures toward Tyler. "He could just as easily be warm inside his house. Drinking coffee, watching television. But no. Every day. He sits out here, waiting, sulks like a spoiled child."

Andre tries not to be petty, but these past three weeks, he's constantly regretted his decision to ask Tyler to join his team. Yes, Tyler's polite and respectful, and he always has a stupid smile on his face. But in Tyler's eyes Andre sees something dangerous, something mischievous, something a little too sly. Tyler obtains the fewest signatures, for which he always has an excuse. And worse yet, he's quick to take offense when Andre ignores his equally impractical and shitty ideas.

"Do me a favor," says Andre, crossing the street. "Don't apologize."

"What are you talking about?"

"Every time we're late, you apologize to him. Sometimes you apologize three times in a row. *I'm sorry. So sorry. We won't let it happen again.* You're pathological."

"Maybe the problem is we're always late."

"Tyler works for us. We pay him well for his time. His time is ours to waste."

Tyler leaves his truck huffing and puffing. His sweatshirt makes him look like a tool, like his wife dressed him this morning, both of which are true. Right now, across town, Tyler's canvassers are waiting at a local diner, where, each morning, Tyler briefs and equips his team. The meeting at the diner is Tyler's idea, an act of public relations, a move to strengthen the perception that this ragtag campaign is his own creation.

"Sorry we're late. So sorry. Real sorry." Brendan shivers through his scarf. "Can we talk in the garage?"

Inside, standing beside a workbench, Tyler says, "Don't know how many names we'll catch today. It being Youth Day and all."

Andre looks to Brendan, and they both blink.

Tyler's face shines. For once, he's the keeper of knowledge unknown to others. He clearly savors the moment, takes his time to explain that Youth Day is a Carthage tradition, the one day each year in which the law allows minors to hunt without tags or licenses. Kids under sixteen can hunt on public and private lands, can each kill one regulation deer.

"My father took me, and his father took him," Tyler says. "I take my sons every year. And one day, my sons will—"

"We get it," Andre says. "This youth hunting day—"

"It's just Youth Day, brother," Tyler says. "Don't y'all have Youth Day where y'all from?"

"Sounds to me"—Brendan can't resist—"like Take Your Daughter to Work Day, but, you know, without daughters. And with guns."

Brendan and Andre make each other laugh, but Tyler is undeterred, shares tales of Youth Days past, silly melodramatic parables about emotionally bereft fathers bonding with deer-slaying sons.

"Local businesses give prizes," Tyler says. "Biggest buck, most coyote pelts—"

"You can hunt coyotes on Youth Day?" Brendan says.

"Folks can hunt coyotes year-round," Tyler says. "Coyotes are a huge problem. Woman down the road, she owned one of those small dogs, you know, a shitshoe—"

"Shih tzu?" Brendan asks.

"Damn coyote snatched the shitshoe from her backyard. Right in front of her. Most folks around here bait traps. Some use antifreeze, but that takes a while to work. I use my own brew." He points toward a low shelf, between boxes of old VHS tapes, where a stoneware jug bears a skull and crossbones drawn sloppily in purple marker. "A few drops on chicken bones. Put the trap in the trees right outside the property line. Brother, problem solved."

Brendan has a line of coyote questions—no matter the subject, the kid has questions—and Andre stops paying attention. Instead, he calculates the harm this silly holiday will cause. Tyler's canvassing team is four: Tyler, Chalene, their eighteen-year-old son, and Tyler's slow-witted friend. Andre needs each in the field. A single absence could hurt his plans.

"I'll leave to you and your people to decide whether to work on Youth Day," Andre says. "But today, and today only, we'll pay your people double. Four dollars per signature."

"That's mighty generous," Tyler says. "But Youth Day is our heritage. It's sacred and—"

"Fine. Triple. Six dollars a name. Today only. Usual verification. Tomorrow, the rate returns to two dollars."

"Well." Tyler purses his lips, grabs his nape. "If it were up to me—"

"Also, for your people that decide to work, lunch is on you." Andre shows a roll of twenties, peels off two hundred dollars, of which, he knows, Tyler will spend forty and pocket the rest. Andre hates that he must bribe his own straw man. "Get your people something special. Not pizzas or burgers or that fried fish shit at the gas station that everyone around here loves."

"Reckon missing one Youth Day won't end the world." Tyler takes the denim pouches. "Shit, I worked two shifts last Christmas."

Tyler releases a deep belly laugh, and soon enough, all three are laughing deeply, as though they're old friends.

The Carolina Casa, a fusion of Southern and Mexican, is the region's fastest-growing fast-food chain. The meals are cheap, swiftly prepared, available at all hours of the day or night, but to Andre, the Casa's spongy, brackish, warmed-over fare represents all that he hates about dining on the road. This Carolina Casa caters to the students who attend Nathan Bedford Forrest High School, which is located one block down the road. All the students must do is pass beneath the roadside billboard on which a nearly nude blonde hugs a chrome pole: *Ladies! College can wait. Earn up to $1,000 tonight!*

Brendan loves the Casa, can't get enough, and the kid's recent video game victory entitles him to spoils, among them gold, glory, and the choice of where to dine for breakfast when they're running too late for the kid to cook.

"Maybe Javier's hoecakes." Brendan reads the Casa's drive-thru menu. "What are you getting?"

Andre settles into his seat, opens the newspaper. The front page features a photo of last year's Youth Day editor's choice: a twelve-year-old boy, plump and cherry-cheeked, balanced atop a bent knee, scoped rifle slung over his shoulder. The boy's holding a slain buck by the antlers, a buck so beautiful that Andre regrets the creature met such a fate. Pictures like this abound inside the paper. Adorable boys, some as young as six, with bloodstained hands.

He struggles to understand this quirky community's sensibilities, the way strangers narrow their gaze to ask if he's from town, and, if so, which church he attends. Last week, a flock of sparrows fell from the sky, at least a thousand dead birds raining across a half-mile radius, bodies pelting rooftops and car tops and the elementary school playground at recess. The local paper interviewed a university professor, the ornithologist swearing that such phenomena are not unusual in nature. No one in Carthage believed him. Some believed it was evidence of a vast conspiracy. Some believed it was a message from God. Everyone agreed that the media and government would never tell the people the truth.

"Let me guess what you'll order." Brendan points toward the drive-thru menu. "You want coffee. No sugar. No milk. Black and bitter."

Andre worries that, between his poor diet and booze, he's gaining weight. Already his clothes don't fit quite right. His entire life, he's never not been lean, never once worried about his shape. Now he worries his colleagues will make fun. Last year, a junior partner, a marathon runner, developed a tumor in her leg, a cancerous mass that took surgeons six hours to remove. Unable to walk or run, she gained thirty pounds. Tried her best, but she couldn't shake the weight. Folks around the firm tease behind her back, but to her face, everyone says she wears the weight well.

"Come on, Dre," Brendan said. "Pick something."

"Why do you care?"

"Because yesterday you ate all my Cancun Cinnabites," Brendan says. "This time, I'm not going to share."

"Do what you want." Andre's tablet chimes twice, and his forefinger slides across its screen, picks the app that monitors the progress of each canvasser. Chalene Lee, in the field for five minutes, has already logged ten names. At six dollars per name, she may set a firm record for the most cash earned by one canvasser in a single day. He scans the app's map feature, sees the exact location of each member of the team. To his relief, all four have deployed to the field. For the past half hour, he's feared a mutiny, feared that Tyler's team would think he's Youth Day's version of Ebenezer Scrooge. Now, with the team in the field, nothing short of a Youth Day miracle, Andre feels relief. God bless us, every one.

Carthage County's only superstore is busier than a mall the day before Christmas. The time's not yet six thirty, but this early, the parking lot is full, with fathers and sons wearing orange vests over camo, passing through the double doors, shopping bags in hand, boxes of ammo tucked beneath their arms. From this spot, on the fringe of the parking lot, hidden beside an open dumpster, Andre and Brendan have a clear view of Chalene in her jeans and campaign sweatshirt. She's the lone canvasser not collecting signatures door-to-door. Instead, she's set up shop here, beside the front door of this bustling superstore, a move that's proven surprisingly successful, perhaps because passersby pity her, this doughy pregnant woman who begs for signatures outside in the cold.

About Chalene Lee, Andre has yet to make up his mind. To be sure, she's bright and gracious, with an enviable work ethic, and now, having said her piece, she's abandoned all complaint about the three-initiative strategy. She's the best signature collector on Tyler's team, averages forty names each weekday, scored three times that many last weekend. Andre suspects she could play a larger role in the campaign, but he worries about the inevitable clash, the moment he gives an instruction that conflicts with the tenets of the Good Book. He doesn't expect to ask Chalene to kill, or to steal, or to make a graven image, but campaigns are a tricky business, and he'd prefer to keep his options open.

"Dre?" Brendan chews a hoecake. "I want to ask a question."

Andre readies for a fresh wave of campaign-finance-related objections. The kid still struggles with the morality of their vocation. To be fair, Brendan doesn't bemoan their tactics every day. Indeed, four days have passed since the kid last lent voice to complaint. These days, Brendan's starting to grasp the political reality, that Americans enjoy lamenting the role of corporate money in politics but that no one cares enough to change the rules. So now the kid's stuck in this precarious position where he's asking the next logical question, that is, whether there's any real point to complaining. The answer to which, of course, is no.

"It's okay if you don't want to answer, and if it's offensive . . . You know what? Never mind," Brendan says. "I need to get some sleep. Forget I said anything. I'm tired. Aren't you tired?"

Andre sips his Carolina Casa coffee, scalds the roof of his mouth.

"I take it back. I'm going to ask. But, you know, I'm just asking. So please don't take offense." Brendan finds a bottled water in a backseat cooler, loosens the cap, hands the bottle to Andre. "Do black people hunt?"

"What?"

"I've never heard of black people hunting. I've never seen a photo or movie with a black hunter. For that matter, I can't think of a single black person who's known for hunting."

"Can you name a single white person known for hunting?"

"Orion. Teddy Roosevelt. Elmer Fudd," Brendan says. "I'm not saying . . . it's not like a racist stereotype. Like black people can't swim. Or black people don't pay taxes. Or black people—"

"Maybe you should stop."

"Perhaps it's an economics thing. Hunting, not taxes," Brendan says. "Maybe African Americans view hunting as a luxury. You know. An expensive form of recreation. The guns. The ammo. The licenses. Plus, butchering and keeping the meat. Those aren't insignificant costs in time, money, labor, especially when you consider the grocer sells cheap ground beef that probably won't make you sick. But, on the other hand—"

"Why do you always have another hand?"

"This town's dirt-poor. Youth Day's an official holiday. They cancel school."

The kid keeps speculating, something about the fallacy of Giffen goods and the Irish famine, but Andre's now distracted. Into the neighboring parking space has backed a police SUV, a jet-black paramilitary-style vehicle more appropriate for a war zone than a bucolic county in western South Carolina. From their position, the cops can see straight inside Andre's Jeep, and though he has broken no law, and though years have passed since he last felt the grip of a policeman's cuff, the mere proximity of these two white men, dressed in black, feels like a blade at his throat. He runs down each way that these cops might cause trouble. He trusts that Brendan doesn't keep weed in the Jeep, that papers in the glove box will prove that the rental's not stolen. But the technology in the back seat—a printer, a scanner, two tablets, and a laptop—all this, he fears, is too flashy for Carthage. Around here, tech savvy might amount to probable cause.

Andre considers his options, resolves that he has but one clear choice. He needs for Brendan to drive away, and he needs for that to happen now without an elaborate academic discussion, without a protest from the rich white kid, whom he considers his friend but who has never—and probably will never—experience a humiliation like a cop's arbitrary stop-and-frisk.

"Maybe it's historical. Maybe black Americans, in the Jim Crow days, were forbidden by law from owning guns?" Brendan picks at crumbs in his lap. "Or maybe black people were forbidden from hunting on public land. You think Youth Day was segregated? Dre, you ever hunt?"

He wants to say, *Brendan, I'm a former felon, I'm prohibited by law from touching a gun.* Instead, he takes a sip of coffee. "Fuck, Brendan."

"I'm sorry. I didn't mean to offend. I'm tired, I—"

"Not that, jackass," Andre says. "This coffee is shit. Can we go someplace where I can get a decent cup?"

"You're such a baby." Brendan licks his fingers, puts the Jeep in gear. The Jeep coasts through the crowded lot as Andre keeps his eyes on the cops, the Jeep traveling a quick half mile before Andre feels at ease.

CHAPTER EIGHT

Youth Day is ending; the sun is setting, and halfway across the county, Tyler Lee and his team wrap up their canvass. Brendan and Andre, each eager to see his own bed, must idle the next hour, and the kid prefers to wait here at the abandoned train depot. The kid likes to see the coyotes and boars and bears that wander around the rails. If he and the kid are lucky, they'll see the pack of wild dogs that sunbathe on platform four, or the family of mean-ass raccoons that have also made the station their home and with whom the wild dogs are at perpetual war. Until wildlife comes, the kid, on his tablet, perfects websites for fake organizations that have endorsed the liberty initiatives. The Atlanta-based Council of Christian Commerce. The Charleston-based Society for American Freedom. These sock puppets mingle online with Carthage's small-business owners, offering *exciting opportunities*, free online promotion and office-supply discounts and inclusion inside an award-winning regional business directory. All the small-business owner must do is endorse liberty. E-mail some friends. Add the campaign's logo to their website.

Brendan double-taps his tablet to load the campaign website, which, like the public perception of the campaign itself, eschews the sophisticated or flashy. The home page is simple: a nice tight picture of Tyler, Chalene, all six sons, each dressed in their Sunday best. The family stands before Carthage County Junior High, the brick-and-mortar public school that the county's elite abandoned decades ago to spite a federal court desegregation order.

The site sees slow yet steady traffic, most of which, the IP addresses suggest, originates outside South Carolina. The website's *Contact Us* page allows visitors to submit a private message to Tyler, but, in reality, it's read by Brendan, who sends a form response. Most messages are spam: pledges of better sex or offers of assistance by political amateurs. The site also receives a steady flow of rants from political fanatics, angry men—always angry, always men—who write long, meandering manifestos rooted in fantasy, misinformation, paranoia, and fear.

Message review is customarily a tedious task assigned to the team's most unpopular intern, but Andre knows the kid derives a voyeuristic pleasure from reading the histrionics. By a six-to-one ratio, these fanatics support the liberty initiatives, with the lone dissenters, too often honest-to-God anarchists, adamant that Carthage should adopt natural law.

"'Slaughter them all.'" Brendan reads today's first message. "'Patriots will raise a twelve-gauge against those liars on the Supreme Court, those usurpers at the UN, and the Jews that run the Federal Preserve. People will not tolerate oppression from Washington overlords.'"

"We should warn the Jewish preservers."

"The message is signed Sherman Camp, DDS," Brendan says. "How can this guy call himself a patriot?"

"Love your country, loathe your government. What could be more American than that?"

"Think he's a real dentist?"

"If you're going to lie, why would you claim dentistry?" Andre says. "In your entire life, have you ever heard anyone say, *That guy's a dentist, so he must know what he's talking about*?"

Andre's surprised by the lack of local reaction. He would expect praise or protest in the local paper, perhaps a letter to the editor or column or editorial, but Carthage County, thus far, has ignored his effort. Interest in the initiatives should be low at this stage, but in his experience, each town, no matter the size, has a community of vocal do-gooders obsessed with local government. By now, the campaign should've captured their attention.

Brendan reads another message. "'The radical progressive experiment must end. It makes us soft, and we cannot afford it. Cut government. Cut waste. Cut all unconstitutional institutions. Keep only what's necessary to preserve order and protect property. Let individuals choose the services they want.'"

Andre laughs. "So does that mean I could buy my own local police force?"

"Why not?" Brendan says. "You're already buying your own local election."

"Sure, make jokes, but right up until this jackass's house burns down, he'll complain at every city council meeting about the waste of funding a firehouse," Andre says. "But let his house catch fire, I'll bet you, the asshole will shame the entire city for having too few firemen. You sure there's no local message?"

Andre thinks, perhaps, folks don't take the campaign seriously. After all, who in Carthage would ever expect Tyler Lee, of all people, to collect fifteen hundred signatures in ten days? Tyler's a high school dropout who's worked mostly backbreaking, bone-wearying jobs. He's the last person one might peg to start a political revolution.

"You don't feel a little bad about the initiatives?" Brendan says. "People around here love hunting. It's an essential part of the culture and the economy. You're asking them to support an initiative that's against their own interest."

Self-interest. Desperate people are terrible at assessing their own self-interest. Last night, Andre navigated the website on which insurers upload Hector's medical records. Hector, this past week, attended three appointments with his physical therapist. The physical therapist's notes caught Andre's eye: *Patient's wife seeks recommendation on alternative therapies. Particularly electroshock. Claims to have a friend who saw this cure ALS.*

He wasn't surprised. Vera has never trusted modern medicine, is prone to embrace random ghetto quackery over a doctor's learned judgment. Two days ago, during their most recent conversation, she shared another therapy idea, one she swore she'd researched extensively. Gold-tipped acupuncture and unpasteurized milk. She quoted straight from a website that offered, as a part of an annual subscription, a weekly newsletter entitled *Medical Marvels That White-Owned Multinationals Don't Want Black Folks to Know.*

"Self-interest is never simple." Andre's phone vibrates against his hip. "Your grandmother's a millionaire a couple times over, and she's still pissed at Reagan for cutting her taxes."

He checks his phone. He's missed a text from Tyler, who says he's running an hour late. The message, complete with three exclamation points and a smiley face, is presumably childish payback for this morning's tardiness. Andre grabs his tablet. "Bet his lazy ass didn't even meet his daily quota."

"I don't mean to start a fight, but maybe if you were nicer . . ."

"To Tyler?"

"I'm just saying the ancient Greeks had this concept of *thymos*," Brendan says. "It's the fundamental human desire to feel respected and recognized. Everyone wants their opinions taken seriously. Everyone wants to feel valued."

Andre studies today's canvass results, concludes that each signature collector has pulled his or her own weight—everyone, that is, except for Tyler. Today Tyler's collected a total of twenty-four names, nowhere near the fifty-five collected by each of the two other canvassers who went door-to-door, nowhere near Chalene, who, stationed outside the superstore, collected a canvass high of one hundred fifty-three.

The television broadcasts Paula Carrothers, the bone-thin six-foot-tall administratrix with razor-sharp cheeks and thick tortoiseshell glasses. She testifies before the county council, the topic: preparations for the biennial reenactment of the Battle of Silver Creek. She suggests, in response to a recent trend of post-reenactment brawls, that the county council allocate extra funds for security, for an ambulance, for overtime to pay the firefighters who, last time, spent half the night extinguishing piles of soiled Union uniforms drenched in diesel and set ablaze. The council agrees with a brief, unanimous voice vote, and with the bang of a gavel, Paula Carrothers has her money.

Andre presses pause, syncs his tablet with the television. This footage, now three years old, will make excellent film, yet another clip in a series in which the county council showers their precious county manager with bundles of cash. He plans to string these five-second clips together to make a digital ad, a montage of Carrothers requesting extraordinary sums. Fifty thousand dollars here, twenty-five thousand dollars there. Perhaps he'll have a little fun, maybe auto-tune each request, maybe mix in the sound effect of a scratched record over the *cha-ching* of a cash register. The size and frequency of the funding, he hopes, will leave voters appalled that their elected leaders handle their hard-earned tax dollars with so little care.

By now, he's reviewed archived footage from Paula Carrothers's first seven years in office, has three more years to go. Thus far, he's been impressed. In her public testimony, Carrothers is consistently thoughtful, framing each issue in terms of how best to serve her community, a polished and considerate public servant if ever he's seen one. She's never without a flag pin, and at the start of each council meeting, when all rise to say the pledge of allegiance, Paula Carrothers pledges a little louder than the rest.

Andre advances the video, starts to study the next county council meeting, this one, like all the others, opened with a guest-led prayer. The newly crowned Miss Carthage County, a twenty-year-old redhead wearing too much blush, reads from inside her bejeweled journal, hands shaking, voice aquiver. She asks the good Lord to watch over these proceedings, to bless the five members of the council with wisdom and courage, but clearly Miss Carthage County is in way over her head. She mumbles, breathes heavily into the mic, trips over words longer than two syllables. The rambling prayer, which feels as though it will never end, is difficult to watch, and Andre, who, like the members of the council, has begun to cringe, wonders what thoughts pass through Paula Carrothers's head. The county manager has a bachelor's degree in finance and public administration, earned a scholarship to graduate with honors from the nation's finest women's college, and now, here she is, forced to suffer the stuttering prayer of a svelte debutante wearing a tiara and a sash.

The beauty queen's rambling becomes unbearable, and Andre removes his earphones. The attic, cold and damp, has the faint smell of burnt plastic—has another surge protector failed?—and a soft hiss remains unexplained. Brendan sits at his L-shaped desk, his back to the flat-screen on which Paula Carrothers appears. The kid's hunkered down with a six-pack of energy drinks and a bag of pumpkin seeds. He's reviewing signatures to confirm that each signatory is, indeed, eligible to endorse the petition. If the signatory is ineligible, the campaign will still submit the name to the county—never know, maybe the clerk won't catch the mistake—but Andre doesn't include these problematic names in his internal tally, which, today, surpassed sixteen hundred, more than needed to appear on the ballot, but far less than required to impress Mrs. Fitz.

His phone rings. It's Vera. He's not sure he can persuade her against alternative therapies, but he can, perhaps, buy some time. Maybe he should channel the ancient Greeks, pretend that Vera's proposal deserves equal consideration. But first, he'll say, he wants to talk face-to-face, maybe ask questions of the friend of a friend who recommended electroshock. Anything to ensure that Vera won't strap his brother to a DieHard until after Andre makes his case. Maybe he'll take the shuttle to DC next weekend. The campaign has plenty of money, but he doesn't have nearly enough time.

CHAPTER NINE

The firm's software-development team has created a Liberty App that supporters can download to stay connected with the campaign. Rally schedules. Streaming videos. Social networking updates. *Join Carthage County, Proud and Free.* The app is generic, an interface seen before, and he wonders whether it will appeal to Carthage's young. Thus far, the online campaign hasn't gotten much traction. He's budgeted another ten thousand dollars for online ads. Every time a Carthaginian uses a search engine, entering terms like *jobs* or *loans*, *Powerball* or *credit score*, the search engine returns a campaign banner ad.

Andre checks his watch, thinks how best to pass the time. He's come to loathe Sunday mornings, the holy hours that he spends alone while Brendan attends Mass and all of Carthage attends church. Already he's completed the day's administrative tasks: written an optimistic letter to PISA, e-mailed a candid status report to Mrs. Fitz. He's grateful that the state doesn't have any reporting requirements. In federal elections, the law requires that candidates and PACs appoint a treasurer, a legally bound accountant who must, under penalty of prison time, track each dime raised or spent. But for South Carolina local elections, where federal campaign finance rules don't apply, and where state legislators eschew all political regulation, Andre answers for spending only to PISA and Mrs. Fitz.

So Andre pursues another distraction, a series of mindless searches that inevitably turn toward Cassie. The results include positive reviews about her new debut album. He selects a video interview, two days old, conducted by a local jazz legend, a beret-wearing saxophonist sporting a goatee. Cassie shines. She's smart, funny, sexy. Her answers are playful yet polished; she speaks with an alluring confidence.

He's starting to write her an e-mail, a flirtatious congratulatory note, *Cass, I knew you had it in you, girl,* when, six minutes into the interview, she tells the jazzman that she's engaged and pregnant. This pronouncement, at first, Andre assumes he mishears. *She has an engagement at the Pageant?* So he replays the five-second bit again and again, each time, breath held, ear pressed against the laptop speaker. Perhaps she misspoke. Perhaps she's joking. Deep down he knows neither is true. He sits back, plays the video to its end, where, as though with the last twist of the knife, the jazzman asks whether she is now truly happy, a question to which the woman Andre loves answers: *For the first time in my life.*

On Instagram is confirmation, an engagement announcement and photo: Cassie, glamorous in white elbow-length gloves and a navy gown; her new fiancé, the hatchet-faced Canadian with a Prince Charming chin, his arms wrapped around her. He reads the page again and again, recognizing each word but failing to comprehend their collective meaning. She's four months pregnant—she doesn't look so—and, though she left him three months ago, Andre knows this child is not his. The night he bent his knee, six months ago in the shadow of Abraham Lincoln,

Cassie proposed a sexless engagement, claimed that celibacy would enhance their wedding night. Had she been unfaithful even then? On the night she wept and said she would love him forever?

He strains to piece together the chronology of her betrayal, and his memory sticks on the last time he saw her, at a crowded Japanese teahouse, where, he now realizes, she lied to his face, ended their engagement under false pretenses. On the back of a sheet of music with a trio of blank staves, she'd handwritten his faults, flaws that included drinking and cynicism, moodiness and short temper, pessimism and mistrustfulness. She looked him square in the eye, claimed, as he choked down grief, that she could not, would not, marry a man who could never know joy. But each painful personal accusation, he now realizes, was a lie, a pitch to pacify a heartbroken sucker. He'd sat there, pleaded, begged, apologized for the way he thought, for the way he acted, *for the way I am.* He promised to change, to become the man whom she wanted him to be, and when she refused, flat-out said that she'd made up her mind, he slammed his palm against the bamboo table, shouting, *I am not too sad for a woman who sings the blues.* She slid his ring across the table and rose to leave, bumping the table's edge, her black tea spilling over her saucer and staining the ivory sheet of music that cataloged his faults.

"Dre? You've seen it?" Brendan, in a linen suit, stands behind him. "Dre, man, you okay? You look a little . . ."

"Seen what?"

"You sure you're okay?"

"Seen what?"

Brendan tosses his keys on the table, spreads today's newspaper beside the keys, leafing through the Sunday edition, which continues this week's coverage of Youth Day. It is a photo album of adorable white children with dead deer. Nothing, so far, surprises. Brendan stops on the penultimate page, and, at first, Andre's unsure on which story his attention should focus. Then he spots, in the lower quarter of the left page, a black-and-white photo of Tyler, arms folded, proud atop the courthouse steps. The headline reads: LOCAL CONSERVATIVE SEEKS REFORM.

"How many times did we tell him?"

"Several times," Brendan says. "No media without your approval."

"Did you know about this?"

"Me? I'm literally with you all day," Brendan says. "But, Dre, if you read it, it's not all that bad. He actually does—"

Andre snatches the paper. The story is not long, an editorial afterthought at best. To Andre's surprise, Tyler stays on message. Tyler speaks about liberty, and the founders, and the founders' love of liberty, and the need to take his country back from out-of-control despots. He says the government has given up on locals like him, that no one in government listens to the common man. For the liberty campaign, Tyler takes sole credit, says that these initiatives were inspired by his love of scripture and history. Collecting signatures, Tyler boasts, is the most patriotic way one can spend Youth Day, because, as he articulates, *Liberty is all about the future and our children and stuff like that, brother.* The feature swallows whole the campaign's statistics about county land ownership, publishes the salary of Paula Carrothers, who, for this story, declined comment. The feature is lopsided. The feature is effusive. The feature is borderline propaganda. In short, the feature is perfect.

Brendan breaks the silence. "Maybe we should remind him—"

Andre snatches the keys from the table, charges through the door, newspaper tucked beneath his arm. The kid scurries behind, shouting, stuttering, down two flights of stairs and out the front door, where Andre turns, clasps the kid's shoulder to ensure his words are felt. Andre says that he will speak to Tyler alone, promises to return once the necessary business is done.

The road to Tyler's house is empty, and yet, as he passes each milepost, Andre feels an intense insecurity behind the wheel. He worries as the rain falls in flashes—waves gushing down his windshield—but he pushes forward, tries to steady the Jeep as he bounces wildly with the rise and fall of the slippery road. He passes familiar stone walls and rickety bridges, short pines and dead oaks, abandoned pickups and a prairie of wilted grass and two vultures feasting upon the carcass of a mule.

At last, the Jeep reaches the Lee home, where, on the covered porch, Tyler and Chalene, swaying in a swing, hold hands. The two wear their Sunday best, Chalene in a powder-blue dress with a Puritan collar, Tyler in khakis, clip-on tie, short-sleeve white shirt. Andre marches across the lawn, plants his feet on the front step. Chalene's face brightens, and, as she rises, clutching her pregnant belly, she says, "Dre. Sweetie. You're early. You want a fried bologna sandwich?"

"What the fuck was so hard to understand?" Andre pitches the newspaper into Tyler's chest. "No interviews without my permission."

"Hot damn, brother. It came out today? In the Sunday edition?" Tyler opens the newspaper, finds his picture. "They said Monday or Tuesday! Baby, come see. I look good."

Chalene wipes her hands, takes the paper with care. This article is the first time her husband's name has appeared in print except for the two DUIs once listed in the crime beat. No wonder she wants to preserve the article: public affirmation that by marrying this jackass, she didn't make a terrible choice. Chalene looks up. "Andre, can I get you sweet tea? You look like you got some sun."

Andre says, "Who gave you permission to give an interview?"

"Whoa, brother! They came to me," Tyler says. "Trust me. This is good. I thought you'd like the surprise."

"We should go inside," Chalene says. "I think the storm's gettin' worse."

"Baby, check on the boys. I'll be behind you," Tyler says. She hesitates but, after Tyler kisses her cheek, retreats inside. "Like I said, reporter came to me."

"You knew better."

"Dre, come on, read it," Tyler says. "This is a good thing."

"You're fired."

Tyler stands, raises his chin to reveal a thick, hairy Adam's apple that bounces with each hard swallow. He steps forward, close enough so that Andre can smell the tobacco tucked beneath his lip. Andre prays this asshole takes a swing, hopes this white boy will throw the first punch. Andre, more than anything, wants a reason to whoop someone's ass.

"Brother, look at the paper. I am this campaign." Tyler spits chew into the bushes. "You fire me, I'll go straight back to the paper, and I'll—"

"Tell them what? That you manipulated your community because PISA paid you a few bucks? Shit. Go ahead," Andre says. "You like seeing your name in print? We'll see how much people like it when you confess to being a Judas, *brother*."

The rain starts to fall, sheets thick as glass, and Andre, on the front step, not yet beneath the covered porch, is drenched in the downpour. He moves to climb a stair, but Tyler blocks his ascent.

"You know what, I did some checkin' on you. Nearly killed a guy. Four-count felon. All-time loser." Tyler spits, wipes his mouth. "DC time is fed time, and fed time is serious time. Even

I know that, *Toussaint.* But I got a question: Can a homeboy with your record even vote?"

"Who needs the right to vote when I control the ballot?"

"People like you, you crack your teeth, you make noise, but you ain't nothing but half a hand," he says. "Seems to me, you should be witherin' in a hole. After what you done. You and your homeboys, you and your affirmative—"

"Tyler! Now, you hush now." Chalene flies through the door, steps between the men. "Now, both y'all quit all this foolishness."

"Get off my property, Toussaint, before I get my gun." Tyler spits as Andre climbs back inside the Jeep. A minute later, Andre's back on the road, compelled by a need to find a dark, empty hole. He pulls beside the road, searches, with wet, trembling hands, the GPS. The nearest open bar is two counties over. Sunday. Blue laws. More reason to hate Carthage. He hoped that once he fired Tyler, he might feel better, but instead, he feels drained of energy and emotion. He knows he just fucked up, unnecessarily put the campaign at risk, another self-inflicted wound that Mrs. Fitz will say was reckless and thoughtless, and, of course, she'll be right.

The floor beneath his bar stool begins to shake.

Andre's pretty certain that he's drunk—one hour, four doubles, who wouldn't be?—but he's also fairly certain that this small, dank hole has begun to quake. He considers whether to panic, whether to drop to the floor and crawl beneath a booth, but he's also quick to realize that the shaking has yet to alarm the bartender, a smooth, serpentine brother with a cluster of moles beneath his eye.

Against the counter Andre lays his palms flat, considers the possibility that his mind is simply swimming. But he's hard-pressed to ignore an abundance of proof to the contrary: half-empty bottles that clink together, neon signs that flicker, a bell above the door that rings as though to warn that the British are near. At the end of the bar, a drunk sable-skinned man with salt-and-pepper hair pauses playing solitaire with a deck of pornographic playing cards.

The rumbling ends, the mere passing of a train, and Andre drains his drink. The bartender pours another generous double, and Andre pays. Five for the drink. Five for the tip. Andre doesn't know how his night will end, but he's an hour outside Carthage, and if his day continues to worsen, he'll need the bartender on his side.

"You sure I can't get you something better?" The bartender checks the label on the bottle of cheap liquor. "First drink on the house."

Andre knows the bartender is running a game, offering to sell pricey booze to a drunk man, the first shot free. But Andre doesn't mind. He respects the effort, an honest hustler trying to make a buck. Andre says, "Things usually this quiet?"

"You know how folks be on Sundays. The angels sitting in the pews, the devils sleeping off last night." The bartender leans in. "Wait 'bout an hour. Party picks up with the last-minute crowd that ain't ready to give up on the weekend."

The bar door flies open, and in walks a cello-shaped woman, maybe thirty, with dusty-blond cornrows and pristine peach skin. Her brows, drawn on and exaggerated, seem to belong to a silent-film star, and her torn collarless shirt hangs over her tattooed shoulder to expose her bra's tattered pink strap.

She slams her bucket bag atop the counter, searches inside as she curses beneath her breath. She empties the bag, unafraid to reveal all her secrets: pepper spray and a diaphragm, chewing gum and tampons, a switchblade and a troll doll and a roll of duct tape. At last, she finds a coin purse, pours her change into a green glass ashtray. She counts her treasure, one coin at a time, says to the bartender, "Whatcha sell me for . . . one fiddy?"

"Directions to the water fountain."

"Come on, James. Is that any way to be?"

"Baby girl, I ain't got no time for your broke ass. Buy something or get out."

She props her elbow atop the bar, rolling her eyes, rests her face inside her hands. Andre, for a moment, thinks she might cause a scene. Instead, she relents, repacking her bag, filches a fistful of swizzle sticks and packets of white sugar. The bartender meets Andre's eye, winks, and throws his neck in the woman's direction. Andre shoots a quick sideways glance, judges the woman in a different light. Isn't there a proverb about picking up white women in a black bar?

"A shot for the lady," Andre says. "Whatever she wants."

The woman, chewing on a swizzle, stops packing. "Finally, a gentleman."

He cups his ear, pretends he can't hear a word, a move he learned in college to get the girls to come closer. She takes the bait, slides over her stool. This close, she smells like grapefruit, a spicy scent that's probably sold in bulk.

"So what's your deal?" She runs cherry ChapStick around her lips.

"I'm just out looking to have a drink."

"*Uhh. I'm just out looking to have a drink*," she says. She mocks his voice and posture. "You white? You talk like you white."

"Funny, you don't."

"Nigga. I am black. Blacker than you, anyway." She sinks the shot he bought. "And don't look at me like that for sayin' *nigga*. I didn't mean it like that. You the one talkin' all proper and shit. Your mama white?"

"No," he says.

"But I bet she was bougie."

"This is the worst thank-you for a drink I've ever had."

"Your daddy bougie too?"

"Wouldn't know." He hears his words slur. "Never met him."

"Lucky. I knew mine. He was an asshole." She points two sharp fingers toward the bartender. "Wasn't he, James? Wasn't my daddy an asshole?"

"That he was, baby girl," the bartender says, and the woman smiles, satisfied. Andre passes on the opportunity to ask about her father. Daddy issues, without a doubt, are the least sexy form of small talk. He wonders, though, what to discuss next. He guesses it's better not to ask whether she has a kid or a job or a man at home.

"Buy me another drink. I want a . . ." She leans over the bar, arms folded beneath her breasts, G-string creeping above the back of her drawstring pants. "Get me somethin' classy. Somethin' with olives or cherries."

"We ain't got no olives. Ain't got no cherries," the bartender says. "This ain't Buckingham Palace."

"Piece-of-shit ghetto bar," she shouts. "With piece-of-shit ghetto service."

"Baby girl, I ain't puttin' up with your tantrums tonight."

She throws away the threat, slides between Andre's legs to reach for a cocktail menu covered in dust. She runs her forefinger across the menu, mouths the words like a child who's just learned to read. Finally, she selects a sour-apple martini, an order that annoys the bartender.

Andre pulls out his roll of cash, pays her tab and an extra-generous tip. For the first time, he realizes that this entire afternoon, he's been spending the campaign's petty cash, money he withdrew from the safe to pay Tyler. Using campaign funds for personal expenses is a career-ending offense. Sure, some junior partners lie, print up fake receipts or enter nondescript cash expenses, but for Andre, stealing from the firm is stealing from Mrs. Fitz. So he tells himself to remember to reimburse the petty cash from his personal savings, which are slight. Between Hector and wedding planning and the expense of living comfortably in DC, he doesn't have a net worth.

The woman gawks at the cash, says, "You dealin'?"

"Why is that your first assumption?"

"*Uh. Why is that your first assumption.* Because that much cash, you bound to be causin' trouble." She reads his annoyed expression. "What? I know things. I ain't Pollyanna from Hicksville. I been places. I've done things. You don't know a damn thing about me. Fuck you."

He thinks that this woman isn't pretty enough to excuse such abuse, though, based upon her confidence, no one's ever told her that.

"You gotsta try this." She presses the brim of her martini glass between his lips. "Taste like shit, don't it?"

He stands, sets a twenty on the bar.

"Oh come on. Don't leave me with James. He'll call the sheriff on me. He's done it before. I'll be nice. I swear." She raises her fist, extends her pinkie. "Don't make me beg."

Andre takes his first drunken step, doubts he can take another.

"I got a present for you." She digs inside her bag, slams an orange prescription bottle atop the bar. "I nabbed these from the rich bitch I work for."

Andre returns to his stool, not because he likes her, nor because he cares about her pills, but because the floor has again begun to shake, and because, in truth, he has nowhere else to go.

In the alley, between two empty dumpsters, Andre and the woman with cornrows have sloppy, drunken, and unprotected sex. Afterward, she asks for twenty dollars, which confuses him. They hadn't discussed money before, and now he wonders whether he just engaged the services of a pro. He's amazed how a cheap moment can so easily be made cheaper. He pays her, and she scribbles her name and number on his sweaty hands.

"Call me later?" She kisses him.

"Yeah. Sure."

"Promise?"

"I promise." Of course, he won't.

In the Jeep, the clock reads 12:05 A.M., and the GPS claims he's forty-five miles from Carthage, an hour-long drive straight down State Route 44. He revs the engine, rolls out of the lot, and before long he's flying down the highway, windows down, stereo blaring, AC on full blast. He presumes that he's too drunk to drive, and, indeed, he is, but this small two-lane road is empty, not another vehicle in sight; no one else, he reasons, could possibly get hurt.

To his surprise, highway driving is easy, relaxing, just keep your foot on the gas and eyes on the road. Maybe, from the beginning, he should have been driving drunk. He pushes the Jeep harder, faster, seventy, eighty, eighty-five miles per hour. He knows he should slow down, that he's driving too fast, that, with each passing mile, he's inviting death-defying risk, but, in this moment, surpassing ninety miles per hour, Andre feels invincible.

The view turns dark as carbon, and he considers driving as far as he can. Maybe he could reach the Florida Panhandle by sunrise and, once there, start a new life. He and Cassie talked about moving to Florida, maybe opening a nightclub. He would manage the bar and staff; she could book the entertainment. She joked that Bogie in *Casablanca* could be his inspiration, with Andre wearing a white dinner jacket and black bow tie, playing chess against himself, and never drinking with the customers. He hated the idea—what did he know about running a club?—but he never told her so. Now he'll have to find new dreams to pretend to love.

He pulls onto the exit that leads to home. In his rearview mirror, a police cruiser approaches, lights flashing. His instincts say to flee, to floor the pedal and start a high-speed chase through the barren streets of Carthage, a thought so childish, so ridiculous, it immediately evaporates from his imagination. But right now, he's the very model of probable cause. He figures he's committed at least half a dozen crimes, predicts the cop will frame him for a half dozen more. He pulls into a vacant lot—what other choice does he have?—prays that he hasn't exhausted all his luck. He hasn't. The cruiser picks up speed, passing him along the one-way road, and disappears into the dark.

Two minutes later, Andre parks on his front lawn. Brendan, standing on the porch, wears the same linen suit, in the same despondent pose he struck this morning, and Andre suspects the kid never went back inside. The kid, pale and gaunt, looks like a parent who spent all night sick with worry, and Andre wonders with whom he has talked. Andre closes his eyes, allows a moment to pass, and when he comes to, Brendan's standing over him, the driver's-side door open, pulling Andre from inside the car. The kid helps Andre take a bold, ambitious first step, but Andre's too heavy, too unsteady, too clumsy, and collapses, smashes face-first into a puddle of tar-black mud. Andre rises quickly, spits the muck from his mouth, imagines his face and chest now black like a bit player's in a minstrel show.

The kid helps Andre inside the house, where Andre says, "Hold up, B—hold up. I got a question. Seriously. B—it's important. Come on, man, it's important!"

"Yeah, Dre. What is it?"

"I hate my life."

"That's not a question, Dre."

In Andre's room, Brendan, with a damp towel, wipes Andre's face, chest, hands, and feet, removes Andre's ripped and muddy pants. The kid speaks words that Andre is too drunk to understand, with a face soft and kind, free of judgment. Andre curls beneath his sheets, too ashamed to express his gratitude, to explain that he's not a lush, that today was simply bad. Instead, as the world again goes dark, Andre says, "I'm sorry, B. I shouldn't've been rude to you this morning."

"Don't worry about that now, Dre."

"No. No. Seriously, B. I was an asshole, and, for fuck's sake, you're my only friend."

CHAPTER TEN

In a dark room, Andre wakes hungover, belly down, hands sweaty, stomach a school of silverfish. He taps a bedside lamp, and a soft glow stings his eyes. He sits up, finds beside his bed an ice bucket with a fresh plastic lining and on his nightstand a glass of water in which shaved lemon peels float. Tinfoil on the window blocks the sunlight, and across the room, in the corner, a comforter with the colors of the Irish flag sits bundled atop an upholstered chair.

Slowly, carefully, he rises, peeling himself from sticky sheets, dons pants before bumbling into the parlor. He's dizzy, doesn't remember a damn thing about last night, doesn't remember how he got home, can't explain why he feels like he got his ass beat. Headache. Fever. His face feels numb, his torso tender. He squints against the sunlight, barely makes out Brendan cooking brunch. The unmistakable aroma, pork and onions in a greasy skillet, makes his nausea worse.

Brendan hands Andre a glass of cold cranberry juice that he gulps down in three quick swallows. He's no longer thirsty, but he still feels sick. "I'm going back to bed."

"Check your e-mail." The kid refills the glass. "The Boshears want to meet."

"Write back." Andre heads toward his room. "Tell 'em we'll meet next week."

"E-mail wasn't from Victoria," Brendan says. "E-mail was from Nana."

Andre imagines the interstate game of telephone: Tyler calls the Boshears, the Boshears call PISA, PISA calls Mrs. Fitz, and now Mrs. Fitz has called him. He should've seen this coming. Now he'll have to call his boss and explain his side of this story, a version of events that, in the light of day, doesn't feel all too compelling. *Yes, ma'am. I fired our straw man because he took the initiative and snagged a successful feature in the local paper. No, ma'am. I don't have a backup plan.* Maybe he'll embellish—*Ma'am, I swear to God, that redneck called me a nigger.* He's told bigger lies to get out of smaller troubles.

Andre takes a seat at the table, finds, spread before him, today's newspaper. He sips the juice, squints at the news type in search of reactions to Tyler's unauthorized interview. But no response appears within the smudged, ad-heavy pages. No editorial. Nor follow-up feature. Nor letter to the editor. No one cares. He skims the comics, the sports section, the crime beat that lists criminal sentences. One man, age forty-two, received six months, stayed and suspended, for fondling his fourteen-year-old niece; four teens, exact ages and names withheld, received community service after pleading no contest to taking indecent liberties with a blacked-out classmate with initials KS.

"Pick your cure." Brendan presents a plate in each hand. On the left plate, tomato slices, scrambled eggs, oyster crackers, and a white spine of lettuce. On the right, sausage, bacon, eggs, canned beans, potatoes and onions, ham and tomatoes. Hangover or not, who eats like this?

"About last night . . ." Andre takes the leaner plate. "I needed to—"

"You don't owe me any explanation." Brendan grinds pepper on the tomatoes. "But if you need to talk. Well, you know."

The past twenty minutes, the two have been stuck in the Jeep, watching a freight train run, at a glacial pace, through this trailer park. Andre imagines all the personal property that the neighborhood boys must have flattened on these rails—pennies and bottle caps, soda cans and butter knives, house keys and little sisters' favorite dolls—and he imagines the lonely little girl who sits by her bedroom window, wondering on which train she'll one day hop, her only real chance to escape this small town and to make something of herself, a huge risk, she knows, but a risk, even at this young age, that she realizes she must one day take. East or west, doesn't matter in which direction the train runs. Just as long as she can hop aboard and never look back.

"Let's not waste this opportunity." The kid is passionate. "We don't need a second straw man. We can run a transparent campaign. Respect the voters. Respect their intellect. We'll tell folks that we represent PISA, that a mine could spur local investment, some short-term jobs. Studies show—"

"Jesus, B," Andre groans. The kid knows he's sick. Why is he picking this fight now? "This county has a fifty percent high school dropout rate. You think anyone gives a shit about academic studies?"

"Dre, you're missing the point. We make our case on the merits."

"That's a great campaign. *Vote yes for millions of gallons of cyanide in your drinking water. It may kill your kids, but, heck, it might also kill your mother-in-law. On Election Day, you decide.*"

"That's better than all the secrecy."

"First, it's not secrecy. It's privacy. And people have the right to participate in our democracy without—"

"PISA is not a person. Bribery is not participation. By definition, secrecy is . . ."

A wave of nausea hits Andre, and he buries his face deep in his lap. He feels light-headed, dizzy; he might faint. For the first time, he suspects that last night he consumed something trickier than off-brand booze. The kid says, "Need me to pull over?"

"The height of Jim Crow. Segregated water fountains. Lynchings. The whole white-hood-wearing, cross-burning shebang." Andre sips his water. "Black business owners would fund white candidates who supported civil rights. And these black entrepreneurs gave their support anonymously, because if local whites learned—"

"You're seriously comparing billion-dollar international conglomerates with blacks during Jim Crow? Dude! In grade school, did you not watch *Eyes on the Prize* every February like everyone else?"

"Here's your problem," Andre says. "Anonymity or secrecy—call it whatever you want, but it's long been part of American politics. And not only black folks in Jim Crow. You think dark money didn't further the political fortunes of gays, of women, of your people?"

"Irish?"

"Stoners."

"We prefer *cannabis connoisseurs*."

"The entire marijuana legalization movement is full of anonymous money," Andre says. "Dark money isn't just about big corporations. Anonymous money benefits anyone who wants to share a message but who fears the message might harm the messenger."

"Dude, spin it however you want," Brendan says. "But blacks, gays, cannabis connoisseurs, each of those groups has reason to keep their identities secret. People in those communities express their political views, and those people lose their jobs, lose their freedom, lose their lives. What the hell is PISA afraid of losing?"

"We're sticking with our current plan."

"And what exactly is our current plan? We still need a registered voter to submit the signatures, and you fired our straw man."

"Here's my plan. We sit in silence for the rest of this ride." Andre turns on the radio. "'Cannabis connoisseurs'? Really?"

"Yeah, I know. But what did you expect from a bunch of stoners?"

On the eastern shore of Lake Santee, two dozen men pray. The men form an imperfect ring, in the center of which a purple-robed man preaches. The wind, strong and wild, whips the preacher's words away, casts them down shore toward a cottage-style boathouse, where a sign delimits public from private. PUBLIC BEACH ENDS HERE. NO TRESPASSING. WE HAVE GUNS.

Andre and Brendan stand on a cliff's edge that overlooks the entire scene. Victoria, on the private beach, waves. She points up the hill, toward the mouth of a sandy path, draws her forefinger through the air as though tracing the trail. The wind lifts the hem of her dress, and, blushing, she retreats inside the boathouse.

"Before we head in," Andre says. Seventeen years have passed since his release and making this disclosure hasn't gotten any easier. The past few weeks, the kid's been good enough to avoid any awkward discussion about Andre's criminal past. But now Duke Boshears probably knows, and Andre can't predict what the fool will say. "Here's the deal. You might know. I have a criminal record. Two years in, three years out. I was young, sixteen, homeless. I was runnin' with older boys, and I found myself in this criminal situation, and someone got hurt. Not making excuses. I was wrong. I regret it."

The kid runs his tongue across his teeth, and Andre wonders what's passing through his mind. Over the years, Andre's learned to predict a person's reaction based upon the listener's political bent. Conservatives tend to shrug, to acknowledge that they too, at sixteen, raised hell, that, but for the grace of God, they too could've ended up imprisoned. Liberals never admit personal failure. Instead, lefties prefer to rant about the criminal justice system, to mount their soapbox and to show off their knowledge of racial disparities in policing, prosecution, and sentencing. The kid, Andre guesses, will do neither, and, indeed, Brendan leans forward, ear turned, as though awaiting more. Andre says, "You did know, didn't you?"

"Dude. It's the twenty-first century. Of course I knew," he says. "I did an extensive background check on you when I learned you'd be my mentor."

"When did I become your mentor?"

"And we should definitely talk about that, because, Dre, in the mentoring department, you could do better. But, yeah, so what? I Googled your name."

"I'm not complaining," Andre says. "Makes perfect sense."

"And then I used those search results and cross-referenced the information with a private database of federal criminal offenders. Got your birth date. Mother's name. No father's name. Then I paid a two-ninety-nine sketchy fee. Learned you have a brother, Hector. He's got medical issues, and he's married to Vera, and boy, that's a criminal record. They live in a bad neighborhood. Is that racist to say? That part of DC is like one hundred percent black, but it's also like one hundred percent violent. Not a causation. But correlation, I'm sure, but still, dude. That neighborhood. Al-Qaida training camps have fewer annual casualties."

"Yes. That's racist. It's true, but it's also racist."

"You were a part of a special pilot program. Your three years of parole, you were enrolled in college. A second-chance scholarship paid all your expenses. You finished in four years, with honors. That's how you met Nana. She endowed your scholarship."

"Please stop."

"You've had one job since graduating college, and that's with Nana. Do you really speak Arabic? Oh, and dude, we gotta work on that credit score. How'd you manage to get a loan to buy a condo? Was the bank manager a friend of Nana's? Yeah, bet that was it."

"Don't you have better things to do than stalk people?"

"I respect your privacy. Privacy is important. But it's public information and a prudent precaution. You could've been an axe murderer with shitty credit," Brendan says. "Now I know I was half-right."

The kid has a point. Online opposition research is essential to modern campaigns. Criminal records. Public debts. Sarcastic comments written on disreputable message boards. But Andre rarely researches people in his personal life. Yes, he's researched Cassie and his mother, neither yielding helpful results, but he's never researched Brendan, or Mrs. Fitz, or Vera, or Hector, not because he respects their privacy, but because he cares so little about their private lives.

The kid says, "And, if I can be honest with you, when I read the criminal complaint, I was a little freaked out. I was like—"

"The criminal complaint is online?"

"For like ten bucks. As is the arresting officer's affidavit. As is your booking photo. Were you sporting a 'fro with sideburns?"

"Like I said, I was sixteen and homeless."

"Were you sixteen and homeless in a 1970s blaxploitation film?"

Andre drifts away, considers the news that the complaint now appears online, hates that he's lost control over his own personal narrative. These past seventeen years, he's taken great care to polish the retelling of his past, emphasizing his youth, embellishing his circumstances, omitting any reference to the fifteen thousand dollars or Dylan Miller. Now he must revise his own story, review the complaint and mold his account to those facts in the public sphere. He wonders whether that's possible. The facts are bad. Dylan Miller could've been any of his clients' sons. Andre says, "You still freaked out?"

"Dude, of course I am. It's insane that you help billionaires buy elections."

"I swear to God, B. I'm not talking about the job. I'm talking about the conviction."

The kid hesitates, ponders. Seems not to have asked himself this question, says, "No. No? No!"

"The first *no* would've been good enough."

The wind picks up, throwing itself in harsh and loud somersaults across the beach. Flecks of sand whip against flat rocks, and low, delicate waves crash against the shore. Andre raises his hands, shielding his face, wishes he had worn warmer clothes. He wonders whether the praying men, in white buttoned shirts and khaki pants, are bothered by the cold, wonders whether the benefits of prayer include a Lord that keeps them warm.

"Dre, seriously though, one more question."

"Yes, B, it was a 'fro. That winter, I grew a 'fro. Happy?"

"Okay. Two questions. Second question: why are we talking about this now?"

Andre straightens, inhales. "Tyler Lee Googled my name and . . ."

"Paid the two-ninety-nine sketchy fee. Hmmm. Yeah. So Duke Boshears knows."

"You can wait here if you want."

"Let's face it. Any conversation with Duke and Victoria is awkward." The kid grips his nape. "Their marriage is like a tontine where happiness is the prize."

"Does anyone understand anything you say?"

"I won't leave you hanging. Ever. Whither thou goest, I will go. Like Paul said to the apostle Mark, 'We be bros forever.'" Brendan proudly lifts his fist, expects a fraternal bump, but Andre has had enough, turns his back to pursue the path that heads down the hill, the kid's fist left raised in the air.

"Dude, you are a horrible mentor," the kid shouts downhill. "A horrible mentor with well-below-average credit."

The inside of the boathouse is a half-submerged heated garage that shelters a floating small houseboat. Why do cash-strapped rich people always own the coolest toys? Victoria kisses his cheeks with unnatural lips, and he again questions why a former beauty queen would undergo such drastic plastic surgery. She is the perfect hostess, offers refreshments, provides a boathouse tour that ends beside a picturesque window that overlooks the praying men.

"Them? Oh. One of those men's fellowships. Born-agains returning home," Victoria says. "You know, grown men who want one last chance, who sign a pledge that they won't drink, that they'll be good fathers, that they won't knock around their wives. Then they feel all proud of themselves. Go 'round town walking with their chest out, bragging. *Gee, look at me. I signed a piece of paper saying I won't beat my wife.* Like the governor should give 'em a medal."

She steps onto the houseboat, which bounces atop choppy waters. To Andre's surprise, the boathouse can't keep out the rough water, and he wonders whether a boathouse that keeps the elements at bay would have cost extra. Victoria gestures for her guests to board, and Andre tastes his breakfast rise up his throat. To be sure, he fears neither drowning nor the boat's collapse, but he's hungover, and the boat and the waves and the rocking and the yawing, it's all too much to bear.

Duke Boshears emerges from inside the cabin, sunglasses backward around his neck. He crosses the boat deck, beer can in hand, adjusts a fishing pole cast into the lake. Andre questions the ethics of fishing indoors, feels it's unfair to the bass.

"Come on," Duke says. "Make yourself at home."

Now both Boshears stand, staring, patiently awaiting their guests. As the moment grows more uncomfortable, Andre weighs a list of excuses not to board: childhood trauma, muddy shoes, his ancestors' experiences with white people and boats. He thinks, perhaps, that the truth will do, but while he's analyzing that strategy's pros and cons, Brendan steps forward, says, "Maybe we could sit over there?" pointing at a picnic table in the boathouse's corner. "I get motion sickness."

The picnic table is an excellent choice, beneath a vent that blows warm air. Andre, eager to end this conversation, summons a faux enthusiasm, emphasizes the campaign's success: an effective and efficient canvass; more than sixteen hundred verified signatures, more than enough to appear on the ballot; an internal analysis that suggests all three initiatives enjoy broad public support. To his surprise, Duke Boshears offers effusive praise,

Good news, well done, I completely agree, while Victoria sits stone-faced, arms crossed. Andre assumes she's upset about Tyler, but she isn't.

"These liberty initiatives." She grips the table's edge. "I saw them in the paper. First I heard of it, and I thought . . . well, never mind what I thought. I was surprised. That's what I'm trying to say. I was surprised."

"No one's asked me, but I say you've got a genius plan," Duke says. "You know, my second campaign, the one for state senate, I ran on liberty."

"Sweetie, please, you ran on being a redneck. Don't confuse the two."

"Don't mind her. She's in a mood. Go ahead, tell 'em. Tell 'em why you're in a mood." Duke's like a boy taunting his little sister. "Paula Carrothers and Vicki here are thick as thieves. Paula's godmother to our two girls. I tell Vicki, this campaign ain't personal. Politics is business with blood."

"I'm not in a mood. I'm just surprised." Victoria's face turns bright red. "But, yes, Paula is a friend, a dear friend. She's also—"

"A fucking cunt." Duke looks at Brendan. "That's a Scottish phrase, ain't it? *Cunt*?"

The word, and the casual vitriol with which it is spoken, has horrified the kid. The only question is how Brendan will respond. The obvious answer is that *cunt* isn't a phrase. It's a word. And probably not a Scottish word at that. And above all else, a word that men should never use, unless a pistol is pressed against their head, and, quite possibly, not even then. Andre, with a stare, begs Brendan for restraint. *Right now Duke is our friend.*

"It's that you said you'd consult us on major decisions. To me, this seems major." Victoria struggles for words. "I understand you're professionals, and I don't doubt you know your business. But Paula works hard. Real hard. And she cares deeply about this community. Last year, she created a program for girls—"

"See? There it is. That's my problem with Paula. Or, should I say, one of Her Majesty's problems," Duke says. "She spends taxpayers' money on her own personal pet projects."

"How is a weekend clinic for pregnant teenagers her own personal pet project?"

"We got a bazillion GD churches in this town, some of 'em richer than Midas. Let one of 'em pay the bill." He punches his open palm to emphasize his point. "Taxpayers shouldn't foot the bill for little girls that don't have the sense to keep their legs closed."

This statement sets off an argument, and the Boshears bicker, her voice flush with rage, his voice thick with sarcasm. Clearly the two have had this fight before, perhaps about one of their own, talking in circles, Victoria urging Christian compassion, Duke demanding fiscal responsibility. By the time the squabble ends, Victoria's upset. She bites her lower lip, takes a moment before speaking. "Mr. Ross, I would very much appreciate if you could . . . I'm trying to say . . . This county is run by incompetent men. The sheriff. The school superintendent. Our treasurer has a seventeen-year-old mistress. Is there any way you . . ." Her voice breaks. "Please."

She turns her face to stare through the window at the men who promise not to beat their wives. She doesn't need to be told the obvious: that this type of campaign is less likely to succeed against a man, that a healthy share of the electorate simply resents a powerful woman, that, by virtue of being smart and successful, Paula Carrothers is the ideal foil.

"You just don't understand," Victoria says. "Paula's the one who made it."

Andre endures a long silence, doesn't question Victoria's loyalty. If she planned to expose PISA's campaign, she would have done so by now. Yes, Miss Vicki loves her childhood friend, but clearly Miss Vicki loves her wealth and status more.

On the public beach, the preacher in purple wades into the water, and a bearded man, maybe in his forties, follows behind. The bearded man, dressed in white, hesitates, as though fearful that he might be swept away. The pastor takes his hands, guides him into the lake, where together they pray. The bearded man falls backward, plunging beneath the surface, and rises seconds later, drawing deep gasping breaths, sins forever washed away.

CHAPTER ELEVEN

Brendan and Andre play video games through the night, another unanswered set of Brendan victories, another awkward set of Irish song-and-dance. The kid takes a break from gloating, opens his window, a cigarette tucked behind his ear. On the sill, beside a baby-food jar filled with copper screws, the kid sits, a sliver of pink sunrise aglow against his back.

"Can we talk for a sec?" The kid pauses, either to carefully choose his words or to surrender to his THC-induced fog. Andre wonders from where Brendan gets his re-ups, suspects that the kid has a connect somewhere between here and Charleston. Hopes that the kid isn't doing anything reckless. From experience, Andre knows the troubles that can befall a rich white kid who stumbles into the wrong neighborhood.

"You have to forgive Tyler," Brendan says. "We don't have options. We need a local registered voter to submit an affidavit attesting to the validity of our signatures. That's the written law. For better or for worse, Tyler Lee is our man. He's the face of our campaign. He's on the website. He—"

"Appeared in the newspaper when I told his dumb ass—"

"What can that possibly matter now?" Brendan says. "Dude. You gotta make your peace with him, and you gotta do it now. We don't have another choice."

Andre drops his chin, sucks in a huge breath. He knows he should just walk away—let this moment pass and come back tomorrow—but his fists have tightened, his jaw has set. Et tu, Brendan? Tyler Lee does an interview, an affront that still pisses Andre off, and no one gives a damn? Cassie cheats. No one cares. Mrs. Fitz gives this bullshit assignment. No one cares. How many different ways can one man be disrespected? No. On principle, he will not eat any more of their shit. So, when the kid sings the same refrain, *we must, we have to, we have no choice*, Andre strikes back. "You've no idea what the fuck you're talking about."

"Dre, I'm not an idiot. I know—"

"What? What do you think you know?"

"I know that my grandmother doesn't give out third chances," the kid says. "No matter how much she loves you."

"You gonna snitch? Tell your grandmother?"

"What? No. I didn't say . . . I would never . . ." Brendan springs to his feet, points his forefinger like a dagger at Andre's heart. "That is not me, and you know that is not me. Say that again, Dre, I dare you. Say that again."

The kid, his face a mask of pain, returns to his perch on the windowsill. Andre sometimes forgets that he's not arguing with Hector or his juvie friends. With each of them, he could levy any accusation, could utter an insult that cut straight to the bone. In those worlds, among friends, words held little value. Intentions, actions, loyalty, these were the measure of a man. Outside juvie, the world is different. Outside, friendship is different. Outside, respect is different.

"I'm sorry. I know you would never . . . I'm sorry, B. Really, I am."

"Maybe you should stop drinking," Brendan says.

"I know."

"You're a mean drunk."

"I know."

"And sometimes you're mean when you're sober too."

"I'm sorry."

Brendan plucks the cigarette from behind his ear, lights it, takes a long, thoughtful drag. Andre inhales the smoke, relaxes to consider the merits of the kid's request. He knows that Tyler's pardon is inevitable, that if he doesn't forgive Tyler now, then in forty-eight hours, he'll receive this order directly from Mrs. Fitz. She too will fault his fragile ego, but mostly, she'll repeat her favorite truism: sometimes, in politics and in life, you gotta dance with the gal that you brought to the ball.

The Jeep pulls beside a short school bus with a bumper sticker that reads JOHN 3:16, parked outside a barn. Brendan points to a wire chicken run, where two dozen dyed chicks—blue, green, bubblegum pink—peck pine shavings. Above the run appears a neon sign: BABY CHICKS. 2 FOR $5.

"Dre." Brendan hands over an envelope fat with cash. "Please remember—"

"Jesus, Brendan. I'm here. I'm meeting him. I'm making nice."

"—everyone's opinion deserves respect."

Inside, the barn smells of mesquite and fresh-baked bread, and the clamor of a busy kitchen rises above the sizzle of a grill. The restaurant, open five minutes, is without customers, and the interior resembles the trendy artisan bistros once popular in

Georgetown: clean, sunlit, whiskey-barrel tables, plank countertops. The owner, an old black man with Poseidon's beard, fills a tin pail with cellophane-wrapped syrup candy. "You waitin' for Chalene?"

"No, sir. Tyler. Tyler Lee?"

"Don't know nothin' about no Tyler, but Chalene's here." He points toward the bathrooms, one labeled ROOSTERS, the other HENS. "She's in there. Hopefully she ain't makin' a mess. Ask me: pregnant women always makin' a mess. I'm keen to ban 'em from my establishment."

Andre picks a table, stays standing as he wonders whether Tyler Lee will make an appearance or whether the coward has sent his wife, which is, without doubt, a characteristically chump move. With each mistrustful thought, Andre's impatience grows more intense, and he finds himself guessing at the motives that persuaded Tyler to choose, of all places, here. He bets that Tyler knows the owner, that Tyler aims to show that the Lees have a black friend, a proposition so juvenile, so offensive, that by the time Chalene steps out of the bathroom, wiping her hands on her prairie dress, Andre seethes.

"The money we owe you from the canvass." Andre tosses the fat envelope on the table. "It's all there. Count it."

"I didn't ask you here to . . . This isn't about money." She shoves away the envelope, sits, folds her napkin in her lap. "Please try the trash-can chicken."

"Is Tyler coming?"

"Please. I thought . . ." She rushes to her purse, unfolds a sheet of spiral-torn paper, begins to read. "When you came to our house on Sunday—"

"Listen, Chalene. I don't know what Tyler's pulling—"

"He don't know I'm here. I asked you here. I wanted to

say . . ." She looks down at the paper, starts from the beginning. "When you came to our house—"

"Oh for fuck's sake, Chalene. Will you please take the damn money?"

"I ain't finished," she shouts, voice breaking, as she brings her fists together, crumpling the paper. Her first tear falls, and Andre panics, thinks his best option is to turn around and race through the barn door. But instead he stands paralyzed, uncertain whether he's been harsh or he's the victim of the unstable hormones of a pregnant white woman.

"All I wanted to do was apologize. I spent a lot of time writing this." She's sobbing. "But you and my Tyler, pulling your penises out, spraying your testosterone all over the place. Stubborn men. Makers of your own misery. Jesus would not approve."

No one has ever made this particular accusation. He takes a moment, confirms that he's not offended. If such rudeness repulses the Son of God, then Andre's got bigger troubles than being short with a pregnant woman.

"I been praying over what to do, praying real hard about what to say, because I am real sorry about what my Tyler said." She gasps for breath. "I wrote down what's in my heart, and I practiced saying it in the mirror. And now, you . . . you're being . . ."

"An asshole. You're right." He sits. "I'm an asshole. Go ahead. Say it."

"How can you be in politics and be this frustrating?" she says. "Aren't elections about getting people to like you?"

"That's a common misconception. Elections are about getting voters to hate others." He realizes, too late, that the question was rhetorical. He glances over his shoulder, sees the staff enjoying the spectacle. The owner shakes his head, as though to say, *That does it, no more pregnant women.* The chef chuckles. The busboy winks. The butcher gives an encouraging thumbs-up. Andre hides the envelope beneath a napkin as the waiter approaches.

"Sweetheart," the waiter says. "How can I make your day better?"

Chalene wipes her eyes, orders the large-portion chicken spaghetti, extra spicy, extra cheese, with a large sweet tea. She orders a side Caesar salad, with sardines if in stock, with salted ham if not. Andre orders the special, chicken bog, the cheapest meal on the menu. When the waiter leaves, Chalene says, "He's judgin' me. Isn't he? Or am I crazy?"

Andre bites back the urge to say, *Yes, he's judging you, and yes, you're crazy, and now, thanks to your tearfest, he's judging me too.* Instead, he leans forward, whispers, "I'll stiff him on the tip," and after she giggles through tears, he says, "You come here a lot?"

"Oh goodness. Who can afford it? But the baby's been craving their spicy chicken spaghetti." Chalene pats her napkin against her flushed cheek. "With my last two, I had these cravings, spicy chicken spaghetti, and I tried fixin' it at home. Tried reverse-engineerin' the recipe like they do on TV. Never could get the spiciness right."

"I thought you might know the owner."

"Mr. Dix? No. I guess I know him. Small town and all. But I don't know him better than anyone else."

The waiter returns with Chalene's sweet tea and a basket of ash cakes, compliments of the staff. She says a quick blessing as the waiter leaves, quotes chapter and verse before tearing into her first cake, then a second, a third, smearing globs of honey butter across each cake, each bite savored with as much pleasure as the first. She's the happiest woman in South Carolina. And there's something about her satisfaction, about the exuberance with which this small, frail mother-to-be eats, that's a pleasure to watch.

"Can I read what I wrote now?" She licks her fingers, opens the notebook paper. "Please."

"I wish you wouldn't."

"Fine. But all I wanted to say was my Tyler was wrong. He knew better. Should never've talked to that reporter. Should never've said anything about your past," she says. "We have all made mistakes. We have all sinned. We have all come up short of the glory of God."

She has more tears in her eyes.

"Forgive and forget," he says. "That's my motto."

"Crazy thing is, my Tyler and me, we met in prison. You know that?" She breaks another ash cake in two. "His uncle was doing fed time. Dummy shot up a postal van. My family, we lived in Spartanburg; my daddy led a prison ministry. We'd travel 'round the state tendin' to convicts' souls. My Tyler and me met in line on visitors' day."

"Tale as old as time."

"Never imagined I'd end up here. You know, I was born with Jesus in my heart, and I always knew I'd serve Christ. I used to have big plans. I dreamed of making disciples in China. You know they stone Christians there?"

He wonders why he would possibly know that.

"Most folks don't. Terrible mess. Terrible. I pray for them every day. Send 'em a few dollars every month." She covers her full mouth. "I even write my congressman once a month."

Writing a congressman. That's quaint.

"Fourteen years old and I had it all mapped out. I even got a part-time job, saved up to buy these Chinese-language cassettes. I can still recite the Lord's Prayer in Mandarin and Cantonese."

She takes pride in this accomplishment. "But time passes. I met my Tyler, and after our first pregnancy—that was our first miscarriage—I sorta gave up."

He gives a sincere sympathetic nod, thinks to confess that when he was a boy, he aspired to be a kingpin. Partners in crime with Hector. Even once he left juvie, with a second-chance scholarship to college, he studied business, thinking that, one day, he'd create his own criminal empire. The modest ambitions of an eighteen-year-old with a rap sheet.

"I was *that* girl in high school. Bride of Christ, the kids called me. I tried to save the students, the teachers, the principal," she says. "Heck, I'd leave little Post-it notes with Bible verses in the janitor's closet. I just couldn't understand why folks wouldn't embrace Jesus's love, you know? I mean, it's like winning the lottery."

"You must've been popular."

"I never got invited to parties." Her voice fades. "Still don't."

He hears a ripple of shame in her admission, and imagines Chalene, fourteen and dimple-cheeked, in her school hall campaigning for her Lord. He thinks she'd be a great campaigner—adorable, passionate, sincere, and persuasive—so he wonders what exactly went wrong. Maybe there were no South Carolinians left who needed to be saved.

"Most folks around here are part-time Christians," she says. "You know the type. Go to church every other Sunday, say grace if they remember. They don't put Christ at the center of their lives. They never study the Word. They never tithe. Never follow His direction. But I don't judge."

He sees why her Jesus campaign failed. Can't win votes by blaming voters.

Chalene steals the last ash cake, and Andre watches her through a new lens. She could triumph on a campaign trail, this pregnant mother of six, wholesome and noble, motivated by a sincere desire to better her community. With the right molding, she could become a superstar. If he asks her to campaign now, she'll say no, but if he asks her to take a smaller step, perhaps to submit and certify the sixteen hundred signatures, then maybe he could later persuade her to do more.

PART III

THE COUNCIL VOTE

CHAPTER TWELVE

Ulrich Plantation sits atop a plot of harsh, unpliable earth, but the plantation's founders—three brothers, horse thieves banished from Bavaria—built a legendary furniture-making operation, producing cabinets and curio desks, exquisite pieces that fetched a handsome price at auctions around the world. The plantation remains the pride of Carthage County and has received such distinctions as the Centurion Award from the Daughters of the Confederacy, which recognized Ulrich Plantation's "continued dedication to the truthful preservation of our nation's proud cultural heritage." The plantation hosts birthday parties and weddings, corporate retreats and field trips, and, for the amusement of tourists and guests, the curators have preserved the sawmill and workshop, stable and barn, chapel and forge. But the grandest preservation remains a marble-pillared mansion surrounded by tall oaks draped with Spanish moss.

In the master bedroom, Andre regrets letting Brendan talk him into hosting this rally here. *Dude*, the kid pled, *a liberty rally at a plantation, that would be the ultimate in ironic.* Anywhere else such a rally would cause a political firestorm. Counter-demonstrations, angry op-eds, black students chanting lyrical slogans. But in Carthage, no one cares.

Through binoculars, he surveys the vast open meadow where today's rally is held. In two days, the county council will vote on his liberty initiatives. If the council fails to adopt the three, then six weeks later, the initiatives will appear on the spring ballot. Andre doesn't expect to win the council vote—PISA has principles: the company will buy an election but dares not bribe a council—but he needs to energize his base, to inspire passionate supporters to spew venom at each member of the county board. Thus, he's organized this event, the latest in a dozen rallies meant to motivate supporters with free barbecue and live bluegrass.

The turnout is strong, maybe four hundred, a fair number of whom are men, angry men, angry white men, some of whom wear costumes: colonial minutemen, Confederate officers. One guy's a Jedi knight. Andre recognizes some regulars, hard-core true believers who want the liberty initiatives to succeed but only as a precursor to a much larger, more radical political revolution.

Andre spots Brendan standing beside a picnic table on which sit platters of smoked meat, molded gelatin, racks of pies, and Tupperware bowls full of all manner of mayonnaise-based sides. The food, Andre's learned, is key to outreach. The good people of Carthage prefer a good meal to a good message, and, thus, he provides this feast. He imagines trying to host a successful grassroots rally with only fat-free vegan fare. Carrot sticks. Chickpeas. Homemade hummus and pita chips. Maybe in Boulder or Berkeley or Burlington, Vermont, but south of the Mason-Dixon line, Negro, please. A campaign that offers sides without heart-stopping globs of creamy mayo doesn't have its finger on the electorate's irregular pulse.

Brendan chats up an olive-skinned beauty, a goofball grin across his face. The kid's got zero game, but that doesn't slow the belle, who clearly digs Brendan. She taps his wrist, laughs at his joke, strokes his cheek to wipe away flecks of pollen. Yet the kid doesn't take the hint, which Andre doesn't completely understand. Part of Andre thinks, Jesus, B, just kiss the girl and be done with it.

Andre wishes he were down there, on the ground, able to interact with the crowd. In all his years of political consulting, he's not discovered a substitute for firsthand intel, direct dialogue with voters about their passions and prejudices. Most Americans are eager to share their opinions. All one must do is ask. But Andre, sequestered up here, accepts the reality that a black man at this event would draw unwelcome attention.

"I brought food." Chalene sneaks up behind him. "Didn't mean to scare you."

"You didn't scare me."

"Fixed you a bit of everything." She sets the packed plate atop a desk, doesn't care that grease or sauce or runny mayo might stain a two-hundred-year-old antique. She's nearly seven months pregnant, fingers like Vienna sausages, wrists like a Louisville Slugger. On the edge of the four-poster bed, she kicks off her shoes, sets her swollen feet atop an ottoman. "I should've never let you talk me into this."

She closes her eyes, releasing a please-notice-me, please-pity-me sigh, and Andre patiently awaits her complaint. Chalene, he's learned, is a first-rate campaigner, a master of see-me, touch-me, feel-me retail politics. She remembers your sick mama's name, reminisces about last year's county fair, swaps embarrassing stories about failed church solos. And yet despite these political gifts, Chalene suffers from a crippling fear of public speaking. Get a group larger than ten or twelve, and she panics. Today's crowd is her largest. He's not surprised when she starts in, feigning illness, like a kindergartner trying to skip school. "I'm gonna throw up sick all over the podium."

"Brendan forgot to bring the podium."

"Now I'm gonna be up there naked." She removes a rib from his plate, says a blessing before clearing the bone. "This can't be good for the baby. Stress is poison to the womb. I read that. Stress causes more birth defects than drinking and smoking and crystal meth combined."

"What pregnancy books are you reading?"

"I had this dream last night. A nightmare. I'm giving one of my speeches and sweat kept stinging my eyes. I was up there blind as Bartimaeus," she says. "You know insomnia's bad for the womb. It's the second leading cause of—"

"Please stop reading pregnancy books not written by doctors."

"Here, pray with me." She licks her fingers, extends her open hand. "Come on, you know the prayer's stronger with more people, and hurry up, I gotta pee."

"Can't we go five minutes without you talking about peeing?"

"I'd rather go five minutes without having to pee." She flicks her wrist, moves her open hands closer. "Shug, come on, please. It'll be quick."

He hesitates before giving in, like he does each time she asks for his hand. These past weeks, he's learned that Chalene will pray with just about anyone, and she'll pray over just about anything. She is constant and steadfast. He's seen her pray for a successful speech, for a successful rally, for a successful campaign. She's prayed for him, for Brendan, for her husband and six sons and unborn child, for her pastor and postman, for her neighbors and nurses, for the special-ed students she shuttles between home and school, for the owner of the local bowling alley, who helps look after her kids. For herself, she asks for wisdom and health, for compassion and mercy, for the strength to carry on throughout each day.

Now, eyes closed, lilt soft, she prays for His guiding hand to bless her speech. She trembles, nerves beyond control, a slight yet familiar quake at her thick wrist. Andre resists the urge to interrupt, to reassure her that she has no need for concern. Yes, for the first time, she'll deliver a brand-new speech, a complete replacement of the old stump speech that has, thus far, served her well. But he also wants to remind her that she's rehearsed this new speech in the mirror, before her children, on the school bus. More important, he wants to reassure her that this new speech, which she wrote herself, is pretty damn good. A thoughtful meditation that links American freedom and Jesus Christ. Starts with Galatians, cribs from America's greatest religious thinkers: Edwards, Bryant, King's "Letter from a Birmingham Jail." *We know through painful experience that freedom is never voluntarily given by the oppressor; it must be demanded by the oppressed.*

Her trembling stops, and Chalene ends her prayer, requesting that Christ find His way into each man's heart, a plea he's certain is aimed at him. She keeps her head bowed, eyes closed, tightens her grip around his hand. A prickly silence rises between them, interrupted by the abrupt clearing of her throat. He knows what she wants, and he's tempted to wait her out, to engage in this battle of wills. But, in the end, he decides against picking a fight with his straw man, who right now needs a reassuring friend, not an uncooperative asshole. So, like each time before, he surrenders to her passive-aggressive proselytizing, saying with a quick, reluctant breath, “Amen.”

On the ride home, Andre receives an updated poll.

The good news: the liberty initiative’s public-awareness campaign has worked. Through direct mail and social media and targeted online ads as well as good old-fashioned word-of-mouth, a staggering nine of ten county residents say they’ve heard about the initiatives, and an impressive seven of ten can name all three. The good news gets better. Among the county’s voting-age population—that is, Carthaginians older than eighteen—the liberty initiatives are decisively popular.

The first initiative, the Bill of Rights in public buildings, is universally beloved. Women and men, young and old, Baptist and Methodist and Appalachian snake handler, everyone in Carthage worships the Constitution. The third initiative, to reduce Paula Carrothers’s salary, also enjoys broad public support, and, for the first time, the auction of public lands now commands the approval of a majority of Carthage residents. All of which is to say: Andre’s confident that if the election were held today, and each eligible voter cast a ballot, they’d win in a landslide.

But therein lies the rub.

The bad news is that not everyone in Carthage will vote. In fact, six weeks from now, the overwhelming majority of eligible voters will avoid the polls. Thus, the firm’s pollsters have also predicted the outcome of an election that includes only likely voters, and these voters, the pollsters conclude, are utterly unimpressed.

Among likely voters, the posting of the Bill of Rights remains overwhelmingly popular. But the majority of these same voters oppose the auction of public lands, and they’re evenly split on reducing Paula Carrothers’s pay.

"Um, Dre, I got a question." Brendan takes the highway exit. "Honestly. Truly. 'Cause I'm curious. I'm just asking."

"Is this another black-people question?"

"Sorta. Does it bother you that some people at the rally were . . . dodgy?"

"You mean the Jedi?"

"I'm just asking, 'cause, you know, some guys at the rally were . . . you know." The kid whispers the accusation: "Racists."

A red light stops the Jeep. Beside the road, parked in a lot, a pickup blasts gospel music, bed full of animal pelts. The truck's owner, a haggard one-eyed trapper, sits atop a crate, reading, his scarred face shaded by a wide-brimmed straw hat. His spray-painted sign says: TANNED PELTS. HUMANLY CAPTURED.

"One guy gave me his card, introduced himself as a congressman in the New Confederate States of America." Brendan digs into his back pocket, retrieves a flimsy business card with smudged text and bent edges. The kid says, "Guy spent ten minutes explaining how taxes are illegal."

"I don't get it."

"Well, he said the federal government doesn't have the power to—"

"Not that. I meant, if you're gonna be an elected official in a fictitious government, why be a legislator?" Andre says. "Why not appoint yourself king or emperor or lord protector? North Korea and Iran both have supreme leaders. That's a title I could get behind."

"Dre, I'm serious."

"You think this New Confederacy holds elections? If this campaign fails, I may need new clients."

"There's a market that's easy to corner. Twenty-first-century Confederate politicians," Brendan says. "But I guarantee they'll make *you* work for free . . . and against your will . . . and in violation of the Thirteenth Amendment, which, by the way, they say wasn't properly ratified."

"Still beats being a graduate student."

"How is this funny? This guy is literally, literally, a card-carrying bigot."

"That's just a PR problem. We could fix that." He stops before confessing that he's fixed worse. Holocaust deniers. September eleventh truthers. What can Andre say? Politics attracts broken men. "Give the guy a break."

"And you covet their support."

"B, what do you want from me? A campaign can't always choose its base."

Brendan's phone vibrates, and Brendan replies to his incoming text, typing away, so immersed that he doesn't notice the stoplight turn green. A dump truck behind them honks, and Brendan checks his rearview mirror, presses send, then steers the car ahead. The kid says, "You hungry?"

"Didn't you eat at the rally?"

"Too busy working."

"Yeah. I saw."

"I promise, Dre. It won't be long."

CHAPTER THIRTEEN

Andre stretches his arms, jamming his middle finger against the Jeep's low ceiling, and watches Brendan pace inside the fast-food joint. The kid's spent the past five minutes patrolling the space beneath a banner that advertises deep-fried cream-cheese-stuffed jalapeños, checking and rechecking his phone, face full of apprehension. The Casa's nearly empty save preschoolers celebrating a birthday. A fat clown with face and lips painted, sitting in an adjacent booth, nears the end of his cigar, while a young mother in cherry-red curlers plays on her phone. A gap-toothed boy licks a ketchup packet. Another boy picks his nose. The lone girl, a pale, sickly sight, bangs her forehead against the table.

The fat clown extinguishes his stogie, lights another in one smooth, swift motion, head tilted back, rainbow wig crushed against his polka-dotted shoulders. Look at this asshole, smoking feet from a dozen kids, a literal bozo who doesn't give a damn that, because of him, the birthday boy's parting gift to his friends might be carcinoma.

Andre checks his watch—a little past four—brings his

thumb to his forefinger, counts the tasks he must complete tonight. A long list that starts with written updates to Mrs. Fitz and PISA, both of whom will have seen the latest poll, both of whom will express frustration with his mediocre progress. So, how should the e-mail start? *Dear Mrs. Fitz, It's my sad duty to acknowledge that I'm fucking up this simple beneath-me campaign.* Tonight, he must also approve both radio ads and the remarks Chalene plans to deliver to the county council.

The list of tasks keeps growing, and a sensation, like a belt, tightens around his chest. His face feels hot and flushed, like there are a thousand pinpricks against his cheeks. One heartbeat, then another pounds inside his ears. In juvie, he trained for moments like these: deep belly breathing, rubbing his own earlobe, repeating a mantra. But all he can think to chant is *I'm fucked. I'm fucked. I'm so fucking fucked.* Which, of course, doesn't help. He tells himself that the poll is wrong, though he knows, from deep experience, that doubting a poll is a sure sign of delusion, a rookie's retort—swear by the polls when the news is good, distrust the poll when the news is bad. He struggles to understand how he could sink eighty grand into these initiatives and, thus far, not persuade most likely voters. He needs an answer soon, because in twenty-four hours, Mrs. Fitz will ask that same question.

Where the fuck is Brendan? They need to get home. Andre has work to do, and right now, he craves a drink. Why doesn't the kid ever act with urgency?

He's reaching to smack the horn when, inside the Casa, a frail, slow-moving woman, wearing sunglasses and a head scarf, approaches the kid, leans in close to whisper in his ear. Her dress is denim, the kind of do-it-yourself patchwork project that might seem trendy on a younger woman but, on her rail-thin frame, looks pitiable. The woman turns, signaling for the kid to follow, which he does, to an empty spot kitty-corner from the birthday party. This new location is neither private nor hidden; from the street, through the spotty, grit-streaked window, anyone can observe the two.

She opens her purse, retrieves a paper lunch sack, and for a moment, she and Brendan simply stare at each other. The kid fumbles, producing his wallet, withdrawing a bundle of bills, and the two pause, unsure who should initiate this trade. In clear frustration, she snatches the cash before shoving the paper bag into the kid's chest. And just like that, the deal is done. She exits the Casa, slow yet determined, counting the cash, and disappears into an alley.

The kid rushes out of the Casa, bumping the chair of the ketchup-eating boy, who begins to cry. Brendan doesn't slow or say excuse me, but makes a beeline for the Jeep, where, once inside, he tosses the small, crumpled bag behind his seat.

Andre is stunned. Please, please say that you didn't just do a buy out in the open for anyone to see. The Casa probably has cameras, and Andre counts at least a dozen witnesses. He's astonished the kid would be this reckless.

"Need anything else before we head back?" The kid grins like a schmuck. "Dre. You okay?"

"Let's just get back to the house." Andre tries to keep his cool—rubs his own earlobe, takes a deep breath, repeats a calming mantra—but he can't help himself. "And why don't your dumb ass put your shit under the seat? I'm not trying to catch a possession charge for your grade-school bullshit."

"Oh, that? Good call, Dre." The kid reaches back, grabs and opens the paper bag. He starts pulling out little baggies and pill bottles, like a child on Halloween inspecting his own stash. Andre looks around, then snatches the bag, shoves it beneath the back seat. The kid says, "Just a couple party favors. Something to get through the final weeks. I bought enough to share. That cute girl at the rally—"

"What is wrong with you? Don't have all your shit out in the open. It's bad enough you bought this shit in front of all those strangers. Now you're opening the bag, pulling shit out." Dre points above the door. "And there's a camera right there filming us."

"Dre, calm down. It's no big deal. I do it all the time."

"Brendan. Right now. I really need for you to shut the fuck up and drive."

Andre might as well have sucker-punched the kid, because that's the precise expression Brendan wears. Andre expects an argument, but the kid starts the Jeep, and the two pass through Carthage in silence, the kid's white-knuckle grip fused around the wheel. This is not the silence Andre has intended, but this silence will do for now. Andre finds his tablet, scans the radio ad copy that Chalene's drafted. She's written a couple lines he likes—*God's people must be as faithful to the Constitution as we are to our Lord.* She's also written lines he doesn't like, with phrases like *righteous nation* and *the Creator's creation*, each appearing three times.

"No." The kid raises his knee and stomps on the brakes, hard enough to make the Jeep jerk, swerve across the median of the four-lane highway. Andre is thrown forward, tablet dropped, palms slapping the dash, eyes fixed on an approaching big rig that brakes hard, so hard that a flurry of sparks ignite, brief flashes of electric fire exploding beneath an enormous undercarriage. The truck swerves, the tractor one way, the trailer the other—Andre is certain this is how he will die—as the roar of the big rig's engine vibrates the inside of his skin. The truck straightens, passes—a near miss—yet the big rig driver is pissed, blasts his horn as he disappears down the highway.

Andre screams, "What the fuck is wrong with you?"

"Why are you such an asshole?"

"You trying to get us killed?"

"I deserve to be treated with respect."

"You want respect?" Andre fears his heartbeat will never slow. "Seriously? You just hit the brakes in the middle of a highway."

"You treat me like . . . ," Brendan says. "I don't understand what I did wrong."

"Then, clearly, you are not listening."

"Dre. I get it. I made a mistake. I shouldn't have bought from a stranger in public. And I know that I'm probably only making it worse now, but . . ."

"But what?"

The kid fights back tears, makes a lost, defeated expression that Andre hasn't seen since juvie, the expression of the new delinquent who just received his first public beatdown, a literal stomping from a bully, the sad yet defiant expression that says, *I won't give you fuckers the satisfaction of seeing me cry.*

"You don't trust me," Brendan says in a soft, watery voice. "You think I'm some spoiled pretty boy. You think I'm a naive poser who doesn't understand how the world works. I don't know how to persuade you that I'm not that person."

"Look, Brendan—"

"Sometimes, I think you don't even like me."

The silence pains Andre.

"Forget it, Dre. You're right. Let's get home."

"We should get off this road quick," Andre says. "That big rig driver will probably radio the cops, and we don't need anyone searching our Jeep."

The kid veers the Jeep back into their lane, passing into open country, where a lone swan sails across a pond full of lily pads.

That night, Andre paces beside his attic desk. Downstairs is silent. The kid hasn't left his room since their return. Andre wants to fix this, needs to fix this, not because he fears the kid might call Mrs. Fitz, but because he wants to do what he knows is right. But fuck if he knows where to start. Saying *I'm sorry* seems inadequate. Andre sometimes forgets that Brendan's twenty-two. All boys that age are a little dumb. A social worker in juvie said it had something to do with an underdeveloped prefrontal cortex.

Perhaps Andre should explain all the pressures consuming his life. But even to save his career, to make amends to a wronged friend, Andre observes limits. He will not, under any circumstances, discuss Cassie, because he values his dignity more than any friendship or career. He simply couldn't fathom looking Brendan in the eye and admitting that most nights he dreams of Cassie and that most mornings he wakes with his face wet with tears.

Perhaps he should share the time his mother got committed and Andre moved in with Hector, who had long since left home. These days, Pershing Avenue is a hip, trendy DC neighborhood, the type of gentrified community that GS-15s adore, with farmer's markets and charter schools and film festivals in the park, but twenty years ago, Pershing was a bona fide slum. A neighborhood at which junkies looked down their nose and where no one gave a damn about two teens, eighteen and sixteen, who lived alone.

There, on Pershing Avenue, the brothers played video games and freestyled and fucked random girls. They owned a black-masked mutt named Obi-Wan Kenobi, and they stood sentinel over a closet full of weed, which had come with the house, cellophane-wrapped bricks abandoned by the previous occupants as though they were an armoire that no one could figure out how to fit through the front door.

Hector made his living running cons on college boys, especially freshmen with Mommy's money and Daddy's pride. The same college boys with sagging pants and pristine sneakers who slept beneath *Scarface* posters, who threw around clumsy gang signs, who blasted profane rap music through the open windows of their black paid-for SUVs. The marks were easy to find, with their personalized gangsta-themed web pages. The relationship started simple. Heroin. Ketamine. E and GHB. Hector provided cheap club drugs without markup. Start with a taste. Build a rapport. Delay a small profit today for a big prize tomorrow. But selling the mark drugs wasn't enough; you had to offer the mark a thug life. Then you had to offer praise, plenty of it, like one would housebreak a puppy. *Good boy. Who's a good boy? You're such a good boy.* Gotta roll the college boy a blunt. Maybe let him call you his nigga. Maybe gift his dumb ass a gun. Definitely introduce him to a fine but trifling ho over there, a princess with a big ass, titty tat, and cell phone bill. But each time increase his buy. Not too much. Not too quick. Five hundred dollars. Eight hundred. Nine hundred. A thousand. Let them trust you with their money. Then you make your move.

Give me five G's today. I'll give you ten G's tomorrow.

These college boys, fancying themselves part 007, part Natty Bumppo, approached life recklessly, lived each day according to a series of selfish, simplistic creeds. *Bros before hoes. Survival of the fittest. You only live once.* One mark, a ginger-stubbled golf prodigy who always wore his visor backward, this chump loved to say, *The way I live, I only need to live once.* Fool thought he was funny. Bet he wasn't laughing once he realized that Hector had never given his real name, nor brought him to his real home, nor given him a phone number or e-mail address that wasn't easily burned.

For sure, Dylan Miller didn't see the con coming. That

gullible Mayberry motherfucker didn't have a clue. Didn't have any friends, which perhaps explains why he followed Hector around like a lost pup. For six weeks, Hector worked Dylan, filled his eighteen-year-old head with fantasies. Shootouts. Big cash. Seedy underground clubs with Romanian dancing girls. Finally, when the day came for Hector to make the ask, Dylan refused to invest five G's. No, that greedy motherfucker wanted to invest fifteen. *Go big or go home.* Hector tried to talk him out of it, explained that a bank might ask questions about a withdrawal larger than ten. Dylan didn't care, clasping Hector's shoulder. *Ten G's ain't nothing. Trust me, my nigga. You only live once.*

The next week, Dylan brought the cash in two Adidas duffel bags. Ten minutes later, Hector disappeared through the back door, a duffel bag in each hand.

Hector pulled this trick with a half-dozen college boys, each with access to a trust fund or an inheritance. The boys were smart enough never to call the police, or, if they did, the police didn't care. Both corrupt and honest cops will root against the wealthy college boy who just got bilked for five G's.

Fate, however, brought Hector and Dylan together six months later, when, by chance, Dylan came upon Hector outside a Wizards game. The fool thrust his forefinger in Hector's chest, cursing, crying, *Dude, you were my friend.* Now, to Hector's credit, Hector walked away, got as far as Gallery Place before Dylan grabbed his collar, stretching Hector's favorite shirt, an expensive tee that featured a contemplative Malcolm X.

Andre's thought a lot about Dylan over the years, and he has yet to figure out Dylan's plan. College boy didn't have a gun, didn't have a friend. All those gangster movies Dylan watched, and Dylan didn't learn a damn thing. Dylan shouldn't have been surprised, after stretching the Malcolm X T-shirt, that Hector threw a mean-ass hook that, a doctor would later say, shattered

Dylan's jaw and knocked him out cold. Now, to be fair, the incident should've ended there, but instead the assault continued, and, in the next eighty-four seconds, captured on a Metro security cam, Big Brother lost control, exercising a suppressed rage—the sum of his every indignity, insult, failure, and frustration—punching, kicking, spitting, shouting, *Who the fuck do you think you are*, and, finally, stomping, knee raised high, heel slammed hard, with the force of a jackhammer and the wrath of a jealous lover.

To this day, Andre believes that Dylan Miller deserved to get taken for fifteen G's. *Trust me, my nigga. You only live once.* But, goddamn, no one deserves a beatdown like that. A beating that left Dylan comatose for months and paralyzed below the neck.

See here, a wealthy white boy, an honors student at that, getting a beatdown, in the middle of the day, on a public street, outside the arena, on a day the Wizards won. Please, that's some shit that decent white folks won't abide. Local affiliates played the full eighty-four seconds, grainy black-and-white footage. *Some viewers may find the following footage disturbing.* Crime Stoppers posted a five-thousand-dollar reward. The mayor held a press conference, called the perp a superpredator.

Andre never learned who ratted them out, but four days after the fight, a little after midnight, a SWAT team cut the power to the bungalow on Pershing Avenue. The team stormed the house, shattering a window before tossing a flashbang inside, breaching the front door with a battering ram, screaming, scurrying, a sudden whirlwind in a small, confined space. These assholes, they put thirteen bullets through Obi-Wan Kenobi—dog wasn't causing no trouble, dog was locked inside a crate—shoved their submachines in Andre's face, slammed him against the floor. Thank God, Hector was in the shower, nowhere near the Glock he kept beneath his pillow. Andre lost his dog that day; he's grateful he didn't lose his brother.

The cops, the fucking cops, they tore up the bungalow on Pershing Avenue. Took the battering ram to the plaster walls, as though the brothers hid secrets inside, which, in truth, they did. The cops ripped up floorboards, shredded mattresses, smashed the butts of their rifles against the television, the Nintendo, the Sega Genesis, as though each act of senseless destruction could earn the cop a prize. They confiscated the guns, the cash, all the weed, and, as helicopters circled overhead, they took the brothers away in chains.

At the police station, the officers set them in separate interrogation rooms. Cops came in and out, never the same cop twice, maybe twenty, thirty cops over what felt like hours. The cops were fucking with him; of this, Andre was sure. Sometimes coming in, lighting a cigarette, blowing smoke in his face, and leaving without a word. One cop splayed across the table photos of Dylan in the ICU, saying, *For fuck's sake. Whoever did this is gonna suffer.* That asshole left, replaced by another, a bald, gold-toothed man, who poked his head through the door to say, *Oh you're right, they're gonna love his car-a-mel ass.*

Round after round. Hour after hour. Men with badges and holstered sidearms. Some men not much older than him. One claimed to have eyewitnesses. Another claimed to have fingerprints. One more claimed to have DNA. And yet they never asked a single question. Andre demanded a lawyer, a phone call, permission to take a leak, and, when the officers denied him all three—*Naw. That ain't gonna happen, little man*—warm piss trickled down his leg to puddle on the concrete floor.

Finally, the last cop entered, a plump-cheeked, silver-haired dowager who, if she were an actress, would've been typecast as a black Mrs. Claus. Ruth removed his cuffs, massaged his wrists, offered warm nutmeg cookies—to this day, the best cookies he's ever tasted—and, when Andre complained about his treatment, how the officers murdered his dog, how he'd asked for an attorney, how they'd made him piss himself, she shook her head, offering sympathies, saying, in a sweet, sincere tone, *Oh, you poor dear.*

For an hour, he and Ruth made small talk: the NBA, pizza parlors, his favorite video game. *Oh, that's a good one*, she said, *my grandson enjoys that one too.* She asked about his mother, his old life, his favorite subject in school, before, at last, saying, "I suppose we should chat about Dylan."

"I don't know nothing about that."

"My job is simply to find the truth."

"Truth is I didn't do it."

"I believe you," she said. "Though we did talk to Hector."

Ruth retold the story of Dylan Miller with exacting detail. She knew the original scam was for five thousand. Dylan suggested fifteen. She retold the story sympathetically: *The media, they make Dylan look like an angel, but he wasn't, was he?* She knew everything, except, she said, for why the beating took place. Ruth didn't ask why Andre beat Dylan. Instead, she played the video, all eighty-four seconds on a loop, shaking her head in dismay when Dylan snagged the Malcolm X T-shirt. *Dylan shouldn't have done that.* On this point, Andre agreed. Perhaps, she suggested, the video made a case for harassment or self-defense.

"You must admit," she said. "That person in the video looks like you."

"I guess."

"Hector thought so too," Ruth said. "He's such a sweetheart. Smart. Helpful. We thought it might be him, you two look a lot alike, but he says it looks like you."

"Can I talk to Hector?"

"Hector left hours ago," Ruth said. "He told the truth, and we let him go."

"Can I go home?"

"Once you tell the truth."

Andre was tired and hungry and confused and reeking of piss, and now he understood that Ruth would never let him leave this room. Not until he said what she insisted he say. And, for this reason, Andre signed her confession. *I, and I alone, attacked Dylan Miller.* He, at age sixteen, assumed that, because he was innocent, he wouldn't go to jail. Assumed he could straighten this mess out later. Thought perhaps, once he received a lawyer, he could clear his name. But the system conspired against him. His trial lawyer, a jackleg plea lawyer without an ounce of professionalism who wore a rumpled brown suit that smelled of cigarette smoke, who had oil-black dirt beneath his nails, this guy came at Andre straightaway—*They got video and a confession, our best bet is to plea.* No way Andre would trust this motherfucker. Andre asked one thing of this lawyer—track down Hector—and that simple task took months, a reunion that didn't occur until the day Andre needed to decide whether to plea.

Hector, on the other side of glass, spoke into a phone. "You need to take these charges."

"I didn't do it."

"What the fuck that got to do with anything," Hector said. "You say you do it. You go to kiddie jail. One year? Eighteen months? You're sixteen. You'll be out in no time. A little in-time is good for someone soft like you. Take the plea."

"We gotta get a new lawyer."

"You ain't listening," Hector said. "Cops took our money."

"Have you talked to Mom?"

"Shit, you know she ain't got no money neither," Hector says. "She also say you should take the plea."

"We should play for time," Dre said. "Something will come up. You could dig around, come across some info that's worth something."

"If you don't plea now, that Dylan motherfucker might wake up, and with that brain damage, who knows what he'll say?" Hector looked over his shoulder. "Take the plea. Cops don't care if they caught the right man. They just need the case closed. You plea, this's all over."

"Over for who?"

"What you want, Dre? Huh? You want me to take the fall? Something I didn't do? Shit. I got a record. That means, what? Thirty. Forty years with sentencing enhancements. Habitual criminality and shit. Probably send my black ass to prison in fucking Montana. Fucking Montana!"

"My lawyer says you lied on me."

"Is that what you want?" Hector said. "Me in Montana till I'm sixty?"

"You gonna testify against me?"

"After all I done for you," Hector said. "Selfish. Think only of yourself. You think you would've survived without me? You owe me. Take the plea, ingrate."

Hector slammed the phone, walked away, the last time the two would speak for years. The next day Andre took the plea.

Now, a drink in hand, the attic nearly dark, Andre decides against sharing this story. He hates thinking about that time. If he starts to tell the story, then he'll have to share the whole story, which, no matter how much he hopes to atone, he will never do. He can't explain why he took the charge for Hector, at least in a way that Brendan will understand.

CHAPTER FOURTEEN

The next morning, Andre has a videoconference with a neurologist, an attractive, green-eyed Sikh with a Boston accent. The doctor, warm and patient, provides answers that emphasize the positive. Hector, she stresses, retains considerable motor control. He does not yet need a respirator, nor does he need a feeding tube to prevent choking when he swallows, but he may need one soon. She makes one surprise diagnosis. Hector, she says, is clinically depressed, an observation to which Andre thoughtlessly replies, "No shit," an asinine comment for which he immediately apologizes. The doctor has written a prescription but worries Vera will not administer the medication. Vera has taken offense at the diagnosis, claims that, despite the illness, she and Hector make each other happy, an assertion she roared while waving her finger in the good doctor's face.

The videoconference has nearly ended when Andre hears a ruckus in the kitchen. Andre abruptly folds his laptop, cutting off the doctor midsentence, and hurries into the kitchen in time to catch the kid racing into his bedroom. He thinks to shout an apology, but the kid's already gone, the door slammed behind him.

Andre drums his forefinger against Chalene's dinner table, staring at a splayed Bible open to Revelation, anything to avoid the hard, threatening stare of the Lees' fourth son, the twelve-year-old with bronze skin, emerald eyes, and thick raven hair. The boy has bushy black brows, sports what Andre thinks is a grown-man's stubble.

The boy has a story, of which Andre knows bits and pieces, fragments gleaned from overheard calls, unguarded moments, pleas in Chalene's spoken-aloud prayer. The boy—what is his name?—was an eastern European orphan, a product of an unnoticed civil war, when a wealthy local family picked him out of a catalog and took him into their home. The boy arrived with problems—aggression, nightmares—and, except for a perfect pronunciation of American profanity, didn't speak a lick of English. That first month, he broke his new brother's collarbone. The next month, he bit off his sister's earlobe. His family pursued every conceivable treatment—prayer; medication; talk therapy; exorcisms, both Catholic and Pentecostal. Nothing worked, and six months in, his father woke in the dead of night, found the cellar flooded, the family's cat drowned, and the boy, all of five years old, standing naked in Wellington boots, yawning, a half-eaten peanut butter and syrup sandwich in hand.

Send his possessed ass back, recommended their pastor, who, that Sunday, delivered a sermon entitled "Understand When You've Been Beaten by Satan." The family reached out to Chalene, who, days before, had delivered a stillborn child, this time a girl whom Chalene had held and hugged and loved until the nurses said she had to let go. The boy still has issues—he is a constant in his mother's prayers—but Chalene claims God's grace has changed his heart.

Outside, his brothers smash bricks against pavement, pausing occasionally to yell inside at the boy, *Fucking Gypsy.* Andre is troubled that the boys would use an entire class of people as a slur, and he debates whether he should say something to Chalene—from where do the boys get this? Maybe she doesn't know that it's offensive. But there's a hitch—and Andre hates to admit it: in truth, the boy does look like a Gypsy. Straight out of *National Geographic.* Cap his head with a scarf, drape him in a too-short vest—God forbid he pierces his ear—and this twelve-year-old could crisscross eighteenth-century Romania in a bow-top wagon.

A thud on the sliding glass door. One of the twins drops his shorts, presses his bare, pale ass against the glass. The teen swings his hips, streaking the glass, fists raised, middle fingers extended.

"Thomas Gabriel." Chalene enters, snapping her fingers. "Pull up your pants, and stop dirtying my glass."

Chalene turns toward Andre, shrugs—*Boys will be boys*—and Andre dislikes the change he sees. She's chopped her hair short, too short—she looks like a death-row inmate prepped for an electric chair—and he considers invoking the clause in her contract that prohibits radical changes in her appearance.

"Dre, I gotta show you something." She opens a cardboard box atop a kitchen counter. Inside are yellow rubber bracelets, five hundred in all; half say *Constitution*, the other half *Christ.* "I used the campaign's credit card."

"That's what the card is for." Which is mostly true. He hoped she'd purchase necessities—childcare, transportation, a trip to the salon. Instead she buys Christian swag.

She continues to justify the purchase—*God and county. Isn't that our theme?*—and he tunes her out, staring at her head, wonders whether pregnancy causes all women to have such dry, flaky scalps. He weighs whether he should compliment her, offer false praise to build confidence, or whether he should offer a blunt, truthful assessment, a move to correct course before she grows comfortable looking like a child soldier conscripted to fight in a foreign war.

"Where's Brendan?" she says.

"He had a stomach thing."

She pauses, reads his face. "Dre, what did you do?"

"Me? What makes you think I—"

"Whatever you did, apologize." The yellow bracelets slide up and down her forearms. "Listen, I don't know Brendan all that good. But I do know three things about him. First, I know he's a papist."

Which answers from where her sons get it.

"Second, I know he's sharper than a fox's tooth."

He's terrified of what she'll say next.

"And third," she says, "I know he loves you. Honest-to-God loves you."

He feels relief.

"Fine, don't believe me, but I see it. *Dre this. Dre that. Let's ask Dre. Dre will know what to do.* Whatever you did, just say you're sorry." She signals the Gypsy to take out the trash. "Trust me. I've raised six boys and a husband. The sooner you apologize, the sooner this too will pass. Otherwise, that's a horse on you."

The Gypsy takes the trash, opening the glass door, passes Chalene's twin boys, the close-knit sixteen-year-old conspirators who speak in whispers, the two now sharing a cigarette beside a burial plot. The backyard is unkempt, tall grass and weeds, cigarette butts scattered among gopher holes, but the graveyard, behind a lattice fence, is clean and cared for. Four small slates mark four small mounds, two sons and two daughters, the babies who never drew breath, yet who were loved, named, set here to rest. Chalene catches Andre gawking at the graves, and he feels embarrassed to have trespassed upon her pain. He says, "I'm sorry."

"It's okay," she says, though he senses it's not. At a loss, he says the one thing that comes to mind. "I love your hair."

"You do not."

"I do. Seriously. You look like a kick-ass Christian warrior." The compliment makes her whole head blush. "You're Carthage's very own Joan of Arc." He thinks, but does not say, Joan of Arc right before the English burned her at the stake.

Two hours into rehearsal, Andre second-guesses whether Chalene should make tomorrow's speech. She's having trouble focusing, trouble enunciating, trouble recalling the essence of a two-minute statement that she's written herself. She insists upon memorization, refuses to read an index card, having learned from some evangelical blog that political statements, like an elegant sermon, are best delivered without notes.

"I need more practice," she says as her phone vibrates. She reads the text, sets the phone aside. "From the top. 'God can be known through the experiences of the people.'"

"'The American people.'"

"What?"

"The line. It's 'God can be known through the experiences of the *American* people.'"

"Right. The American people. What did I say?" She rests her hairless head against her kitchen table. "Fudge."

He itches his own scalp, an unconscious act of sympathy, wonders whether he should, at least, recommend that Chalene do something about the flakes. He's proudly borne a shorn head for nearly a decade; he could have given Chalene tips, chief among them, *A nearly shaved head, with a crown like yours, simply won't work*. When she ignores another vibration of her phone, he asks, "You need to go?"

"'God can be known through the experience of the American people.'" She repeats it, once, twice, three times, before transitioning into her full statement, which goes well for the next thirty seconds until a crash, as loud and unexpected as thunder, breaks her train of thought. In another room, a son—Andre can't tell which one—wails, sobs, which sends Chalene down the hall.

Andre wonders whether he should leave. She needs a good night's sleep. Maybe then she'll nail tomorrow's speech. Atop her microwave, a plastic-wrapped book on whose cover appears a handsome fifty-something white woman standing akimbo. From the photo alone Andre knows the book is Chalene's. Say what you will about Chalene Lee, but she reads like a monk, three or four books each week, each page scrutinized in search of hope, wisdom, and inspiration. He'd call his straw man well-read except the books she reads are all the same, checked out from her church library, autobiographies of middle-aged white women who overcame personal adversity through faith and love of Jesus Christ. From sinner to starlet. From harlot to Harvard. From county jail to Southern belle. Rags-to-riches narratives that surely ain't read for suspense.

But Chalene loves these memoirs, takes pictures with her phone of her favorite lines. Just yesterday, she devoured the tale of a forty-year-old woman, four kids, living in a trailer park in West Texas, who for years straddled a pole, and, from time to time, in moments of shameful desperation, practiced what Chalene described as light prostitution. This story seems indistinguishable from every other book Chalene has read: a series of trials and tribulations—bad boys, bad choices, bad behavior—a sinful spiral that smashed her against hell's rock bottom, a dizzying, harrowing experience that was, in turn, followed by a miracle, yes, a miracle!, the personal intervention of the Lord Jesus Christ. And now, just look at her—this small-town ho turned CEO—she owns a chain of wash-and-folds that makes millions each year. Only in America. Only through the love of Jesus Christ. Indeed, His Word is true. Amen and hallelujah. God can be known through the experiences of the American people.

Her phone rattles against the table, and Andre peeks between the curtains. Tyler sits in his truck, with a white-tailed deer strapped with bungee cords to the roof, typing another text message, and, sure enough, her phone rattles again. Andre hasn't spoken to Tyler in three weeks, not since the two reached a fragile accord in this room, shaking hands, splitting a beer, each sipping from his own pewter stein. Neither Tyler nor Andre apologized. Neither mentioned the past. Instead, the two spoke of the future, their shared vision: Chalene, county, Christ.

"No broken bones. At least as I can tell." She closes the box of yellow bracelets, Constitution and Christ, and he wonders whether anyone will wear these silly things. In his experience, such trinkets are popular with younger voters, particularly college students, the eighteen-year-old zealots so confident in their newly acquired beliefs that they wear their political views as fashion accessories. But grown men and women in Carthage? Will they embrace this silly rash-inducing gimmick?

"You're going to be great," he says. "Tomorrow. The council hall. I'll get there early and sit in the back."

"Bring Brendan."

"I can't promise."

"Fix his favorite meal tonight. Apologize. Everything will be all right."

"A good meal and all's forgiven?"

She raises a shoulder, as though to say, *You'd be amazed how dumb men are*, as her phone rings. She presses ignore, takes his hands, and, with eyes closed, they pray.

In juvie all the delinquents requested kitchen duty. The boys read teen magazines on whose covers starlets struck a pose. Inside, the pages also featured tips to seduce any beauty—clean beneath your nails, play it cool, don't be a cheap son of a bitch but don't be her chump neither—good, practical advice, but no tip appeared more often than learn to cook. A superb meal, advised each magazine, presented more seductive power than washboard abs and a fly-ass car. Andre never requested kitchen work—the heat, the noise, the reminder of his mother, who never visited—but, right now, he wishes he had.

He spreads ingredients across the makeshift counter. Fresh cod. Russet potatoes. Sea salt and egg whites and two kinds of oil, not to mention a dozen spices that were neither easy to find nor easy to pronounce. He skims online recipes, most featuring at least one offensive Irish stereotype, each recommending that he soak the potatoes overnight. One website, TrueIrishCuisine.com, offers a shortcut, parboiling, a foreign concept whose name alone suggests that he's way out of his league. Each recipe will take forever, with no guarantee of success.

The sliced potatoes splash into boiling water, a moment that reminds him of Cassie, the slim-hipped beauty who could never resist any fad diet that required boiled produce. Boiled cabbage. Boiled carrots. She once drank boiled beet juice each morning for a week. Didn't lose a pound, but temporarily stained her teeth a purple hue. He imagines her sitting at this table, snacking on parboiled potatoes, sharing the details of last night's gig: the drunk asshole in the front row, the club owner who grabbed her ass, the shitty, tone-deaf act for whom she opened. *Dre, I swear, I'm better than those white boys.* He wonders whether he'll ever know why she left, whether he did one specific thing wrong or whether she simply buckled beneath the constellation of his faults, and part of him fears that he will never feel whole until he knows the answer for sure.

He cuts the fire, leaves the kitchen to lie down. He doesn't feel like cooking anymore, thinks he wouldn't have fixed a good meal anyway. Tomorrow, he'll find a better way to make amends with the kid.

CHAPTER FIFTEEN

The next morning Chalene calls frantic, pleading, begging, *Dre, I'm sick. Please don't make me give this speech.* He tries to reassure her, to explain that tonight's two-minute statement is a low-stakes formality, a check of the box. He, however, fails to provide comfort and she swears that her Tyler refuses to attend the council meeting if Andre is there. *You're both such children.* To ease her angst, he promises to avoid the council chamber. Instead, he'll watch the meeting live-streamed, an invited guest at the home of Duke and Victoria Boshears.

The Boshears estate impresses, a lush, spellbinding landscape, acres of well-cut grass and smooth, calming slopes. The road winds upward between two plump hills, toward a three-car garage and grand two-story manor, which causes Andre to wonder whether the Boshearses' finances are as dire as Victoria claims.

Andre bangs the cast-iron knocker hard enough that he

fears he's asserted some form of alpha-male dominance. He hopes not, hopes that this evening will lack the customary Boshears drama. The council meeting, polite conversation, maybe a salty snack, that's all he wants. An old black woman wearing a lime-green tracksuit opens the door, face blazoned with a half-astonished, half-annoyed stare. He feels the need to apologize, or, at least, to explain, *I don't know my own strength*, but as he nears explanation, from somewhere deep inside the house booms Victoria's voice. "I told you. I told you, I told you, and you didn't listen, Duke. You never listen."

"Miss Vicki!" the old woman yells. "That man you want is here!"

He enters the foyer, a palatial space with a cinnamon warmth, and instinctively cases the house. The rock-cut candy bowl sitting atop a handcrafted trestle table, filled with apple-peel potpourri—pawn that bowl and you might buy yourself a decent winter coat. Does this house have security? Andre doesn't see a keypad, nor wires around the window, nor sensors around the floor. Not even a silly sticker fixed onto the front door.

Victoria makes a grand entrance—a hug, a kiss on each cheek—brings with her the scent of sweet wine. He says, "Am I interrupting? If now's a bad time . . ."

"Why would you say that? Let me show you around."

Victoria plays the perfect hostess, provides a first-floor tour: dining room, sitting room, anteroom, and den, each room full of dead animals stuffed and mounted against the wall. *This house has been in my family for six generations.* In the music room, an elegant, intimate space, the tour ends. Piano, cello, oboe, and harpsichord. The walls are smooth and round, the ceiling domed and high, a hemispherical shape that, he assumes, enhances the acoustics.

"Growing up, every night before bed, we'd make music.

Mother loved hymns. I played piano, much better than my sisters. Go ahead and laugh, but it's true. I received a scholarship to Vanderbilt's conservatory. But I left after first semester. Missed my parents. Missed Duke." She plays a few somber notes. "How is it fair that our destinies are written when we're that damn young?"

She points toward a big plush armchair and a platter of food. Boiled eggs and sweet cheeses and olives and anchovies. She takes the matching armchair, fills two crystal goblets with wine, presses polite conversation: the weather, a novella she's read, *I trust Mr. Fitzpatrick is well.* A refill of her goblet, another pour into his, though he has yet to take his first sip. She pauses to perform a party trick, forefinger run around her goblet's moist brim to produce a peal of music that swishes and swoons around the curved wall, gaining speed, growing louder and stronger, an amplification that turns the goblet into a symphony. Andre can't keep a straight face. He is as delighted and as impressed as a newborn playing his first game of peekaboo.

"Hon." Duke interrupts her performance. "Didn't we agree to host in my den? The TV's bigger there."

"We're watching a council meeting, not a Hollywood blockbuster." She finds the remote control, presses a button, and a section of curved wall slides away. Reveals a television, stereo system, shelves stacked with albums and cassettes and compact discs. "We're comfortable here."

She presses another button, and the council chamber appears on TV. The live-stream splits the screen, one camera capturing the five empty council seats, the other capturing both the podium and the audience's first two rows. A sudden panic takes Andre—where is Chalene?—and he fears his straw man has decided to stay home. He reaches for his phone, starts to type a text, *Where the fuck are you?* when he notices that each person in those first two rows bears a yellow bracelet. Constitution and Christ.

"Andre," Duke says. "Where would you like to watch?"

"We're comfortable here," Victoria says. "Aren't we, Mr. Ross?"

Andre refuses to be drawn into this passive-aggressive pissing match. Is this how they raised their kids? Andre predicts a short-lived standoff, predicts that Victoria will prevail. She has a steeliness about her, and these past seventeen years, he's learned to never underestimate white women in their sixties. They are, as a demographic, unusually resolute. Andre takes his first sip of wine, a smooth twenty-year-old blend that is, indeed, phenomenal. Which is another thing he's learned about white women in their sixties: they know their wines.

"Andre, you're doing fantastic work." Duke finds a chair. "I'm really impressed. I'm thinking about running for governor. If I do, I might let you advise my campaign."

"Sweetie. You can't afford your payroll taxes," Victoria says. "I doubt you can afford the fees of a professional campaigner."

"Come now. Andre here and I are friends." He pats Andre's knee. "I'm sure we'll work something out. How much is PISA paying for these initiatives?"

Andre takes another sip. The terms of the PISA contract are confidential. Andre doesn't know the precise sum. The client and the senior partners negotiate the price. For sure, PISA fronted the $350,000 campaign budget, and, of course, they pay expenses—airfare, rental car, the shithole in which he now lives—but he doesn't know the variable rate that the firm charges for his and Brendan's time, nor does he know the firm's baseline profit margin.

Onscreen the countdown clock vanishes, and the councilmembers take their seats. A prayer, the pledge, a call to order.

The chairman, a jug-eared octogenarian, conducts the roll call. All five members say *present*, white men wearing polo shirts and khakis. The chairman notes, for the record, that also present is Paula Carrothers. She takes notes at a desk within arm's reach of the council. She looks as though she's recently cried, and Andre wonders whether she's playing the victim for the crowd.

The chairman announces that tonight's agenda includes but one topic, for which the council will now hear public comment. A rush to line up behind the podium, each person wearing yellow bracelets.

"What's the point to this?" Victoria says. "We know we're going to lose the council vote."

"It's the law." Duke drinks from her goblet. "The council's gotta reject the initiatives first. Isn't that right, Andre?"

Andre says, "Title five of the state code . . ."

"Title five says . . ." Duke raises his finger, drains Victoria's goblet. "Once the council rejects the initiatives, the initiatives must appear on the next ballot. That's six weeks away. Go ahead. Ask him. He'll tell you I'm right."

Victoria turns her body toward Andre but keeps her stare on Duke. "Did we try to persuade the council?"

"Pssh. Don't bother." Duke refills her goblet, drinks. "I tried for six months."

"Did a professional try?" she says. "Someone who knows what he's doing?"

"Baby, you're not listening. That's what I'm saying." Duke helps himself to the platter, scoops olives and eggs and anchovies into one cupped hand and funnels the mix into his mouth like a pelican gobbles a shoal of fish. He says, mouth full, "I tried to talk to them. Stubborn know-nothings. They don't understand the economy. Don't understand how to create a friendly business environment. Especially your friend Paula Carrothers."

The first African American reaches the podium, an attractive, plump-faced bohemian wearing bell-bottoms and a crocheted hat. She announces that she's a local poet, shares her latest verse, a series of sonnets that place a stress on syllables where stress doesn't belong. She calls herself an educaTOR, claims her childhood was spent in AppalaCHIa, says she has never fallen for the false promises of AmeriKA. The liberty initiatives, she says, are propaganDA, the product of Southern bigotry and international corporaTIONs. That dark money and capitalism are an abominaTION.

Duke clears his throat, warming up for what, Andre predicts, will be a racist rant. Instead, Duke says, "Isn't that Lloyd Merriweather's little girl?"

Victoria blanches. "No."

"Sure it is. I'd know her anywhere. What's-her-face? That's what's-her-name. Ashley." Duke's confident. "That's Ashley."

"Ashlyn Merriweather died last year. Ovarian cancer. Left behind a husband and two sweet little boys. I went to her funeral, sent the family a check."

"Sweetheart, look at her." Duke folds both big hairy feet atop the coffee table beside the food. "Tell me that's not Ashlyn Merriweather."

"Duke, sweetheart, you're getting your black people confused. Again."

Andre feels a pang of pity for Duke. The guy didn't mean any harm. He can't help that he's an asshole, a disability for which Andre has growing sympathy, though even Andre realizes that Duke really should stop drinking Victoria's wine and put his callused feet on the floor. If Duke Boshears were a smart man, then he'd get his own goblet and change the subject. But Duke Boshears is not a smart man, and thus he says, "This check to her family, first I've heard of any check. How much did it cost me?"

"Not much. A trifle. I drew the check from your life savings, and I didn't want the check to bounce."

The poet's time expires midstanza, *rigged elecTION*, and the chair, banging his gavel, forces her to abandon the podium. A few folks boo her. Two senior citizens heckle, but Andre considers the poem a gift. Tonight, he'll overlay audio of the poem atop old footage of Paula Carrothers nodding her head in agreement, movie magic that will take an hour to create. He could blast a link via e-mail to supporters, with a subject that reads, *Paula Carrothers invites her socialist friends to speak*. The perfect slash-and-burn clip.

Three more commenters, white men wearing yellow bracelets, before Chalene, wearing a dress she's made herself, appears.

"Her hair," Duke says. "Andre, you should have done something about that. She looks like a lady who likes ladies. And that dress. Did she make that from a motel curtain? Was that deliberate? Part of a strategy? To make her look like trash? Are we losing the trash vote?"

Andre expects Victoria to mount a defense, but she says, "Oh, bless her little heart."

Chalene starts her statement, stuttering, fidgeting, and Victoria worries aloud whether Chalene is sick. Andre doesn't know. These past three weeks, Chalene's delivered electrifying stump speeches, bringing followers to their feet, and she's never appeared this shaken.

"I find it interesting," the chairman interrupts. "We rejected a bid from a company for the land sold in this initiative. Didn't make much news. We get lots of requests to build on that land,

and we always say no. But now, all of a sudden, here you are, askin' us to auction off that same land."

Chalene allows the chair to finish his thought, and only after she's assured that he has does she resume her statement. But she's lost her place, starting at the wrong spot, jumping midsentence between paragraphs, as though the text has unraveled in her mind.

"What are you babbling on about?" the chairman continues. "Tell me: I see these events you throw. See 'em on your slick web page. And I see all that food and rental space. I gotta ask: where's the money coming from? Look at you; no offense, darlin', but you can't even afford a decent dress."

The chairman pauses, provides the audience an opportunity to laugh.

"I hear you've been running around with a fella. A black fella, I hear, though I don't mean that in any bad way. I don't know whether it's personal or professional, don't know whether he makes his money dealin' or pimpin'. But I would caution you to remember your First Corinthians. 'Bad company corrupts good character.'"

Chalene says, "The rules say you're not supposed to ask questions."

"Sweetheart, I make the rules, and I say your time is up." His tone's sharp as shattered glass. "Now sit down."

"That's not fair."

"You don't get to decide what's fair."

"I didn't get to finish."

"Sit down and shut up."

Tyler Lee storms into the camera's view, and a sheriff's deputy rises, hand on sidearm, occupies the space between Tyler and the chairman. A photographer snaps photos. Folks murmur. The chairman, surprised, bangs his gavel.

"You're a big man, yelling at a pregnant woman." Tyler's face purples. "You're all incompetent buffoons. You talk, and you talk, and you talk, and you never get nothing done. You think you're better than us, think you're elite, think you're slicker than owl shit, but you ain't nothing but whores for sale."

A gasp. A few laughs. A thin smattering of applause. The chairman bangs his gavel. "We will restore order in the chamber. Sergeant at arms—"

"You weak, 'fraid-of-your-own-shadow capons. Milksops. Thinking about yourselves at the expense of us. Our forefathers are spinning in their graves. What have you done for Carthage? Nothing. You sit by and people lose their jobs. Our country is getting poorer and sicker 'cause of people like you. That's treason."

"—remove him."

Two sergeants at arms, in tight blue blazers, assume a position on either side of Tyler. The two strike quickly, like vipers, their tight, bruising grips like fangs sunk deep into Tyler's biceps. Tyler does not go easily—not when his wife's honor is on the line; he yanks free, yelling, "Get off me, you servile puppy dogs." The gauntlet is thrown, and the sergeants have the clear advantage. They are two, taller, quicker, thicker, fitter, fifteen years younger and each carrying a baton. One, two, three, they count aloud before resuming their assault, lifting Tyler off his feet, throwing him to the ground, pinning him against the carpet, his arms twisted behind his back, their knees pressed against his jaw and spine—treatment that, by God, Andre has always assumed law enforcement reserved exclusively for young black men. Tyler resists, kicking, screaming, flailing, a fight that Andre respects but knows, from experience, is a complete waste of strength. And in the blink of an eye, the sergeants at arms prevail, handcuffing Tyler, dragging him offscreen, the sheriff's deputy following closely behind, stun gun in hand. Offscreen Tyler releases a staccato burst of screams, not once, not twice, but three times—even Andre, no novice in the ways of excessive force, is horrified—and all the while the chairman sits back, smirking, amused by Chalene's tears.

CHAPTER SIXTEEN

Andre is a pupil scolded before his entire class. His teacher's reprimand is sharp, blistering like lashes against his back, scarring his thin skin, an aggressive and unsparing assault. Mrs. Fitz unfurls her fist, finger by finger, cataloging each of his campaign's faults: failure to build a coalition, failure to seek consultation, failure to adequately prep his straw man for the council's inevitable resistance. Failure after failure. She chronicles each from a list that she knows by heart.

"You know how I spent this morning?" she asks. He knows the answer. She's told him twice, once in an e-mail and again ten minutes ago, at the start of this real-time long-distance thrashing. "On the phone with PISA. The CFO, the CEO, COO, every smug overpriced attorney in Manhattan. We'll be lucky if they simply fire us. Lucky if they don't file suit alleging breach of contract or, more fittingly, complete and utter incompetence."

She's clearly been awake for hours—he can see it in her face, in the plum-colored bags beneath her eyes—and yet, at seventy-something years old, she roars like a lion.

"How many years of experience? A generous budget. How many IQ points between the two of you?" She stabs her finger at Andre, then at Brendan, who sits by his side. "And you can't put this local initiative to bed. Even before this disaster at the council—and let's be clear, that performance yesterday was a complete disaster—you were barely neck-and-neck. How, Andre? How? How, when you have a war chest and the advantage of experience? This should have been fish in a barrel."

He thinks—but does not say—her critique is unfair. The campaign has been smart, his message superb. A resonating theme. A charismatic straw man. Powerful rhetoric. No one can say he hasn't properly framed the issues. No one can say that he hasn't built a solid base. He's run a textbook dark-money grassroots campaign. A case study in street-corner democracy. And yet he must concede that, despite his best efforts, she's right: the campaign is not a runaway success.

"You had two objectives: Win the election. And do it quietly. And what have you done? Neither." She shivers. "You've made a fine mess of things. That's what you've done."

"But, ma'am." He sees, for the first time since this scolding began, an opportunity to present his defense. "I think we can—"

"I am not finished." She's five hundred miles away, speaking via videoconference, and he flinches as though she's raised her hand to strike. "You must listen."

"Ma'am. I apologize."

"Apologize? A lot of good that does me." She opens a tin, pops a mint into her mouth. "I thought you were on an unlucky streak. Thought if I gave you one more chance, gave you one simple referendum, then perhaps, perhaps, you could turn it all around. I should have known better. Should've known it was—"

Someone in Washington clears their throat offscreen, and Mrs. Fitz takes a pause. Andre wonders who's on the other end, standing in the shadows, listening, and he hopes that it's her personal assistant, who is his friend and ally. If that cleared throat belongs to someone else—a founding partner, or, God forbid, a rival associate—then Mrs. Fitz has decided to abandon her protégé. He's desperate to ask, *Ma'am, is someone else there?* but knows that such a question will invite more scorn.

"How much cash do you have left in your coffers?"

"About two hundred thousand dollars."

"Mercy mercy me." She waves around a stack of his weekly reports. "Any amateur could've caused the same mess for a quarter of the price."

He keeps his face forward, away from the kid, who sits quietly, in his pajamas, just out of Andre's eyeline.

"Nana. Can I say one thing?"

"No," she says. "Your hands aren't clean either. I only have myself to blame. The two of you together."

Andre's phone rings, sends a bolt of panic through him. He thought he'd turned it to silent. His face flushed, he fumbles inside his pocket. It's Chalene, who's called twice this morning but has yet to leave a message.

"This campaign needs a fix," Mrs. Fitz says. "A complete relaunch. You've got what? Around six weeks?"

"Yes, ma'am." He's eager to share his plan. An aggressive campaign. Push polls. Whispers. Faux endorsements and robocalls. Tried-and-true tactics. Right now, people may dislike Tyler and Chalene, but he guarantees, by the time he's done, they'll dislike Paula Carrothers even more. "I recommend—"

"No. No. No. Andre, stop. Stop. Son, you must stop," she says. "We are way past your recommendations. We are—"

"But—" He sees her eyes set aflame. "I apologize."

"I spoke with the others. We agree. Someone new must bring order to your chaos." She foreshadows what he knows is next. Her expression softens, her voice turns tender, the executioner's calm before the fall of the axe. She says, "I'm assigning a new team leader."

He imagines all the people whom this decision will make happy. The people invested in his failure. Rivals at the firm, for sure, but, for reasons he can't explain, he resents the inevitable I-told-you-so of Duke Boshears.

"Dre. Don't think this brings me joy, because I don't feel joy. But you have six weeks left, and your numbers are . . . this is a business. I don't take joy in this."

"I would never think that of you, ma'am. Never."

"Your straw men. George and Gracie? You'll need to get rid of them. They're damaged goods. Make sure they keep their mouths shut. Maybe send them on a cruise. Make them disappear until the campaign ends."

"I'll see to it."

"And, for God's sake, both of you, clean yourselves up. You look like . . . merciful heavens." She closes her eyes, shakes her head. "Even the longest day must end."

She taps a button on her keyboard, and the flat-screen goes blank.

"She's never spoken to me . . . I mean, I've heard her speak that way to others, but never to me," Andre says, turns to meet the kid's unsympathetic stare. "B?"

The kid rises, heads downstairs saying, "Good luck, Dre."

That evening, pacing Chalene's porch, he rehearses what he'll say. His message is simple, no need to complicate the issue: PISA seeks a new direction. We appreciate your contribution, but, in light of recent events, PISA wants change. If we win, which we will, then PISA promises to keep a well-paid post open for Tyler.

The Gypsy opens the front door, chewing, a turkey leg in hand. Andre assumes, at first, that he's interrupted a birthday party. Loud music. Loud talking. The glow on the Gypsy's face is bright. Inside, Andre finds all six sons feasting at the kitchen table, jolly and merry, the biggest banquet this house has probably ever seen. Plates and platters of food cover every inch of table space and countertop, with excess desserts, pans of pudding and pastries and pies, placed wherever there's room.

"I told you." Chalene kisses his cheeks. "Toussaint Andre Ross. I told you!"

"Don't call me that." He wants to get this over with. "I talked with PISA."

"I like Toussaint. Sounds respectable. From now on, I'm calling you—"

"Chalene, PISA has reevaluated the campaign."

"All this time I felt the burden of your doubts." She smiles as though her next move is checkmate. "But see what can happen. This is proof. Undeniable scientific proof. The power and the glory of trusting your troubles to the Lord Jesus Christ. Praise His name."

"Yes. Praise His name. PISA thanks you for your contribution."

"When doubts filled my mind, your comfort gave me renewed hope and cheer. Behold." She opens a shoe box, a treasure chest of cash and checks. "I lost count. Sweetie, how much money is in here?"

"Five thousand eight hundred fifty-three dollars." The Gypsy speaks with a mouth full of bread. "And a little change."

"Between us"—Chalene leans in, whispers—"he probably skimmed a little off the top. He's good at math, the best of all my boys, but you know, he has that thieving disability. If I had to guess, we have at least six grand. Don't worry, I'll make him give it back." She restores her normal tone and voice. "What do we do with all this money? With . . . how much again, sweetheart?"

"Five thousand eight hundred fifty-three dollars and change."

"Thank you, dear." She shakes her head in cynical disapproval. "Do we have to report it? This is our friends' and neighbors' money. And folks will send more. A couple people called, said they put checks in the mail. These folks, they don't have much, and they gave what they could. I want to do this by the book."

"This came in today?" The house phone interrupts his thought. "From who?"

"Everyone!" Her cell phone rings too. "Sit. Enjoy. Praise His name."

She answers her phone, snaps her fingers and points toward the couch. He resents the command—he's not the family dog—but he sits, nonetheless, beside a stack of newspapers, on which appears, on the front page, right smack in the middle, Tyler Lee at yesterday's council meeting. The staff photographer has captured an extraordinary moment, an action shot—is this when Tyler called the chairman a milksop?—a perfect snapshot of Tyler's face full of frustration and rage and passion, fists raised, *Christ* bracelet on one wrist, *Constitution* on the other.

In every election, one photo defines the contest. A candidate tripping over the curb. An incumbent's disengaged stare. The all-too-familiar embrace of a married candidate with his arms around a woman not his wife and half his age. More often than not, the photo—and the narrative it represents—isn't the product of a campaign's best effort. Instead, the moment occurs naturally, captured by a stringer or on a supporter's phone, and the photo resonates, speaking an inexpressible truth that, somehow, articulates a campaign's perceived strength and weakness. This photo, yes, hot damn, Chalene's right. This photo is a miracle. Tyler's angry—no, more than angry, he's genuinely pissed, ready to fight, ready to lay down his life, to battle on behalf of God and Carthage.

Chalene hangs up the phone, which, she says, "hasn't stopped ringing. Everyone saw the paper, and they see my Tyler." The phone rings again. "The picture's everywhere. A gal from church says it's now her husband's screen saver. Our pastor put it on the church home page."

"This picture?"

"Oh, and you'd be proud, I've been handin' out voter registration cards, and, oh! The bracelets." She raises her wrist to show hers as the phone continues to ring. "These two are all that's left. I passed out my last set an hour ago. Everyone wants them. I ordered more. Used the credit card. Is that okay?"

"Chalene." His patience is exhausted. "What are people saying?"

She answers the phone, and Andre skims the paper. Inside, at the jump, is the poet. Her photo is equally angry, equally aggressive, and yet hers is unflattering. Have they darkened her skin? The text beneath her photo is surely a gross misquote. He knows why the editors picked this shot—they practically stole his idea—and he's not naive enough to resent the bigoted blessing.

These photos, he knows, represent the only facts that people will learn about last night's council meeting. God bless social media. Good for pictures; terrible for truth. Most folks won't watch the full meeting online, and most folks won't read the full story, a short fifteen column inches that offers a shallow summary.

Andre flips through the newspaper, expects a sidebar or op-ed, some piece of investigative journalism that questions the link between PISA and the initiatives.

Nothing.

Tyler wanders inside from the backyard, shirtless, wears a camo apron and jester's crown. He carries a platter full of thick steaks, marinating in a puddle of blood and grease, in all about three hundred dollars' worth of well-marbled beef.

"Dre, brother, you're here! Sit down. Grab a plate." Tyler wipes his hand against his apron, grabs Andre in a big bear hug. "Brother. I'm telling you. It's been a madhouse. Folks in and out all day. Bringing food and money. Things are different. You can feel it in the air. Like status electricity."

Tyler finds the largest steak, plops it atop a paper plate for Andre. Tyler's all smiles, with a newfound confidence and swagger. Andre takes his seat, unfolding a linen napkin, watches the steak juices soak through the paper plate.

"Tyler." Andre pokes the meat that is burnt yet bloody. "Question."

"Italian dressing, brown sugar, a little bourbon."

"Today's article in the paper."

"What? No, come on, brother." He slams down his steak knife. "Man, I knew it. I knew it. There's just no pleasing you. I didn't do nothing wrong, and you come here, in my house, and—"

"No. No. Tyler. The article's great. You did great. I couldn't be happier." On Tyler's face relief turns to pride, as though all his life Tyler's sought Andre's praise. "But I've done this for a while, and now, twice, you've received especially favorable coverage from the local newspaper."

Tyler casts a glance over Andre's shoulder, and Andre turns in time to catch Chalene's face. Andre regrets that he asked, because without a doubt, the two share a secret. In politics, you never know what secrets people might keep: family secrets, secret families—the bigger the secret, the bigger the sin.

"Boys," Chalene says, "take your plates out to the patio."

The boys complain—too hot, too dark, too many bugs—but Tyler, with a clear of his throat, hastens their retreat.

"The publisher, the paper's owner." Chalene slides into Tyler's lap, and the two exchange an obnoxiously long kiss. "We worship with the family."

Is that the secret? No. Of course not. Otherwise the boys could've stayed. He suspects that she's about to share dirt, dark salty poisonous dirt that one sprinkles in their nosy neighbor's yard to kill their rosebushes. Maybe, oh, just maybe, one of them had an affair, which wouldn't be a complete surprise. Probably Tyler. All that time working with half-naked hoes. Of course he strayed. Of course he surrendered to temptation. Name one red-blooded American male who wouldn't have. Goes to show, though. This marriage has always felt too solid, too healthy, too happy, and too strong. Two people couldn't possibly love each other this much for this long.

"It's the same family that adopted our Lucius." Her voice breaks as she gestures outside at the Gypsy. "That family wanted to send my angel back to that godforsaken war-torn land where they don't even worship the Lord Jesus."

He's disappointed. He wanted something salacious, but he realizes this revelation's worth. The newspaper—the only print media in town—owes his straw men. These past few weeks, Chalene's shared every banal family secret. Andre even knows the vaccination history of the family dog (only rabies, everything else is luxury). Why didn't she share this? He suppresses his irritation, saves for another day a discussion about relevant information.

He slows the Jeep, checks his cell. The battery is dead, and he wonders whether Mrs. Fitz has returned his call. He has, in the past hour, sent a half-dozen texts, phoned four times, each time leaving a message explaining that the campaign's circumstances have changed. The council meeting represented a watershed, the real moment this campaign began. He recommends, before she assigns a new team lead, that she put a new poll in the field, confirm what he sees on the ground.

"Please, Mrs. Fitz," he says. "Just one more chance."

He turns the Jeep, brakes hard at the mouth of his driveway. Directly before him, right there in the middle of his pebbled drive, a coyote lies on its belly, pawing a cottontail rabbit, muzzle bloody, teeth tearing at flesh and fur and bone. Andre flashes his high beams, but the coyote refuses to relent. Andre sticks his head through his window, yells, "Get the fuck out the way," to which the coyote raises its nose, baring its fangs, and growls.

Again and again, he honks the horn, until at last the coyote rises, seemingly more annoyed than intimidated. Andre slowly advances the Jeep—inch by inch—but the coyote stands its ground. The standoff, however, is short-lived, as the coyote, tail raised, snatches the rabbit, trots down the road.

He seizes the moment, dinner plates in hand, sprints onto the porch. There, beside the open door, a dull-edged, world-worn footlocker with a broken hinge. A stretched-too-tight belt—orange and green and white—keeps the bloated footlocker shut, and a dog-eared sticker makes plain to whom this luggage belongs.

The screen door closes, and he follows the fresh scratches etched onto the wood floor, passing through the vestibule and into the viewing room and to the base of the stairs, passing the mounted predators' heads that he once resented, finding, along the way, the kid's flotsam and jetsam: a face towel and dice cup, a tote bag and balled-up pair of socks. Andre collects each, like a father tidying up after a careless child, cradles each item in the crook of his arm. A short climb up the stairs, and he's paralyzed by a fear of what he might find.

"Please, B," he whispers to himself. "Please don't go."

He slides open the door, advances to Brendan's room. Finds the space empty save a stripped bed and a television that sits atop a pyramid of milk crates. The faint stench of a cigarette irritates his eyes, and he traces the scent up into the attic, where the smell is strong. In the dark, sitting on the ledge of an open window, the kid is pensive, ash-tipped cigarette in hand, face pale in the moonlight. Andre reaches for the light, but the kid says, "Don't." Pauses, then says, "I called you."

"My battery." Andre sets the dinner plates atop the conference table, removes the tinfoil. Fried chicken. Slabs of ham. Corn and tomatoes and beans. "Chalene sent more calories than a sane man should eat. She packed that honey cake you like. Let me grab you a Guinness."

"My mom called." The kid takes a drag, then hands the cigarette to Andre. The kid knows Andre doesn't smoke, but Andre senses he must take this hit. To his surprise, Andre enjoys the sudden inner warmth, sweet and spicy, the tickle of his throat. The kid says, "That's the last one."

"We'll find more. We'll go to Charleston. Make a day of it."

"No. It's my last cigarette forever. After this one, I'm done." The kid reclaims the cigarette, forefinger brushing Andre's wrist. "About an hour ago. They . . . the firm . . . the partners . . . they were supposed to meet."

Andre braces for bad news, understands the packed bags beside the front door. The firm must have called, and the founding partners must have recalled this team. He has no right of appeal. Their decision is final. Infallibility is the best perk of seniority. He never thought his career would end like this: midcampaign, in a shadowy, smoke-filled room in a derelict house in a backwoods town that he's happy to leave behind.

"B," he says. "As soon as we get back, I promise that I'll take full responsibility."

"What? No, man, Dre," the kid says. "The security guy called my ma. What's his name?"

"Sabatino?"

"Yeah, yeah, Sab, I like him." He takes a long puff, holds the smoke in his lungs, which must surely burn, then exhales. "He found her passed out at her desk."

"Wait, Sab found who?"

"Someone started CPR right away. Used one of those portable defibrillators. But by the time the paramedics got there . . ." The kid takes his last drag, drops the smoldering butt to extinguish it beneath his heel. "Dre, man, we gotta go back to DC. We gotta bury my nana."

PART IV

GOODBYE

CHAPTER SEVENTEEN

No one quite remembers when Fiona Fitzpatrick joined St. Benedict of Palermo, the District's only African American Roman Catholic church. Most likely, she joined twenty-five years ago, during that period when she considered abandoning political consulting to scratch an itch and run for office herself, to become the first elected white mayor of Washington, DC. She ultimately decided against a run—her friends, the polls, an exploratory committee each predicted a humiliating defeat—and most folks assumed that she would return to her former parish, a small, elite Georgetown congregation where she'd worshipped for nearly thirty years. But Fiona Fitzpatrick didn't. She stayed here at St. Benedict's, and she received communion, and she baptized grandchildren, and she mourned the loss of her first and then her second husband; and here, on a cold, wet day in spring, is where the people who loved her say goodbye.

The two-hour funeral Mass ends, the choir singing, one last bold, jubilant performance accompanied by a string quartet, the formation of a haunting harmony that soars like seraphs through the sanctuary; all the while clergy, black men in cream robes, lead the exiting procession with a little extra soul in their step. Her six sons and two eldest grandsons guide her casket up the aisle, a solemn parade followed by a cadre of family and dignitaries.

Andre's been stoic the entire ceremony. It's been six days since Brendan shared the news, and Andre has yet to surrender to emotion. But this closing hymn, this damned awe-inspiring hymn, both beautiful and breathtaking and sung by a choir that is sincere in its grief—My God, Mrs. Fitz, you would've been proud—this hymn rumbles like a peal of thunder trapped inside his chest, and he wonders whether all funeral Masses are this grand, this full of pageantry and regalia, tradition and spirituality, hope and loss. He wants to believe that the answer is no, to believe that the church has done something special for its most faithful of daughters. Sure, Mrs. Fitz would've complained. This service, she would have said, was too long, too loud, too much of a fuss. But, in his heart, he has to believe she would've been happy, or at least content.

The casket disappears through an archway, and the cathedral springs into motion. Hundreds of mourners fill the aisles. They shake hands, exchange hugs, check their phones. The other associates pass him without acknowledgment, and he wonders how best to interpret their silence. He thinks maybe they simply don't know how to respond to his sorrow, that they don't know how to comfort the usually stony black man now wiping tears. Perhaps they think it's better to simply leave him be. Or, possibly, they know something he doesn't.

"Lovely service, wasn't it?" Mr. DeVille, the firm's other senior partner, stands beside Andre. "And that homily. Boy. Pitch-perfect. Eloquent. Funny. Touching. Such nice things the father said. I should be so lucky. You think Fiona wrote it herself?"

Andre buries his chin in his chest; the last thing he needs is for someone to see him giggle at his mentor's funeral. But the moment has also made him aware; a small group of important people, the firm's most senior staff, are huddled beneath the archway, watching. Andre wonders what they expect. Will Mr. DeVille fire him here? It would be a savvy move. Anywhere else, Andre might cause a scene. Stomp his feet. Pound his fists. Throw a chair. For sure, he'd raise his voice and curse the old man out, but here, in Mrs. Fitz's church, moments after her funeral Mass, even Andre wouldn't dare.

"Don't mind the vultures," Mr. DeVille says. "Why don't we walk? This probably isn't the best place to talk shop anyhow."

The two make the short trip into a nearby vestry, a small room with round windows that overlooks journalists snapping pictures of mourners. Her funeral has attracted international attention. The *Post* ran a lengthy obituary that quoted a former president. *She was to me a trusted advisor and loyal friend.* The story was chum in the waters, beckoning scores of protestors, groups now assembled across the street, kept at bay by candy-cane-striped sawhorses and uniformed police. One group protests capitalism and corporate money in politics. Another is a coalition of homophobes, members of an anti-Catholic, anti-gay, anti-Semitic Missouri-based church that travels around the nation in white minivans to mock families' grief. To Andre's disappointment, the homophobes win the prize for best demonstration. These assholes came to play. The other group has no sense of order or direction or flair. It feels as though the anti-capitalists woke up this morning, forged a Doodle poll, and chose between this protest and brunch. They're not even standing together, diminishing their strength, scattered among trees and trash cans and random onlookers in plastic ponchos. They should take a page from the playbook of the homophobes, who have not only formed a solid block, but also positioned themselves strategically in front of the news cameras. Their banners even include a short, easy-to-remember call to action: *Friend us on Facebook, follow on Twitter, or find out more at . . .* But the anti-capitalists, their signs are lousy: long, busy, confusing. One man—who's either homeless or a college professor—has written a sign in Latin. Another woman's sign is a photo of a vagina—possibly hers, but, God knows, possibly not. A third protestor, a punk-rock diva wearing a miniskirt and satin tie, her sign must have fifty, maybe sixty words in small sloppy print.

"That woman's sign has more words than *Anna Karenina*," says Mr. DeVille. "But I suppose that's a good thing. If our opposition ever organized, we might both be out of a job. I—"

"Am I out of a job?" Andre blurts out, and regrets the interruption. But what are they here for, if not to settle this question? They are both busy men. No need to draw this out. "I'm sorry, sir. I didn't mean any disrespect."

"I've received a briefing on Carthage." The old man whistles. "Messy, isn't it? I've read your memos. Talked to PISA. Studied the finances. Fiona wanted to replace you as team lead, and I think she—"

"Sir, with respect, I don't think she understood—"

The old man sets his jaw, raises a brow, an expression that says, *That was the second time you've interrupted me. I dare you to try a third.*

"I'm sorry," Andre says. "Yes, sir. She did want to replace me."

"I asked Vinnie to put a tracking poll in the field. Apparently, you're ahead. Fifty-five/forty-five. Likely voters. That stunt at the county council. The man electrocuted in front of his wife. Turned the tide, didn't it? People were on the fence, but now they're mad, and rightly so. That video made me mad."

Andre thinks that if Mr. DeVille knew Tyler, then Mr. DeVille might feel differently, might feel the sizzle of a hand Taser is precisely the public reprimand that a jackass like Tyler needs.

"I see no need to replace you," Mr. DeVille says. "You can keep your team as is. It's you and an intern, right? But understand, we can spare no more resources. Money or staff. You must win with what you have."

Mr. DeVille doesn't say what Andre presumes. This reprieve is not an act of mercy. Most likely, Mr. DeVille couldn't find a volunteer to take over the campaign. Not this late in the game. Not this small backwoods campaign without an ounce of prestige. Andre's colleagues, the firm's other junior and senior associates, are many things: ambitious, cunning, and shrewd. They are not fools.

To be safe, he waits a little longer in the vestry. Not too long, only long enough to ensure that he won't bump into anyone he knows. To pass the time, he checks his phone, hopes for a message from Brendan. The two haven't talked since the night Mrs. Fitz died, the same night that Andre drove the kid to the airport.

He leaves the vestry, tiptoeing between pews, careful not to disturb a praying woman, makes his way to the cathedral's front entrance, where, beside the door, is a picture of Mrs. Fitz. Across the street a few protestors collect their things, their numbers now small. The cameras have left, as have the homophobes, no doubt off to ruin another solemn occasion. Only three anti-capitalists remain, scruffy white boys with designer scarves and blond dreads, laughing, high-fiving, slapping each other's backs. Now they can enjoy that late brunch. Andre doesn't wish to spoil their good cheer, but he's tempted to ask what exactly they think they've accomplished. *Did you advance your cause today? Is corporate money now and forever banished from American politics?* He knows what they'll say, what they always say: *We made our voices heard.* He hates that answer, which invites the reply: *Well, good for you. Too bad you don't have corporate money, because then your voice might have been heard a little louder.*

Andre descends St. Benedict's granite steps, tries to hail a cab, the first two passing, the drivers not bothering to hide their skepticism. Two more empty cabs pass before one stops. Inside the cab, which is cold and smells of pot, he dials the kid again, gets his voicemail. He can't win without B, and, deep down, he doesn't want to. The kid, he hopes, has forgiven his sin, but they haven't discussed it, haven't hugged it out bro-style, which leaves Andre to question why the kid hasn't returned his calls. But what if lingering resentment isn't the reason? What if Brendan simply needs more time to grieve? Mrs. Fitz passed only six days ago. Is it too soon to ask the kid to leave the comfort of kin? Andre doesn't have much experience with this kind of loss. Perhaps for once, Andre should choose honesty, explain that he needs Brendan, that the two could support each other through this time of loss and sorrow, and perhaps Andre's better off starting with the God's honest truth: *Goddamn, B, I miss her too.*

Andre could work for a lifetime and never afford a house like Mrs. Fitz's. A two-story stone-and-clapboard nestled on a ten-acre Northern Virginia estate. He's had some good times here. Thanksgivings. Christmases. His first celebration of Easter. But now, standing in her front yard, Andre hesitates to enter. He knows that he shouldn't feel anxious, but he remains unclear on whether, in the end, he enjoyed her favor. Andre doesn't wish to cause a scene, doesn't wish to make a grieving family feel unease. But he's scheduled to return to South Carolina—his flight leaves in, can that be right, hours?—and because he needs to know whether Brendan plans to return too, he'll risk their whispers.

"Dre. Thank God you're here." Gracie Fitzpatrick flies through the front door, gives him a peck on the lips. "It's madness inside. Six sons and six wives. Twenty-two grandchildren. Eight great-grandchildren. A baby that refuses to stop crying." She counts each on her hand, one by one, by name. "And, if that wasn't enough, a pack of aunts and uncles and cousins crossed the Atlantic for the service."

"Proof that family transcends international borders."

"Proof that everyone assumes they're a beneficiary of her will." Gracie, in her thirties, has a classic beauty: eyes dark with mascara, flawless skin, raven hair pulled back to reveal a long, elegant neck. "Last night there was a fight. Can you believe it?"

"Everyone's emotional. Arguments are bound to happen."

"Not an argument. I mean a fight. Fisticuffs." She shadowboxes with her elbows tucked in. "My brother, Sean, got popped right in the nose. The whole thing was a mess. Blood and snot. We had to fetch a physician."

Andre struggles to remember which grandson is Sean. Is he the one whom both Brendan and Mrs. Fitz mocked, the twice-divorced, rarely sober mooch who never finished high school, who never held a steady job, who, now thirty, still harbors delusions that one day he might become an international rock star?

"Don't pity him. If that's what you're thinking," she says. "Sean had it coming. He thinks he's funny. Kept asking the extended family stupid questions about Ireland. *You ever seen a leprechaun? How often do you say begorra? Do you know the words to 'Danny Boy'?*"

"Is Sean okay?"

"Who knows? But I know one thing: if he heals too quickly, he won't learn his lesson." Gracie channels her grandmother. "I mean, I love my brother, I do, but let's face it, he's a bum, a bona fide asshole. Nana, God rest her soul, thought so too. Speaking of bona fide assholes, how are you?"

Eight weeks ago, of all Mrs. Fitz's kin, Andre knew Gracie best. She's her grandmother's favorite, the unmarried millennial socialite who sacrificed her own love life to move in here after Mrs. Fitz's second husband died. Gracie's a critic and dramatist who, last year, produced an acclaimed performance, a high-concept piece entitled *How Spiders Learned to Dance*, which debuted at the Kennedy Center.

She escorts him inside, where half the firm stands around, chatting up senators, ambassadors, former cabinet secretaries, and a former Speaker of the House. In the anteroom, huddled beside the open bar, the firm's three newest junior partners, phones in hand, whisper, probably wondering whether they should stay longer or whether they've put in sufficient face time. At the base of the master staircase, three shaggy blonds, boys no older than ten, wearing black ties and black suspenders, leap from the bottom step, their polished loafers slapping against the marble floor.

"Stop running!" Gracie says. "Cousins from Waterford. They've never seen a house this big before. Brendan told them somewhere hidden around here, there's a passage to Narnia. Dummies have been searching the house for three days."

Andre lets loose a laugh that causes some to stare.

"It's not funny. They've punched holes in three wardrobes. Some of those were antiques." She pinches his arm. "I shouldn't be surprised. You and Brendan together, good grief, for eight weeks in the middle of nowhere. Amazing South Carolina's still in the Union. Whose bright idea was that?"

He smiles politely, doesn't share Mrs. Fitz's final admonishment, her regret at having ever paired the two. He wonders whether Mrs. Fitz really meant that. Perhaps she expressed not truth but frustration. He hates not knowing, considers asking Gracie—*Did she mention me near the end, did she think me a disappointment?*

"How are you holding up?" He realizes he hasn't asked. "Anything I can do?"

"You can eat a gluten-free vegan lunch." She points toward the crowded dining room, to a catered feast. "I bet it's awful."

"I'm happy to," he says. "First, though, is Brendan around?"

She gives her grandmother's knowing stare, and for a moment, he expects her to say no. He feels the burn of shame, wants to ask another insecure question: *Did he tell you that I was needlessly cruel?* But she points at patio doors that open onto the backyard, where a greenhouse stands.

He kisses her cheek, crosses the lawn alone, passing a blossoming tulip tree that he planted years ago. The exercise blistered his hands and nearly broke his back. Mrs. Fitz lured him here on a Saturday, promising to discuss a potential presidential contender who wanted to establish a ground game in Nashua. Of course, Andre came running—who doesn't want to win the New Hampshire primary?—even brought cheddar-and-onion bagels, her favorite, from the Georgetown baker she adored, only, as soon as he walked through her door, to experience the bald-faced bait-and-switch. *Shall we chat outside while we plant a tree?* Like a fool he agreed, assumed that the whole project would take, what? Ten minutes tops? What the hell did he know about planting a tree? A black kid from Southeast simply assumes that trees plant themselves. Twice he pinched his skin between post and driver. Twice splinters pierced his palms. Mrs. Fitz stood sentinel, issuing orders, judging his work, obsessed with getting the tree to stand perfectly upright. *I won't have a crooked tree causing my guests vertigo.* In the end, tree planted, they sat upon the earth, eyeing the sunset, drinking honey-sweetened tea, eating bagels now as rigid as smoked beef, the first picnic of his life.

Of all his memories of her, this is his favorite.

The greenhouse reeks like a stagnant pond. The humidity, the stench, the steady trickle of water that would drive any sane man mad—he struggles to understand this greenhouse's appeal. When Mrs. Fitz first announced she planned to take up aquaponics, he confused her intent with aqua aerobics, blue-haired biddies bouncing around a public pool with floaties around their arms. Now he must give his mentor credit. The garden impresses, pleasant to see and good for food. Peppers and peas, cucumbers and kale, potatoes and plump green tomatoes ripe on the vine.

Brendan sits atop an upturned crate, hunched over, eyes stuck on the ground. The kid, sweaty and pink faced, looks like he's lost a fight: hair disheveled, shirt untucked, top button unfastened, tie undone. The kid chugs an Irish ale sloppily, with brew seeping around the curves of his lips.

"Careful," Andre says. "You don't want to ruin your suit."

"Not my suit." The kid wipes his mouth. "Borrowed it from my cousin Sean."

"Is that the same Cousin Sean who got popped in the nose?"

"Who do you think popped him?"

"You? Busted his nose? That before or after you asked to borrow his suit?"

"Once you beat down a punk, you don't need to ask his permission for anything," the kid says. "Didn't you teach me that?"

Andre doesn't remember that specific lesson, but he can't deny the statement's truth. Sounds like something he might say. Almost certainly the kind of streetwise maxim that he learned from Hector or in juvie, a truism that Andre, drunk and chatty, might have passed along during an all-night gaming session.

"I hope I taught you other things too."

"One day I'll write a book."

The kid fishes behind him, trembling, retrieves and lights a cigarette. The smoke tickles Andre's nose. A sneeze. A cough. A quick *ahem* to clear his throat. Brendan seems to enjoy Andre's discomfort. The kid takes another prolonged puff, blows the smoke toward Andre's face. Andre ignores the insult, blinks hard to clear his irritated eyes, says the first thing that comes to mind, which he immediately regrets. "I thought you quit smoking."

"Dre." Brendan checks his phone. "I have a lot of work to do."

"I've tried you every night for the past four days." Andre hears the exasperation in his own voice. "I left two voicemails this morning."

"We've been busy."

"Too busy to return a text?"

"I swear to God, Dre. You're worse than a girlfriend."

The kid takes another puff, blows the smoke upward, the poisonous vapor evaporating around a bush of navy beans. Andre assumes cigarette smoke isn't good for vegetation, but who will complain if a dead woman's tomatoes taste like ash?

"Our plane leaves in four hours," Andre says. "The firm has paid for our tickets. You made a commitment. To the firm. To the client. To your grandmother."

"Who do you think you are?"

"Tell me what to do. Whatever it takes to go back to the way it was. Please," Andre says. "You want me to beg? I'm begging. You want me to change the direction of the campaign? We'll run the most honest fucking campaign the world's ever seen. Just name it. Name it."

Brendan drops the cigarette, smashes it beneath his heel before kicking the smoldering butt beneath a bench. The kid drains the half-empty beer, hands trembling. Andre worries about the shakes. Maybe a rush of adrenaline, maybe a symptom of grief, or maybe the kid's drunker than Andre thought.

"I made a mistake, B," Andre says. "I'm sorry." And he means it. "You deserved better. You were always . . . you are an excellent friend."

"Dre, it's not just that. Profiting from discord. Working for corporations to manipulate communities. A career in dark money, in secrecy, in legalized corruption. Dre, that's not what I want my life to be."

"You haven't given it a fair chance. I mean, weren't we having fun?"

"It was the most fun I'd had in a long time." The kid's voice breaks. "You were my best friend until you weren't."

Andre feels a catch in his throat. That may be the nicest thing anyone's ever said to him. "Come back. The fun doesn't have to end after Carthage. When I make junior partner—"

"Jesus, Dre. You still don't know. Nana, she had a plan. You and me. The middle of nowhere. Thirteen weeks. She didn't care about PISA. She didn't care about you. She knew you were on your way out. Hell, everyone at the firm says you're falling apart. Ask an intern. Nana wanted you to teach me your tricks. Wanted you to convert me to her cause. Wanted you to show me that fixing elections is flashy and sexy and cool. Dre, she was going to shitcan you and I was your replacement."

"I don't know where you get your information—"

"From her. She told me herself. Before you and I went down south. In her office. This was your last campaign. She was done with you. You weren't worth the trouble. That's exactly what she said. *Not worth the trouble.*"

"I get that you're mad, but your grandmother would never—"

"Oh, Dre. Grow up. She screwed people over for a living. Made a fortune doing it," Brendan says. "Why would you assume that she wouldn't screw you over? Why would you ever think that you're special?"

"Because she told me so."

Brendan laughs, a sincere and deep laugh. "You ask whether

I'm heading back to South Carolina. I ask, what's back there for you?"

Three shaggy blonds, the ten-year-old boys, storm the greenhouse, racing up and down the verdant aisles, cheering, energetic, and gleeful. The boys open cabinets, peek beneath benches, run their little fingers through barrels of soil like cops executing a search warrant. Their search is meticulous; no space escapes their inspection, but, in the end, the effort is unsuccessful, and the boys, exhausted and frustrated, stand impatiently before Brendan.

"Cousin Brendan," the shortest one says, "we can't find it."

"Well, it's not here," Brendan says. "I can tell you that."

"But we checked everywhere else."

"Why would there be a passage to Narnia in a greenhouse?" Brendan says. "Come on, lads, use your heads. Think. Think! Go on ahead, I'll catch up."

The boys fly, spinning through the greenhouse, knocking over a clay pot that shatters into three sharp shards, soil and seeds spread across the floor. The boys don't stop or slow. They simply sail through the door, shouting, laughing, indifferent to the destruction they've wrought.

"Look, Dre—"

"Don't commit right now." Andre pulls a folded itinerary from his pocket, sticks it in Brendan's jacket. "Give it some thought."

"We did have fun. I grant you that."

"And if you don't make the flight tonight, there's one tomorrow—"

"But I've made up my mind."

"And the day after that. And the day after that. The airport never closes."

"Cousin Brendan." The shortest boy holds open the door. "You coming?"

Andre and Brendan stand in silence. What else is left to say?

To Andre's surprise, the kid gives him a hug, a tender, affectionate embrace, brimming with sincerity and sorrow. It is a kindness that Andre knows that he does not deserve, and in this moment, a moment that feels as though it could last forever, Andre understands that he's lost his only friend.

"Maybe I'll call you later, okay?" Brendan wrests himself away and heads toward the door.

"I don't believe anything you've said here tonight," Andre shouts at Brendan's back. "Not about your grandmother. Not about calling later. And definitely not about busting Sean's nose. I know you, Brendan Fitzpatrick, and not a single word you've spoken here is true."

"True? Oh, come on, Dre. Don't be silly," Brendan says. "Truth doesn't matter. I learned that from you too."

Brendan pushes forward, hand in hand with his cousin, two Irishmen on their way to find a passage to Narnia.

The woman in the next seat weeps uncontrollably. Nose runny, mascara smearing, an occasional wail into the bend of her arm. She can't be more than twenty-two, and, best Andre can tell from her brief, breathless phone conversations, she's a recent college grad whose Capitol Hill internship ended without a job offer. Now she's compelled by her parents, on whom she financially depends, to return to South Carolina to resume a life that she thought she'd left behind.

Ordinarily he'd call such a woman ridiculous—White girl, please, yours is not a real problem—but now, seated on a boarding plane, three hours since he left Brendan, he has nothing but sympathy. He shares her outrage, her sense of betrayal and rejection, at having been welcomed into a world beyond her imagination, having been teased that she could build a life here, always in the back of her mind a fear that this life could fall apart with little notice, and finally having those fears realized, learning that no one ever wanted your sad, pitiful ass in the first place.

"Ma'am, you a'ight?" the flight attendant asks with an aggressive mix of indifference and impatience, to which the young woman, eyes pink, face squished, says, "Yes, ma'am. I'm sorry. Thank you for asking."

"Sir," the flight attendant says, "how are you?"

Andre knows what game the flight attendant tries to play, and he refuses to help her score, saying, "A scotch and soda, please."

Andre hopes this young woman's heartbreak has taught her a valuable life lesson—never trust happiness—but, honestly, who, at that age, learns a damn thing? By her age, Andre should have learned another cardinal rule: never trust anyone. Friends. Family. A stranger on the street. Don't trust any quiet motherfucker, and for damn sure don't trust any motherfucker who opens his mouth. But clearly he didn't learn that lesson. If he did, then he wouldn't be sitting here, heartbroken that Cassie deceived him, astonished that Mrs. Fitz renounced him, wounded that Brendan abandoned him. Trust is an essential element of betrayal. A truism so simple, so fundamental, that it should appear inside a fortune cookie.

Now look at him. As pathetic as this heartbroken intern at his side. A pair of disillusioned fools. Chumps on their way back to South Carolina. Brendan had a point: what exactly is back there for him? And yet, Andre obsesses over a better question: what remains for him here in DC? He'd be alone with his thoughts, sulking in a condo that, without a job, he couldn't afford. The decision to return to Carthage, Andre's convinced himself, is practical. A victory, he hopes, will renew his sense of purpose. If ever a man needed a win in his life, Andre Ross is that man. Besides, he's nearly broke, and for a while longer, he'll need to pay the medical bills for Hector, whom Andre didn't visit this trip because, this week of all weeks, Andre simply couldn't summon the will.

The young woman's phone pings, and she reads a text, and her grief springs forth anew. She opens her mouth and bursts with sadness. Passengers on their way to coach stop and stare in horror. Most clearly assume that he's the cause of her grief, and Andre tries his best to mime his innocence. But the passengers, already resentful that he's in business class and they're not, can't ignore the optics. A black man sitting idly beside a pain-stricken white woman. One guy, a white guy in chino pants, is clearly enraged. Tightens his fist. Bites his bottom lip. Rechecks his boarding pass in disbelief.

The plane finally finishes boarding and takes flight through the moonless, starless night sky. In the darkened cabin, the woman continues to weep, and, for the first time, Andre feels the weight of his conversation with Brendan. A low, sorrowful moan fills the cabin, the most soul-piercing yet, and to his surprise, he realizes this expression of torment and sadness is his own. He wants to lean over to the woman, to share his own story in a whisper. *The only person to have ever believed in me has died, and in the end, I can't really say whether she ever believed in me at all.*

PART V

THE FINAL STRETCH

CHAPTER EIGHTEEN

The theme of this year's spring fair, "Cowboys and Banditos," is a bona fide hit. Thousands of fairgoers wear costumes and masks, some with Stetsons and spurs, but most dressed as Mexican bandits. The local superstore kept the bandito costume in stock, buy two, get one free, and thus all the bandits look alike: the same straw sombrero and striped poncho, the same thick black mustache and faux-leather bandoliers. The fairground, which borders the lake, is a twenty-acre cobblestone promenade packed with carnival rides and beer gardens and kissing booths and a pony park where chubby schoolboys can watch their slender brethren ride a Shetland. The liberty initiative has rented prime real estate, two booths, one inside each fairground gate. Word has spread across the fair. If you have a moment, stop by the Liberty Booth. Just let the volunteers look up your voter registration status, and you're automatically entered to win a prize. A drawing, held each hour, promises exciting prizes like T-shirts and e-readers and rifle slings, each embroidered with the campaign's motto: "Carthage County, Proud and Free."

In the fairground's center, on the small amphitheater stage, the liberty initiative has bought time. Half an hour each night, which cost a small fortune but has proven a good investment. Right now, on the stage, Chalene paces, microphone clipped to her blouse, as maybe six hundred fairgoers watch. Andre feared that the campaign might need to plant a rabble-rouser to energize the crowd, but, no, this crowd, with faces new and familiar, is possessed by the Holy Ghost.

"Amen. Amen. Amen. Can I get an amen?" Chalene says, and the crowd, hands flailing in praise, shouts back, *Amen. Amen. Praise the Lord!*

Chalene has carefully crafted this production, with two dozen children, dressed in white, sitting cross-legged onstage behind her. The children's purpose Andre doesn't understand: props, Greek chorus, tenuous metaphor? She's also got a band, a trio of pale-skinned, pockmarked teens, gangly and greasy, who can't keep a beat.

Five nights she's put on a show, each night preaching a different sermon. She still has stage fright, but a crowd this big, she says, is different. Something about not seeing their eyes. Tonight's message asks whether Paula Carrothers is qualified to hold public office. Andre recommended another topic, any other topic would do, but on this matter Chalene harbored strong feelings. *Dre, I delivered five speeches with your themes, now let me do one of my own.* And so, despite polling that suggests the liberty initiative has begun to alienate swaths of women, he relented.

In her sermon, Chalene makes clear that her argument is not personal. She wrings the scripture tight to conclude that the Bible has set forth minimum criteria to hold public office. The Good Book says—and, according to Chalene, it's perfectly clear, just read it yourself, right there in the Books of Samuel—that a public servant must be male, must acquiesce to divine law, and must believe in God's wrath and love. And because Paula Carrothers is neither male, nor acquiescent, nor a true believer in the power of Jesus Christ, she is unfit to lead this community that seeks God's blessing.

"White people are fucking crazy." The voice, from behind him, is smooth and sultry. Andre twists his hips, finds an ebony woman with a huge wavy Afro, worthy of the voice. He recognizes her face, doe-eyed and rawboned with well-cut lips. She advertises as a mystic—palms, tarot cards, dreams, she reads them all. She says, "Professing themselves to be wise. They became fools."

She must need a customer—he hasn't seen anyone enter her tent all day—and if he had the time he might volunteer. He doesn't believe in prophecies, and even if he did, he wouldn't tempt fate by having his future spoken aloud and, thus, written in stone. But these past three weeks, he's needed a friend, so he'd be happy to fork over a twenty just to sit there, in the presence of a stunningly beautiful woman who wants to talk.

"All that anger, all that hate, all that negative juju," she says. "Sure, they'll win the election, and then what? Not a damn thing will change. Not for the better. Not for them."

"You've seen a win in their future?"

"Don't need to see the future, hon. Just need to understand the past," she says. "White people in Carthage, trust me, they can always be counted on to do the wrong thing, especially in groups, especially when they think no one's looking."

She pauses as an old woman and child pass. The old woman is dressed as a sexy, possibly slutty, bandita: too-short skirt, stiletto boots, strapless low-cut corset that reveals flabby midriff. The child, a little boy, maybe five years old, is also dressed as a bandito, his costume embellished: belly padded, skin greased and darkened, a tequila bottle duct-taped to his tiny hand. The mystic gives them a smile, says through gritted teeth, "See what I mean? That's a damn shame."

Andre can't disagree.

"They let the high schoolers pick the theme," she says. "In the past few years, let's see, there was 'Homies and Hoes.' 'The Orient Express.' Last year, 'How the West Was Won.' You believe that? These fucking white people picked genocide as a theme for a county fair."

She isn't joking, but Andre's amused.

"You know what they've never re-created?" she says. "A black man on elephants coming over the Alps to kick white people's ass."

Chalene starts to wrap up, but first she must bring urgency to her cause. The election takes place in eleven days. For the undecided, she says: if you don't vote for liberty, then you'll vote for tyranny. For her supporters: don't forget to cast your ballot. She conveys this message through prayer. Lord, touch the hearts of the undecided. Lord, bless those who cast the ballot in Your name. Lord, we know, as always, that You are watching.

The prayer ends, and she surrenders her mic to Tyler before leading the children and the band offstage, a graceless transition that signals a tonal shift. Unlike his wife, Tyler prefers to remain unscripted, meaning he rarely stays on message. For the next ten minutes, Tyler will speak any thought that drifts into his mind, an uncensored stream of consciousness that yesterday ran the gamut from the bastards in Congress to the bastards in Hollywood to the know-nothing know-it-all bastards who run America's universities.

"You with them?" The mystic gestures toward the stage.

"No."

"Yes, you are. Don't lie to me. I got the gift," she says. "That and, you know, I saw you with them yesterday, talking in the parking lot."

"That wasn't me."

"I didn't mean to get personal, but I've noticed you. That's all I'm saying. Ain't many brothers in Carthage, even fewer helping white folks preach liberty," she says. "You're here each night. Hanging back, watching all this. I'm not judging."

The crowd laughs, and Andre realizes that he hasn't heard a word that Tyler's said. But Andre catches the next two, *political whore*. He and Tyler have talked about this, the need to use code. Call Paula radical, call her shrill, call her uptight or hysterical or frigid or self-serving or spiteful or ambitious or crazy or secretive or shifty, but please, under no circumstances call her a whore. It doesn't poll well, even here in Carthage. Trust me, Andre told Tyler, I've checked. But now Tyler's invested in this rant, blasting Paula Carrothers, who thinks she's so much smarter than everyone else, thinks she's so much better, thinks that because she's got a fancy college degree she's elite. The crowd, men and women alike, cheer, laugh, applaud. One woman, wearing a liberty-initiative T-shirt, claps her hands and cries real tears.

"I'm just gonna come out and ask," the mystic says. "And please, you know, don't take offense."

Andre knows exactly what she'll say. Black man. A conservative cause. He braces for childish name-calling: Sellout. Oreo. Uncle Tom. What business does a black man have advancing this kind of venomous rhetoric, which, not too long ago, justified the subjugation of black men? You think Jim Crow was just about separate drinking fountains? No. It was about language. About words. About angry language and angry words that denigrated and humiliated and provoked violence. Brother, she will certainly say, what are you thinking?

But she doesn't. She certainly thinks it, but she doesn't say it. Instead she says, "I thought maybe, that woman, the crazy pregnant one who knows her Bible . . . I was hoping, I mean, if you know her and all, I was hoping she could—"

Quiet down? Shut up? He would understand either; from time to time, he's thought both.

"—I was hoping she could condemn me." She hands over a black sheet of paper with blood-red print that lists twenty-one Bible verses that explain why Christians should avoid a mystic. "Please, brother. It won't cost you nothing, and I'd really appreciate it. Do me a solid and help a sister out."

"This really works?"

"People come to the fair for thrills," she says. "What's a bigger thrill than risking your soul? I can double my fee."

Tyler, onstage, waves a rifle overhead. He wanted to bring a real rifle, but the fair's executive committee forbade firearms on their grounds. An insurance thing, they claimed, an assertion Tyler distrusts, a policy, he insists, that violates his Second Amendment right. This replica is a compromise, a Confederate assassin's rifle, a Whitworth complete with scope. To Andre, it's a waste of money, a fancy-ass toy that cost a grand to custom-make on the quick. But Tyler swore. *A Whitworth rifle means something around here. You never heard of a Whitworth sharpshooter? What did you learn in grade school?* Andre still doesn't understand, and yet, as Tyler pumps the rifle into the air, Andre must concede this prop has electrified the crowd.

"Trust me," Andre says. "You don't want these white people mad at you."

"I can't pay you, but do this for me, I'll give you a free reading," she says. "A good one."

Andre's curious what differentiates a good reading from a bad. Probably a five-dollar tip.

"Come on, brother, don't be an asshole," she says. "You want to know your future, you know you do. I can sense it in you. All that emotion, all that sadness and anger and fear. I see it written all over your face. You're like a—"

"Yeah. I get it. You see that I've hit rock bottom."

"Oh no, sweetie, I see that you're still falling. But trust me, rock bottom, it's coming soon, and it's gonna hurt," she says. "Tell me honestly, though, why you this sad? What woman's done you wrong?"

"Tell me honestly, what woman hasn't?"

Tyler preaches anarchy. Hates government—federal, state, municipal—even the local school board doesn't escape his scorn. *Evolution? Global warming? Islam? What are they teaching?* He urges revolution, if not at the ballot box, then on the city streets, and for this noble cause, he swears he's ready to give his own life.

"See what I can do," Andre says. "But you gotta let me buy you a drink."

"I sense you're the kind of fella who prefers to drink alone."

"We'll have fun. I promise. You can tell me more about my shitty future."

She ungloves her hand, wiggles the finger that bears a diamond ring.

"Honestly," he says, "that's not a deal breaker."

"Well, it is for my wife."

Tyler reaches the tag line that marks his end. *The revolution is not a part-time job.* He welcomes Chalene and all six sons, each dressed in white, back onto the stage. The family performs their grand finale, the final bow of Appalachia's very own von Trapps, the moment in which each member of the Lee clan flings a baseball cap into the crowd. A pack of campaign enthusiasts—children, teens, way too many grown men—rush the stage at breakneck speed, an honest-to-God stampede over shitty, poorly stitched two-dollar caps made in Saigon.

The Gypsy, with his patent air of menace, sits cross-legged beside a giant stuffed panda in the bed of his father's pickup. The boy whittles a walnut block, big, bold, aggressive strokes of a pearl-handled knife that he won blasting tin ducks at the county fair. Nine pulls of the trigger. Nine bull's-eyes dead center. Nineteen seconds flat. A record, the carny said. *Ain't never seen no one do nothing like that.*

How exactly did this happen? Andre and the Gypsy alone in the back of a pickup. The other Lee sons swore, pantomiming their hands on a Bible, that they had already purchased nonrefundable front-seat tickets to tonight's stadium show, ten dollars each to see dwarfs blasted from cannons, an extravaganza set to fireworks and the marches of John Philip Sousa.

"Tyler wants to show you something," Chalene shouts through the open cab window as the pickup takes an unexpected detour. Tyler shouts, "Brother, you'll love it. It's a surprise."

Fucking Tyler loves surprises.

This new route, on the way to the surprise, leads to the old county seat—a small antebellum plaza that features a town square, where looms the old county capitol, an abandoned courthouse and clock tower that receives little benefit from its inclusion on the state registry of historic places. The square is a ghost town, abandoned for thirty years, yet still has a haunting charm, with cobblestones and kerosene lampposts and century-old hitching rails, antiques of a bygone era that Tyler loves to evoke on the campaign trail.

Chalene taps the cab window, draws Andre's attention toward the old city park, where, planted on a parched and patchy lawn, is a phalanx of campaign signs—VOTE YES! FOR LIBERTY!—arranged in sets of twelve by twelve.

Surprise!

In general, Andre thinks yard signs are a waste. Yard signs are good for raising the profiles of unknown candidates and unspoken issues. See a sign. Learn the candidate's name. Not much more to it than that. Study after study has reinforced this point. But Tyler disagrees, thinks he knows better, rejects both the social science and Andre's experience. *You gotta trust me, Dre. I know my town.* So, to appease Tyler, to show that Tyler's voice is valued, Andre designated Tyler director of signs. Gave him that bullshit title and one thousand dollars. And now, sitting in the truck bed, his gaze set upon a sea of campaign signs staked, probably illegally, in a public park that no one visits—signs that the county will surely remove and destroy in the morning—Andre resists the urge to grab a tire iron and pummel Tyler.

"Look at him. He's stunned." Tyler elbows his wife. "Beautiful, brother, ain't it? I've done good?"

Andre gives two enthusiastic thumbs up—eleven days left, what's the use in arguing? These past few weeks, he and Tyler have gotten along. Hell, Tyler even calls Andre his "buddy friend." Why start a blood feud over a couple hundred poorly placed signs?

The truck crawls forward like a tour bus passing through Arlington National Cemetery, and, to Andre's disappointment, Tyler doesn't return to the main road. Instead, the truck takes the scenic route, a bumpy country thoroughfare along which Tyler has placed more signs. The old train station. An abandoned gristmill. A rusted, wheelless trolley set atop concrete blocks.

Tyler honks his horn, draws Andre's attention to yet another sign, one placed outside a site that doesn't appear on the state register of historic places. A slave cabin, no larger than this truck bed, stands alone in an unkempt field of tall dead grass. VOTE YES! FOR LIBERTY! The sign beside the cabin is large, easy to mistake for a billboard, red and white and blue. Sometimes Andre suspects that Tyler isn't really a clown, that Tyler is a mastermind playing the long game, a sophisticated prankster, a maestro of the ironic, a cynical genius who gets his kicks fucking with Andre. Only through such a lens does Tyler make any sense.

CHAPTER NINETEEN

Andre's created an official-looking notice that evaluates a voter's election history. The notice gives a grade—from A− to F+. *If you don't vote in the upcoming election*, the notice threatens, *your friends and neighbors will learn of your grade and of your failure, once again, to perform your constitutional and patriotic duty, the same duty for which your forefathers fought, bled, and died.* The campaign will mail these notices to likely supporters who, public records show, have a poor track record of getting off their asses and visiting the polls. Some seven thousand registered voters in all, a class with an average grade of D+. The strategy is simple, backed by social science: threaten to shame your base and they'll show you love on Election Day.

Now, seated at a long folding table in Chalene's living room, Andre thumbs through the top box of letters. Erica Aaker to Portia Bushnell. Each letter is disarmingly ugly: big, boxy type, red and black, printed on jaundiced paper, an intimidating aesthetic that merges the charms of a foreclosure notice and a truant's report card. This operation costs about ten grand. Not too expensive, but not chump change neither. The fancy paper. The custom calligraphy. The bright golden seal affixed to each letter's corner. Not voting, he hopes, will represent a form of social suicide, a taboo akin to burning the flag on the Fourth of July.

Chalene says in her kitchen, "I don't like this."

"The letter never actually claims to be from the government," he says. "It's perfectly legal."

"It's perfectly creepy. Makes people feel like they're being watched."

He bites back the urge to ask, isn't this how her religion works?

"Make yourself useful." Chalene sets a relish tray atop the counter. "Fix the table, won't you? Folks will be here any minute."

She's prepared a small feast, a bounty of finger foods with colorful names: ants on a log, pigs in a blanket, porcupine meatballs. He wants to know from where she gets her stamina. The baby's due in a few weeks, and she must experience some prenatal fatigue. Shouldn't she be in bed, resting on her side with a pillow between her knees? But what does he know about pregnancy? Not a damn thing. What he does know: Chalene is a marvel. She wakes each morning long before sunrise, as she says Jesus did in the Book of Mark, and she studies her scripture, says her prayers, journals her thoughts. In recent days, she's also started to record a podcast. She doesn't get much help from her husband, who, right now, snores in bed.

"For you." She sets down one last plate: fried drumstick, honey-buttered roll, October-bean casserole with streaked meat, peaches in sugar water. "There's banana pudding in the icebox, but eat your supper first."

She leans against the kitchen counter, gathering her thoughts, and a sudden presentiment darkens her face. In the next ten minutes, Andre knows that she will run the vacuum, beat the rug, plump the sofa cushions, none of which is necessary—she did each yesterday—but she fears her guests, due at any moment, will think she keeps an untidy home. These guests, eleven married women between the ages of eighteen and seventy-three, usually convene once a week, a sort of nondenominational faith-based support group in which members share stories and seek inspiration. They focus on family and scripture: how to be a better wife, a better mother, a better citizen and better Christian, but recently, their focus has changed. These twelve now meet each night to act as the liberty initiative's campaign staff: phoning friends, e-mailing supporters, stuffing official-looking notices into mustard-colored envelopes, all in the name of Jesus Christ.

Chalene struggles with a heavy vacuum, a monstrous contraption that looks like a relic of a 1960s sitcom, and he goes through the motions of offering to help. She shakes her head, rolls her eyes, says, as she has done each night, in a schoolteacher's tone, "Andre Ross, if you want to be helpful, sit down, say grace, and eat your supper." He obeys her command, though he's starting to suspect that the free meal is a massive con, a ploy to get him to learn Bible verses. The joke's on her. He already knows two verses by heart, the first, *Jesus wept*, the second, *Prepare chains! For the land is full of bloodshed, and the city is full of violence*, which, for nearly a quarter century, has been inked, in blue script, across Hector's back.

He chooses to recite the second.

"Dre," she shouts over the vacuum. "Are you readin' those verses I send?"

He pretends not to hear; the vacuum is comically loud. If she'll play the schoolteacher, then he'll play the class clown. She prefers that he recite any other verse—something less dark, something less violent, something happy and joyful and full of God's love. To that end, she texts a verse each night.

"They're not just some random verses," she shouts. "I put a lot of thought into those, picking out verses specially for you."

Somewhere down the hall, a door shuts.

"Do me a favor, won't you?" she shouts. "Read the devotional. The green one I gave you with the blue clouds on the cover. It's designed for busy professionals like you. Three minutes every morning. Can you do that? Please?"

The last bite of chicken. A swallow of sweet tea. His plate and cup are now empty. Did she say something about banana pudding?

"You're worse than my boys, you know that?" She cuts the vacuum, turns her attention to the sofa cushions, which she punches, hard, fast, angry jabs, as though the cushions owe her money. "Just enjoy being contrarious. At the peril of your soul. But we'll see who's laughing on Judgment Day. You wait and see."

He suddenly feels exhausted. The meal was too large. Too much sugar. He might take a nap, might eat the banana pudding. These heavy meals are worse than Brendan's.

"Is that what you want? St. Peter, at the pearly gate, running his finger down his ledger. And whatcha gonna say? *I couldn't be bothered to take three minutes.* You know the Lord Jesus suffered on the cross for hours." She moves on to beat the next cushion. "Promise me one thing, Dre, promise me that you'll—"

The doorbell rings, ends both the lecture and the cushion assault.

"Remind them. We'll have vans on Election Day," he says. "They need to tell the callers about the free rides. We're happy to take supporters to the polls."

"Vans. Free ride. Ferry folks to the polls. Got it." She blinks hard, as though the action commits his instruction to memory. "Get the door, but don't rush."

He takes his time, each step slow and dramatic, which gets a laugh from Chalene as she hides the vacuum. "Stop being silly and answer the door. And we're not done talking about salvation. I ain't giving up on you yet."

On the front porch stand eleven well-dressed, well-preened women, each with a casserole dish in hand. This, he's learned, is a Carthage custom. If you visit someone's home—even for a moment—you'd better bring food. The women shed their coats, talking, laughing, a noisy group that acts like they haven't seen each other in years, though all were here yesterday. These twelve, wearing matching campaign sweatshirts, are, in their own way, diverse: nursing assistant, laundry-truck driver, assistant preschool teacher.

He knows a fair amount about each woman, far more than they know about him, though they have reached a consensus that he's a down-on-his-luck drifter, a vagabond whom Chalene found like a scared, unwashed puppy beside the road. He must be, they whisper, a lost soul whom Chalene wants to bring back to God. Chalene, he trusts, hasn't shared any details, merely says that Andre is a friend who prefers to keep his own business, a vague, mysterious introduction that has only deepened the women's mistrust. One woman—Daisy, the rash-faced grocery clerk with two sons, both imprisoned, the older for prescription shenanigans, the younger for sexual assault—found Andre's conviction online, a record, which she shared, that revealed his crime, birthplace, age, and true first name. This use of an alternate first name—my God, he's changed his identity—drove the group insane, made the women believe that he has something nefarious to hide. *Sweetheart,* each woman told Chalene, *don't let him near your Social Security number.*

For three months, he worried that folks might learn he's a well-paid, high-powered campaign consultant, but now he rests easy knowing that people think he's simply a bum. And that, to him, epitomizes the kind of place Carthage is. A place where folks will easily believe that a black man with a decades-old criminal record is a wandering rogue but will never—never, ever, not in a million years—believe that this same black man is a political puppeteer running a secret grassroots, corporate-financed dark-money campaign.

Bless their little hearts.

For them, Andre plays the part. Or at least that's what he tells himself. He looks homeless and wild, his skin sallow and blotchy, the bags beneath his eyes tender and swollen. A shave, a haircut—he hasn't had either in weeks. Hasn't felt much like it, not since he returned from Washington.

"Ladies. My sisters in Christ. We should get going." Chalene claps, claps, claps her hands. "We got a lot to get done tonight. Amen?"

Amen.

The women, like deliberating jurors, take their seats around the long, cloth-covered folding table that Andre bought for this specific occasion. Tonight is the fifth straight night of phone banking.

"I've got new call lists for you." Chalene distributes lists that Andre assembled this morning. "Yours should include folks who you haven't reached yet. Some folks might be at the fair, amen, but we're gonna keep trying. Also, we got a new endorsement today. Pastor Caesar of Old Mission Baptist West has joined our righteous cause. Amen."

Amen.

"That brings our total number of endorsements from pastors

to thirty-three. Amen! And remember, we got a van on Election Day. So when you speak to folks, let them know we're happy to give 'em a ride. Amen? Free rides, back and forth, to the polls? Amen? Any questions? Amen? Sisters, can I get an amen?"

Amen.

The women join hands and pray, *Lord bless us as we touch our neighbors' hearts.* Andre, standing outside their chain, seizes his chance and, while heads are bowed, removes his flask, pours scotch into his cup of sweet tea. He thinks he's gotten away with it but catches Chalene cheating, peeking in her prayers, which is surely blasphemy.

The prayer ends with another amen, and the women start their calls. The twelve, using their own cell phones, have a strict purpose, either to persuade undecideds or to remind supporters to get out and vote. He's ghostwritten a voter-contact script, tips and canned lines to launch a polite conversation, but these women want to share what's in their hearts, their insights into their communities, their families, their frustrations, the lack of jobs, the lack of morals, the lack of Jesus Christ in American life, but above all else, these women want to share their anger at Paula Carrothers.

"Shhh. Hush up, everyone," says the eldest member of the Christian wives group, a seventy-three-year-old grocery clerk, a widow with one good eye and one bad ear. "This is it. Isn't it? Wait. You sure this is the right channel?"

"Yes, ma'am. It's the right channel," says the youngest member, the eighteen-year-old with tatted-up arms. She's been married two years, her husband a marine serving in the gulf. She works three jobs, hotel maid by day, 911 operator by night, hospital orderly on weekends. She's tiny, barely one hundred pounds, and wants to become a paramedic. She says, in her most respectful tone, "It's only nine ten. We got two minutes to go."

The room is a powder keg of anticipation, with all eyes upon the TV. In two minutes, the campaign's first thirty-second spot will debut. In the meantime, the team enjoys the first act of some generic police procedural in which a team of righteous federal agents, clean-cut white guys with strong jaws, use guile and cunning to catch the crook.

"Shhh. This is it." The widow thrusts her crooked finger toward the television, and this time, she's right. All twelve women lean in, wide-eyed and bright-faced, as though they are watching Neil Armstrong hopscotch across the surface of the moon. To Andre, this ad is nothing special. In fact, he's a little embarrassed. The campaign lacked the cash to make something fancy, so he hired a Charleston-based crew, a pair of twentysomething film-school dropouts who recorded and cut the ad in two days. Happy children, soaring eagles, the raising of the flag above Iwo Jima—the commercial begins with relics of American patriotism, fades into local supporters shouting: *Carthage County, proud and free.* A wrinkle-faced veteran wearing a garrison cap; a gap-toothed girl selling lemonade; a kind-faced, nonthreatening black woman, who is the commercial's only paid actor and not a resident of Carthage. *Carthage County, proud and free.* The final seconds feature the Lees' friends and family, two dozen supporters, including each woman in this room, standing in a semicircle around Chalene and Tyler, who, holding hands, look right into the camera and say, "Carthage County, on Election Day, vote yes for the only initiatives on *our* ballot. Vote yes for liberty. Carthage County is proud and free."

The women rise in ovation. One woman shouts *encore.* Another shouts *bellissimo.* Another shouts *arrivederci.* One woman raises her hands, begins to praise His name, as though the past thirty seconds were a religious experience. For sure these women have never before seen themselves on television, and, yes, they like it. They are now bona fide celebrities, their faces seen as far away as Newberry. Newberry! Never, in their entire lives, could they have imagined such a thing possible. Thirty seconds of stardom that, thanks to the DVRs and VCRs, they can watch over and over in the privacy of their own homes for the rest of their lives, to show future generations and to proudly boast, *I did this!*

This commercial is one of two. A second commercial features pastors and civic leaders who have endorsed the campaign. In total, Andre's bought sixty thirty-second television spots. Cost about half the campaign's remaining budget, which doesn't include the radio ad buy, a purchase of one hundred spots, the first of which aired yesterday. Each commercial, as well as behind-the-scenes interviews, will also play online.

"Can we watch it again?" Janine with the cleft lip is on her knees, poking buttons on the VCR. "Miss Chalene, does your machine have slow-mo?"

Andre sees his opportunity, quietly catches Chalene's eye and mouths, *Good night.* He considers wishing the women farewell, but he doesn't want to disturb the euphoria of newfound fame. They're already watching it again. He sneaks through the side door, and, on a clear, starry night with a full moon, fishes his keys from his pocket.

"Dre, hon, why don't you come back inside?" Chalene chases after him. "The girls will be gone soon. I'll fix you some coffee. You, me, my Tyler, we can talk a bit."

"I should get home." He spots, over Chalene's shoulder, the widow spying through the curtains. "Nice job today, by the way. You're doing great."

"You look a little tired."

"Do we have to do this every night?" He doesn't yell, but his tone is sharp. "It's late. Of course I'm tired. We've been working all damn day. I want to go home."

She wraps her arms around him, whispers, "I'm praying for you, honey, really I am." He knows her well enough to mistrust this show of affection. What she's really doing is sniffing for booze, and, sure, his breath might contain a hint of scotch, but he's not drunk, at least not legally drunk, at least not drunk enough to fail a sobriety test, at least he thinks.

"We're here if you need to talk." She takes a small step back, keeps her firm grip around his fingers. "Really, call anytime. Even in the middle of the night."

She runs her palms over the top of his head, makes the pained expression that he's come to loathe. This mix of concern and resignation, the face of the big sister he never had, bursting to say, *I wish I knew how to help you*. He doesn't know what he's done to deserve this look. He knows that she means no harm, but damn, he's tired of her pity.

"Did you want to take leftovers with you? I can fix a plate." She stalks him to the Jeep. "There's chicken dumplings. Turkey lasagna."

"See you in the morning."

"What about laundry? You've worn that shirt a couple times, and it looks like it could use a run in the wash. Bring a load of clothes with you."

"I'll come around ten."

"Don't forget to text when you get home." She watches him slide behind the wheel, holding open his door, and as she starts to close it, remembers. "The three-minute devotional. The one with the blue clouds on the cover. I can get you another one if need be. Three minutes, Dre. Three minutes. That's all the Lord asks."

Andre, behind the wheel, misjudges a turn and smashes into a mailbox. This mailbox is the third he's hit tonight, but luckily this one is his. The radio's on full blast, and Andre's belting lyrics, drumming the dash, bobbing his head to this mad, infectious beat. He hasn't heard this song in years, not since juvie, that summer when all the delinquents embraced the jazzy hip-hop hit.

He reaches for his flask, which, to his surprise, is empty. He doesn't remember draining the last drop, and he worries he has no more booze inside the house. For a moment, he considers driving to a crosstown liquor store, but he's exhausted and sweaty and has to piss. Which reminds him to step out of the Jeep, leave the engine running, and relieve himself right there on his own front yard.

A burp. A fart. He feels much better. He starts to wander toward the house, then remembers the engine's still running, which causes him to wander back to the Jeep, where he once again checks his flask, which, to his surprise, is empty. Maybe he should go buy a bottle at the crosstown liquor store.

In the driver's seat, he stares at the Victorian gothic, which is silhouetted by the full moon and looks like a haunted house in a black-and-white horror film. God, he hates living alone in this big empty house. Hates not ending his day with Cassie. Hates not having a friend like Brendan. Part of him wants to sleep inside the Jeep, which he accidentally did last night, and part of him wants to put the Jeep in gear and see how far he can travel before dawn. But the time has come to go inside. He cuts the engine, resolves to move quickly, like jumping into freezing water, one, two, three, and he's off, closing the Jeep door, sprinting, a race premised on the notion that if he moves fast enough, then he'll outrun the inevitable drunken vertigo. Across the yard, up the porch steps, through the front door; he falls once, twice, three times along the way, but otherwise makes pretty good time in this drunkard's obstacle course.

He pushes forward hard, harder, up the stairs and into Brendan's room. There, he sits on the corner of the kid's unmade bed, waits for the dizziness to pass. The television, which he never turns off, is deafeningly loud, plays a DVD of a decades-old soccer match. He doesn't watch the match—if he bothered to pay attention, he'd probably find the video grating—but these days, he's at war with silence. If he had neighbors, they would surely complain about the noise. But he would explain that he needs these sounds to fill this big empty house and to keep him from losing his mind, that he can't stand the air of loneliness and futility and judgment that the silence brings.

He turns up the volume, kneels beside Brendan's bed, fingers brushing past Chalene's three-minute devotional. Blue clouds. Green pasture. The most tranquil fucking scene anyone's ever seen. He pauses to let the next round of dizziness pass, resting his face against the kid's mattress, which smells minty, not a scent that he associates with the kid but a comfort nonetheless. The dizziness passes; he wedges his palm between mattress and box spring, removes a baggie of iridescent gummies. He consumes a strict ration of one, carefully puts the baggie back into its hiding spot, as though the kid might return and notice that someone has raided his stash.

In an hour, the gummy will kick in, then he'll find rest. Not the best rest, but the best possible rest that he can achieve these days. His insomnia has become rebellious, and booze alone no longer brings relief, which isn't a surprise—wasn't it inevitable that his body would develop an immunity?—but he never imagined that this immunity would develop this early in his life. Sometimes, this cocktail gives him wild dreams.

Last night, he dreamed about Mrs. Fitz. A nightmare, really, in which she shamed him, told him to his face that she planned to abandon him. *Dre. You're not worth the trouble.* He still doesn't know whether the kid told the truth or whether he was trying to hurt him. In moments alone, Andre tries his best not to think about Mrs. Fitz—it hurts too much. Even without the betrayal, he simply misses his mentor. But he finds that thinking about her is like standing in quicksand. It's a futile effort that causes him to expend all his strength, sinking deeper and deeper into a dark, terrible place, and, in the end, what will it get him other than a slow death?

A bolt of lightning, a peal of thunder. Is that a train whistle in the distance? Now he's curious, opens the window to step outside, his grip tight around a stone gargoyle ravaged by time. This flat square of roof perhaps was once a balcony with a vast daytime view that extended all the way down to the old train station. These days, he spends a lot of time out here, thinking, listening to passing trains, worried about the days and weeks to come. He's middle-aged, wifeless, childless, friendless, with a fifty-fifty chance that soon he'll be unemployed.

In juvie, he had such grand plans for his life. By this age, he thought he'd have become someone special, a man of consequence and importance. Back then, he'd spend hours lying atop his bunk, imagining a life in which he was rich and famous and, above all else, content. Happiness, even in those days, seemed far too ambitious, but content, yes, that he could do. And yes, he concedes that this vision was mere fantasy, and like every fantasy of every seventeen-year-old boy, it was impractical, and yet, for some reason, it's also a fantasy that he continues to hold dear, the standard by which he judges his own existence. He acknowledges that any rational man would've forgotten this foolish vision, but here he is, alone and drunk on a flat square of roof, certain that that young boy, that younger traumatized and imprisoned version of himself, would surely feel ashamed of what his life has become.

His phone vibrates. Chalene texting tonight's Bible verse. He taps a button, means to hit delete, but instead commands his phone to speak the text aloud. *For his anger endures but for a moment; in his favor is life: weeping may endure for a night but joy cometh in the morning.* He hurls his cell toward a train that whistles in the dark, and the phone's soft blue glow sails across the night sky.

CHAPTER TWENTY

The next morning, he ransacks the house searching for his phone. He's checked everywhere: the bottom of the stairs, Brendan's bedroom, the crevices of each seat in the Jeep. He's tried the online phone tracker, but the battery, he's told, is dead, and the tracker is unable to pinpoint an exact location. Why can't he catch a break? He's on his laptop, trying the phone tracker for the fourth time—because, why not, maybe this time it will work—when he receives an e-mail from Victoria Boshears. *I've tried to call, but I can't reach you. Please come see us. We must talk. As soon as possible. It's urgent.* He thinks the e-mail a fortunate coincidence, because he needs to speak with the Boshears.

When he arrives at the Boshearses' estate, slightly before noon, the horizon is bleak and raw, with distant lightning bolts that break the somber sky. The Boshearses' housekeeper, the old black woman, now wearing a lemon tracksuit, opens the front door barely wide enough to see him. Her face is sour, her stance hostile, her presence as cold and as unwelcoming as the day. She doesn't invite him inside. She makes him wait in the portico, in the misty cold.

"Now, you listen." The old woman throws open the door, wags her finger in Andre's face. "I don't want you causin' no trouble between them. I been working for this family near my whole life, and I ain't never seen them argue like this." She pokes him between his ribs. "You hear me, boy? I'm serious. You will not cause no more trouble."

He thinks to snap back: *Mind your own fucking business.* Thinks to mock her use of the double negative. *So, wait, you want me to cause trouble?* Thinks perhaps he should pull rank, to say that grown-ups must have a grown-up discussion, *a discussion that you couldn't possibly begin to understand.* But he decides against admonishment. Not because any response could make matters worse, potentially jeopardizing his relationship with the Boshears, the couple from whom he now seeks a favor, but because, in truth, he has a grudging respect for the old woman. She must be seventy, maybe seventy-five, and he imagines that those years could not have come easily. She survived Jim Crow, a life, at best, spent as a second-class citizen. And because he respects survivors, old black men and old black women who soldier on through unjust times, and because he will not add to the long list of indignities she must have endured, he answers with deference and respect. "Yes, ma'am."

In the sunroom, Duke Boshears, in his blue boxers and bathrobe, enjoys brunch. He's eaten most of his meal, plate littered with tomato seeds and the skeletal remains of a whole trout, the scaled skin heaped in a pile like dirty laundry on a dorm-room floor.

"Andre, my friend," Duke says. "Please have a seat. Can we get you something? Marie, do we have any biscuits left? Marie makes the best biscuits. Get Mr. Ross here some of your biscuits and chokeberry jam."

The old woman leaves, but not before sending Andre one last disapproving stare: *You best mind your manners.* Andre takes a seat at the glass table beside the remains of a lighter breakfast: eggshells, a crust of toast, a near-empty wineglass.

"Where's your friend? The Scottish fellow." Duke claps Andre's shoulder, gives a comforting squeeze. "I hope he's enjoying our country."

"Brendan? He's fine. He's—"

"That's wonderful. Yes. Wonderful. And let me say, I think you're doing a wonderful job. Really quality work. I stopped by the fair booth the other day. Amazing. I don't know how much you're spending, but you're doing a fine job."

Andre doubts he's here for praise.

"But I gotta warn you—just between us boys—before she comes down." Duke scans the doorway, ensures the coast is clear. "The mistress of the house is upset."

Upset? Andre wants to ask. *Upset with you or with me?*

"I'd play it cool if I were you. Of course you'll play it cool. Victoria says she's never met anyone quite as smooth as you." Duke gives a second squeeze. "But you know women. They hear a little bad news, and they get hysterical."

"What bad news?"

"Vicki, God love her, I love her. Sometimes she needs to vent."

"Did something specific happen?"

"I've tried to explain it all to her, and, like I said, you're doing a fabulous job, but . . . She likes you. She trusts you. She'll accept any explanation you give. But keep in mind, she doesn't share our animal instinct. Men like you and me, political warriors, lions, we're different. I tell her that women shouldn't go into politics for this reason. That men—" Heels clacking against the floor interrupt his thought. Duke winks at Andre, yells, "You sure you wouldn't like some juice? My wife makes it fresh every morning. Nobody makes orange juice as good as my Vicki. Oh, Vicki, honey. Sweetie. Didn't see you there. Look who's here."

She crosses to the table, sits with caution and poise, doesn't look either man in the eye. Instead, she clears her throat, fidgets in her seat, rubs one hand with the other, only to raise her gaze after a deep, prolonged sigh. She's been crying, that much is clear, and Andre's surprised that he feels sorry for her.

"Mr. Ross," she finally says. "I trust you're well."

He sees the strain the kindness costs her, worries about what's to come.

"I had lunch with Paula yesterday," Victoria says. "She's very brave, if you ask me. Enduring the constant criticism. Criticism she doesn't deserve. All that is being done to get her fired and she—"

"Oh, honey. Be fair. No one's trying to get Paula fired. Paula's overreacting like she always does," Duke says. "The initiatives only reduce her pay. Makes her salary fall in line with the community she serves."

Fall in line with the community she serves. The line is straight from Andre's imagination. A line that Chalene and Tyler recite on the campaign trail. A line that Andre focus-grouped, that played well with his key demo, but a line that he never imagined would be embraced by wealthier voters. Andre wonders whether Duke truly believes the populist message, because clearly his wife does not.

"At lunch, Paula was in tears," Victoria says. "She doesn't understand why people need to be this cruel. She doesn't understand what she's done wrong."

"People have the right to speak their mind," Duke says. "If she can't take the heat, she needs to find a job in a kitchen."

"It's unfair," Victoria says. "I read the paper. I read what they say online. People don't care if they hurt her feelings. People don't care that she does her job well. They care about scandal. They care about spectacle."

Andre wonders to which spectacle she refers. Three weeks ago, the last day on which homeowners could pay their property taxes, some jackass paid his nearly three-hundred-dollar assessment in pennies. Literally, one five-gallon jug, which must have weighed as much as an obese man, set atop Paula's desk. Jackass must've collected pennies for weeks, must have visited several banks. The payment took Paula and her deputy all day to count, with the two working through their lunch and late into the night. The local newspaper published a pic; the jackass posted his own photos online. The damn move was a hit, praised as an act of civil disobedience. One letter to the editor compared the stunt to the courage of Gandhi. Now everyone in town pays fees, taxes, and assessments in pennies.

But pennies are only the beginning.

Two weeks ago, a different jackass, probably a bored teen, hacked her work e-mail, published six years' worth of messages from the county server. In truth, the hack produced nothing spectacular; each e-mail was already subject to open-record laws. To read them, all one had to do was ask. Andre forwarded the e-mails, tens of thousands in all, to interns back in DC, who read each one, and who, at the end of their assignment, left impressed with Paula Carrothers, who, they reported, is good at her job. She's kind and compassionate and efficient and thoughtful, they said. She uses her discretion to forgive fees imposed upon the poor, volunteers her time with local charities, and calls in favors to help teen mothers in toxic homes. This praise, of course, did not enter the public discourse. Instead, the local newspaper published a front-page editorial condemning her carelessness and indifference to cybersecurity.

There's more.

Six days ago. A midnight lakeside rally that the campaign neither imagined, organized, nor endorsed. Dozens of men, the second-chancers who vowed to never again beat their wives, burned Paula in effigy. The men doused a scarecrow that wore Paula's patented tortoiseshell glasses, and set her aflame. Posted the whole thing online. The men standing beside their wives and daughters, cheering, chanting, *Burn the bitch, burn.* Not the most original or rhythmic of chants, but the footage was spectacular. Alive with color and passion. A masterpiece with literal fireworks at the end.

He knows more stories—didn't some fool follow Paula around with a camera?—but Andre strains to remember the exact details. He can't possibly be expected to keep track.

"She receives calls at her home," Victoria says. "And e-mails from anonymous accounts. From cowards."

"They're only trying to rattle her. No one's gonna harm Paula," Duke says. "Just a bunch of good ol' boys blowing off steam."

"They send explicit messages. Pornography. *Violent* pornography." Victoria shudders. "I've seen it. They are disgusting. Perverted pictures from perverted men. Pictures of abused and debased women. Some of them just girls, little girls bound and beaten and tortured. Some of those photos have got to be illegal. And do you know what these messages say?"

Andre does know. The campaign is copied on most. And, yes, he agrees. Some of those photos probably are illegal. He doesn't condone the messages, and, yes, some senders are certainly mentally ill. And worse than mentally ill, people who live out of county and, as such, are ineligible to vote. But what is he to do? These messages come from private citizens, and Andre isn't in the business of admonishing folks who have given him their support.

The old woman brings a tray: basket of buttered biscuits, uncorked wine, pulpy purple jam in a pink jar. She fills Victoria's wineglass, runs the back of her hand against Victoria's flushed cheek, a caress as gentle as a mother comforting her ill child.

"Please say something," Victoria says, to which Duke replies, "Paula's problem is—"

"Not you," she says. "Mr. Ross. I'd very much like to hear your thoughts."

He thinks she's now made it difficult to request a favor, which is the only reason he's here. In fact, the favor feels impolite to ask, because he needs Victoria Boshears to publicly endorse the campaign. The post-council-meeting bump has nearly evaporated. The campaign no longer enjoys a comfortable lead. Yes, the latest polls show the campaign ahead, and, yes, he's surprised by the size of the rallies, but the lead barely beats the margin of error.

"Our latest polls suggest we're doing well with white men with no college," Andre says. "They make up a sizable portion of the electorate, and we're winning that demographic about two to one. But they're unreliable as voters. Especially the unemployed ones. Especially in local elections. They simply don't show to vote."

"Good ol' boys," Victoria scoffs. "They'll spend an hour harassing an innocent woman but not a minute to cast a ballot."

"We're gonna need women. And, right now, we're polling a little behind with them," Andre says. "We have an opportunity to make real gains with class-conscious women, mostly white women with some education and white women with relatively higher incomes."

"Good. Good. I'm glad to hear that. I'm glad we agree." Victoria is relieved. "It's in everyone's interests to change the campaign's tone. I know we haven't much time. But we can embrace a less misogynist, less divisive, less deplorable message. Oh, thank you, Mr. Ross, I knew you'd understand. Paula can't handle—*I* can't handle—ten more days of this."

Victoria misunderstands. In fact, she's missed the entire fucking point. But her husband hasn't. Duke's face is a mask of concentration, distant yet intense, as though he's playing out each possible scenario, calculating next steps and probabilities, and only once this exercise is done does Duke return to them, with a slight reluctant nod to authorize Andre to do what must be done.

"What? If you two have something to add," Victoria says, "I wish you would."

"The Lees need to keep our base energized. We can't change their message. In the final days, we need to hammer home our message." Andre dives in. "But we also need new voices to legitimize our cause. You wouldn't have to do much. Record a robocall. Write an op-ed. Obviously, you don't have to speak against your friend, you'd only have to endorse—"

Victoria raises her hand, brings it down fast and hard against his face. He doesn't have time to react, and the slap spins his head, echoes throughout the sunroom. Everyone, especially Victoria, is surprised. She clearly did not intend this sudden burst of violence.

She chokes back rage and grief and frustration until, at last, she gives way, an avalanche of emotion, a loud mournful cry that, in his entire life, he's heard only behind bars. He recognizes it as the same cry made by a frightened thirteen-year-old on his first night in juvie, once his trial is over and all that remains is to serve his sentence. It is a cry without dignity or shame. It is a cry of hopelessness and regret. It is the cry of someone who doesn't quite understand how, of all places, she's ended up here.

Andre casts a stunned sideways glance toward Duke, wonders whether he should apologize or press his case. The damage to Paula Carrothers is done—an endorsement will make Paula's life neither better nor worse. Trust him. The crazies will be crazy no matter what is said. That is the nature of crazy. But an endorsement from the likes of Victoria Boshears, that precious and prized aristocratic endorsement, that could be the tonic that legitimizes this campaign. He decides to pursue both—a quick yet sincere apology and a sharper, more sensitive explanation. Logic and reason, he'll insist, must prevail. But before he speaks, Duke rises, says, "Marie. Please show Mr. Ross the door."

Hector once teased Little Brother that he couldn't take a punch—*Dre, why you always crying, embarrassing me, whining like a punk, like a bitch, like a punk-ass bitch*—but, to be fair, those punches, back in the day, were dead serious, not the whiplash smack of a middle-aged diva but the jaw-splitting blow of a strung-out junkie desperate for a fix.

Andre wonders whether this stinging sensation in his face is sincere or whether he's experiencing a phantom pain. He wishes he could think about anything else. But he can't change his thoughts. All day he's tried. Calm, soothing breaths; cold, stiff drinks; hours of shitty TV. Nothing distracts or permits him to forget. He regrets that, earlier today, he canceled his entire schedule, spent all day here alone, sitting on his stoop, sulking, humiliated.

He wishes he had a phone. He'd call Victoria up, cuss her ass out. Instead, he opens his laptop, starts to type a letter written in Victoria's name—mild, nothing inflammatory, the call to action he would've proposed she sign. *Our governments—federal, state, and local—have fallen short of their promise to preserve our precious liberty.* He likes the alliteration; it lends a touch of class. *Our leaders are corrupt, in service to only themselves. No one speaks for the people or the Constitution.* Maybe he'll post the letter online and forward it to supporters. A banner subject line: *Victoria Boshears joins the fight for women's liberty! Tell your friends!!!* He doesn't need her permission. In fact, fuck Victoria and fuck her permission. What can she do? Write a letter to the editor? Won't get published. Demand an official retraction? He'll ignore it. Hire a lawyer and file suit? Good luck getting relief from the South Carolina courts.

If Victoria's smart—and, of course, she is—once she learns about this endorsement, she'll shut her damn mouth. She must know that Andre's preserved months of e-mails and texts and voicemails, her forlorn late-night pleas in search of hope. *Please, Mr. Ross, assure me that the campaign will win.* Be a shame if those e-mails went public, or, worse, if someone published the unsolicited e-mails from her husband, each over-the-top, buffoonish, desperate for someone to take him seriously. Those e-mails, nasty fucking e-mails that are nothing but betrayals, every confidence that Paula shared with Victoria and that Victoria shared with Duke. In painstaking detail, he's listed each of her failures and faults, created a color-coded spreadsheet: red for failed lovers; blue for failed public policies; yellow for personal imperfections like the eating disorder she developed, yet overcame, in college. *Her father, white trash if ever there was, used to beat her and her little sister. That's why her mother left. Maybe you could use that.* Duke preserves Paula's traumas like one might collect stamps, coveting the opportunity to enlarge his collection, eager to share each collectible with his friends, as though to say, *Look what I have for you to see.*

A pity that Paula ever trusted Victoria Boshears. A pity that Paula hasn't moved somewhere else. The truth is that this election might be good for the county manager. Maybe then she can abandon this ungrateful rattrap, move someplace where people appreciate her. A rationalization, he concedes, but a rationalization that's rooted in a rich soil of hard truth.

He resents that Victoria blames the campaign for Paula's troubles. It's not his fault that Carthage's culture is one of discord and dissatisfaction. The rage and the mistrust and the sexism and racism and homophobia and anti-Semitism each existed long before he came to town. Read the local newspaper. Look at the federal statistics. Three in five men underemployed, opiates more popular than vitamins, the median household income among the lowest in the nation. Hell, the male life expectancy in Bangladesh is higher than the male life expectancy in Carthage. He chose neither the audience nor the theater; he merely produced the show.

He types the final line of Victoria's endorsement: *Through love of Christ and country, we will take Carthage back. On Election Day: cast your vote for liberty.* He recognizes that he's angry, that he's more than a little drunk, and that, by the light of day, he wouldn't think half these thoughts, but this move feels right.

The click of a button, and he posts the endorsement on the campaign website, sending copies to media and supporters, an act that doesn't remove the sting from his face. Yet sending the endorsement feels good. This endorsement is a bright beacon of self-affirmation, a sorely needed confirmation that he hasn't lost his touch, that he remains resilient and ruthless, and that, above all else, he is not, and never will be, anyone's punk-ass bitch.

CHAPTER TWENTY-ONE

In his backyard, beyond T-shirts pinned against a line, lies a small shed that Tyler purchased, some twenty years ago, on credit, a clearance-sale markdown, hail dented and sunburned. Chalene, hungry and ambitious, has commandeered the shed, turned the space into her own private recording studio, where, in the past two weeks, she's planted the seeds of an empire. She records a daily podcast focusing on Christian life: child rearing, scripture reading, Satan resisting, and disciple recruiting. At times, her message is playful and light, at others, devastatingly honest, sharing intense, intimate struggles with remarkable candor: miscarriages, debt, depression, and marital discord. Andre doesn't enjoy podcasts—such shows are the rants of antisocial narcissists—but Chalene's voice is pleasant, her narrative compelling.

Now Andre waits inside this shed. Microphones, mixer, digital recorder, and camera. An entire state-of-the-art studio purchased with campaign funds. Today is Sunday, and Chalene, who still wears her church clothes, is preoccupied at her sound mixer. She is a toddler playing with a busy box, twisting dials, thumping buttons, sliding knobs, amazed by the flashing lights and her own ability to create sound. Around her neck hang headphones, expensive and mahogany, that he swears she's never actually brought to her ears.

"Did you hear?" She sets down the headset, and he assumes that she means Victoria Boshears. "Someone threw a rock through Paula Carrothers's bedroom window. Middle of last night. Shattered glass everywhere."

"She hurt?"

"I didn't ask." Chalene pauses to reflect. "Probably should've. Lord forgive me. Someone would've said something if she'd gotten hurt. Right?"

He hesitates to ask more questions. Knowledge can be a liability.

"The police are investigating." She pushes back against her chair, wraps her arm around her belly. "You think they'll catch whoever done it?"

"No."

"Me neither."

If this were any other campaign, he might issue a bullshit press release. A wink, a nod. *We reject and denounce all forms of violence. Ours is a battle of ideas. We wish Paula Carrothers well.* But the rules here are different, the public anger an asset—don't cool the kettle, feed the flame—and he wonders whether he should make light of the offense. Maybe Andre could purchase a box of smooth stones. Maybe, at the next get-out-the-vote rally, he could present the stones, gifts to supporters, each stone bearing a picture of Paula and inscribed with *Rock the Vote!* Deplorable for sure, but a solid joke his base will love. He's patting his pocket, searching for his phone, which he realizes isn't there, when a thought gives him pause. What if Victoria is right? What if the campaign has gotten out of control?

"I was thinking," Chalene says. "Soon I'll have enough content to start my own channel. I've been thinking about it. Prayed over it. And I think I've got a name. The Carthaginian Christian. What do you think? You think it's terrible. Go ahead. Say it. Make your ha-has."

He does hate it, though he keeps the judgment to himself.

"You're not wrong," she says. "But I want something simple. Don't discourage me. I'm fragile. We don't need to decide today. But I want to launch right after the election. The day after, if we can. I don't want to lose our momentum."

"Have you seen my phone? I think I left it here the other night."

"When are you going back to DC? If you need a place to stay, you can stay here. After that, I can send you things through e-mail. Have you ever filed a trademark application?"

He doesn't have the heart to tell her: *Chalene, dear, we are not friends.* Clients occasionally misinterpret the relationship forged on the campaign trail. Consultants and clients have, after all, fought together like soldiers in a foxhole, side by side, sometimes for years. For amateurs, the presumption of a more permanent relationship is an easy mistake to make. But the morning following the election, he'll board a plane and never see her again. Chalene is not repeat business. She will not run for reelection in six years. She will not move through the ranks of South Carolina politics. She will never lead a multinational conglomerate that seeks to organize yet another clandestine grassroots dark-money campaign.

"Oh goodness." Her hand covers her mouth. "You're just gonna leave us, aren't you? We're mules to you. Good to do your work. Are you just gonna ghost us? Ignore my calls? Delete my e-mails?"

He is stunned. She's read his mind.

"It's my fault. Really it is," she says. "I apologize. I shouldn't have assumed. I thought you and me and my Tyler, we make a good team. I know I shouldn't have assumed. You have your own life. I don't know why I thought different. Damn it, Dre. Sometimes you make me feel so stupid."

"You're not stupid. I don't believe that. I swear."

She turns her face, focuses her concentration on the shed's round window onto a sunless sky and a parched field that seems to stretch toward the edge of the world. At first, she looks hopeless and brokenhearted, as though his betrayal has wounded her faith. He expects her to cry because she always cries: cries when she's happy, cries when she's sad, cries when she sees evidence that God has made a world with equal parts passion and pain. But when she turns to face him, she hasn't a tear in her eye. All she has is an ironclad resolve that he would've never guessed rests deep inside her. She rises, draws in breath, and, with a hardness that he has never heard in anyone's voice, says, "The Lord is my sword and shield. I will not perish in battle."

The pause is long and the silence uncomfortable.

Chalene and Andre stare awkwardly at one another, and he cannot fathom what will happen next. He's a little afraid, a little excited. For the second time in two days, will a white woman slap him? In this moment, he realizes a new truth: Chalene didn't fully know who he was, and he didn't fully know her either. He feels as though they are meeting anew, and he wonders whether this introduction has brought them closer.

"Morning's almost over." Her face goes smooth. "I should fix something to eat."

In her kitchen, she makes fried-egg sandwiches: buttered bread, mayo, three kinds of cheese. The conversation is strained yet polite. Full of information that they both already know: upcoming campaign rallies, volunteers who knock on doors, the calls her team should make tonight. The two strive to avoid a lull. Neither wants to repeat the awkwardness from the shed, and, for this reason, Andre considers sharing the tale of Victoria's endorsement. He doesn't want to share the whole truth, worries Chalene will, yet again, see right through him, as Tyler stumbles, shirtless, half-asleep, into the kitchen to kiss his wife.

Chalene's quick to report the news about Paula Carrothers: the rock, the window, *I don't know whether she's okay. Should we call someone to ask?* Tyler folds his arms, bows his head, a stance that, in any other man, might be mistaken for deep contemplation. For a moment, Andre wonders whether Tyler will confess that he broke the window. Improbable but not impossible. A rock through Paula's window is the kind of thing Tyler might do. A rock through a woman's window is the kind of man Tyler is. Instead, Tyler wags his finger, says, "I wager she threw that rock herself. Betcha she broke her own GD window."

"No." Chalene's hand catches the cross around her neck. "You think?"

"I been talkin' to Weston Martin," Tyler says. "Weston's brother and her were in the same high school class. Says that she was a drama queen even back then. That she always played for attention. You know. Pretend like she was hurt to get out of PE. Limpin'. Cryin'. Stuff like that. Couldn't get boys to notice her any other way. She once came to school wearing a cast. You believe that?"

No. Andre does not believe that she wore a cast to avoid high school gym. Nor does he believe that, last night, she smashed her own window. Moreover, Andre resents that, for Tyler, communal hearsay and forty-year-old anecdotes pass for fact. *Do you believe everything you hear?* Tyler refuses to read a newspaper, or a magazine, or a book—haven't got time, he says, don't trust the media. Instead, Tyler receives all his information, on which he makes important life decisions, from a small circle of friends and neighbors, each of whom is as lost as he.

"I knew that kind of girl in school," Chalene says. "Needs Jesus in her life."

"Everyone knew she's fake. Weston says even the teachers called out her BS."

"The more I learn about her . . ." Chalene shakes her head. "Think it'll work?"

"People know her game, but some people are dumb. Fool me once, shame on me, you know?" Tyler says. "But this is a good sign, yeah? Shows she's worried. Ain't that right, Dre?"

Andre veils his eyes, a precaution against Chalene's reading his thoughts. He can't risk his team knowing that for Tyler, he feels nothing but contempt, and that for Paula Carrothers, his heart has become a reservoir of pity. With a lift of his shoulder—*Who knows with her*—he provides the gesture that satisfies both husband and wife. Now the matter is settled: Paula Carrothers broke her own window. Everyone in town will soon know.

Andre. Tyler. Chalene. The three stand hunched over the kitchen table, studying a large county map like four-star generals weighing competing strategies ahead of a great battle. Instead of miniature tanks or infantrymen, the three have placed bottle caps across the map, one atop each of the county's twelve senior-citizen centers: six residential, six adult daycares.

South Carolina doesn't offer universal early voting. Instead the law permits certain voters, with certain excuses, to cast their ballots in person before Election Day. College students, service members, patients with scheduled surgeries—voters who know that they won't be available on Election Day. But the law also creates a blanket exception for senior citizens, anyone older than sixty-five, and these older voters are essential to this campaign's success. These seniors represent roughly 12 percent of Carthage County's total voting-age population, but in the most recent local election, they constituted nearly 35 percent of all voters. This fact really shouldn't surprise anyone. After all, who else has time on a Tuesday afternoon to visit a polling place and cast a ballot for county comptroller? Housewives, the chronically unemployed, and the elderly, the holy triad that make up the liberty initiative's base.

Early voting, for these chosen few, starts in three days. Seniors can show up, invoke their birthright, and cast their ballots. Which is exactly what Andre needs. For weeks, Chalene and her disciples have swarmed local senior centers, registering the unregistered, whispering in hairy ears, shaking arthritic hands, kissing liver-spotted cheeks, asking about ungrateful grandchildren, the kind of bald-faced pandering reserved for terminally ill dowagers. And despite the shameless self-interest, the plan has worked. Seniors in Carthage adore Chalene. Something about a cheery woman in her third trimester that's like a fresh Social Security check in hand.

Chalene now drags her finger across the map, from one bent bottle cap to another, estimates the time required to travel from the Southern Baptist center to the Methodist daycare. Twenty minutes. Depends if you hit a light. Only half the centers own a shuttle or bus. To be safe, she says, the campaign should rent an additional van.

Tyler and Andre agree.

They're nearly done, but first, the three must decide which centers to visit today. One last opportunity to rally and flatter the base. Chalene wants to visit four centers, spend an hour at each, but Tyler worries that she's taxing her health. Four hour-long campaign stops is a lot. Plus, she plans to deliver a sermon tonight at the fair. Plus, she'll host another meeting of her Christian wives group. Plus the envelopes she'll stuff, calls she'll make, doors she'll knock on. To say nothing of the daily burden of raising six ill-behaved sons. For even the spryest candidate, this schedule is punishing, but for a pregnant woman, yes, Andre agrees, she does too much.

"I know my own body," she says. "I'm not a rose petal."

"What if we send the gals from your women's group?" Tyler's voice softens, his words clear and calm, tone sensible. "Miss Patti. She'd be great."

"Patti?" Chalene scoffs. "Patti? Really, Patti? You think Patti's a good idea? My goodness."

Andre and Tyler exchange glances. Each knows where this argument will go. Chalene recently read a feature about a middle-aged woman, forty weeks pregnant, who ran the Boston Marathon, and as she crossed the finish line, her water broke. When it comes to childbirth, Chalene is strangely competitive. But this conversation, Andre senses, is not about competition. Tyler says, "Dre, give us a minute, won't ya?"

"We're too busy," she says. "Toussaint Andre Ross, don't you move one inch."

"Baby. Be reasonable," Tyler says. "The doctor said—"

"I know what the doctor said. I was there." She fans herself with a campaign flyer. "He said I should rest when I need to rest. Doctors. Goodness gracious. I have half a mind to ask for my money back. *Rest when I'm tired*. Jiminy Cricket. He went to medical school for that."

"That's not what the doctor said, and you know that's not what the doctor said." Tyler sends Andre an exasperated glance—*Do you have to be here for this?*—then says to Chalene in a whisper, "You know what he said about you-know-what."

"My body is fine."

"Your body is not fine." Tyler raises his voice. He is an angry bull. Snorts, chuffs. He might charge. "Be reasonable."

"Tell me to be reasonable one more time."

"I don't understand how you can . . ." Tyler takes a huge gasp of air, digs his bitten nails into his own breast. "Why would you take any risk?"

"Dre," she says. "I wanna say something different at each stop."

Tyler roars, slams his fists against the table, crumpling the map before ripping it from the tabletop, knocking over a sugar bowl and sending all twelve bottle caps soaring, ricocheting across the room, a sudden explosion that leaves, in its wake, a razor-sharp silence. Even Tyler is stunned, his face now pale and wounded, his breath a heavy pant. His gaze shifts back and forth between Chalene and Andre, and in the moment that follows, Tyler seems to shrink into himself. He is a preschooler who's thrown a tantrum and is now surprised to learn that he commands the room. Tyler faces the glass door that frames four small graves, the final resting places that he dug with his own hands.

Chalene goes to her husband, whispers in his ear. He kisses her lightly, and they wipe away each other's tears. She rests her face upon his shoulder, and the two join hands, staring through thin glass, seeming to accept the inevitable truth that in the coming days, they will experience either joy or sorrow, and that no matter the result, they will face the future together, as they always have, as husband and wife, as friends and lovers, as soul mates and equals, comforted by the knowledge that their fate is all a part of God's grand plan.

CHAPTER TWENTY-TWO

Carthage's blue laws prevent alcohol sales on Sundays. The lone exception is a local pharmacy, which sells liquor for medicinal purposes, twenty-four/seven and without a prescription. Andre's on his way there, traveling this back road, with its arches of Spanish moss and lattices of bloodweed, that is a scene straight out of a horror film. On nights like tonight, when the moon projects a beam that sets the fog aglow, Andre imagines that the ghosts of slaves, their bodies mutilated and disfigured, lie in wait, eager to ambush passersby who journey this dirt road that cuts deep into the wilderness.

The pharmacy is a Quonset hut that stretches into the hillside, and he slowly pulls into its unpaved parking lot. Tonight, three shitfaced white teens—not old enough to drink, but big enough to cause trouble—tailgate inside a pickup, passing around a flute-shaped bottle, cigarette stubs at their feet. Chained to the rear bumper is a pit bull, a beast of pure muscle, with a faded white mask and a brown patch around her right eye.

To avoid the teens, he considers the pharmacy's drive-thru,

but he needs a prepaid cell phone, which he hopes to find inside. He's searched everywhere for his cell, which he's pretty sure the Gypsy stole. He leaves his car, keeps his head down, as the boys elbow each other and whisper. They don't bother to hide their mistrust. Nor does the pit, which barks, lunges, stretches her chain leash.

Inside the pharmacy, sleigh bells attached to the front door announce his entry. Behind the counter a fat cashier brings an oxygen mask to his face, exposing a forearm that looks diseased, a stretch of skin with hills of red bumps and plains of dead skin. Andre nods and, stepping over a fallen mop, heads toward the back, where the booze is racked on shelves welded onto solid rock. He's scanning the selection when he hears Chalene's voice inside his head. *I'm praying for you.* Two bottles of Dutch gin, he guesses, will last awhile. To be safe, he grabs three.

Two rows later, past an aisle of hatchets and knives, past another aisle of sunglasses and greeting cards, he scans the electronics section. The pharmacy keeps inventory that he can't explain: a TV/VCR, fax machine, Walkman, and dial-up modem. Who the hell needs a floppy disk and what the fuck is a Betamax? All this junk and no phone.

He reaches the checkout counter, cursing beneath his breath—*Fucking Gypsy. Stole my phone.* Of this, he's certain. At first, he doesn't notice the customer ahead in line. His attention is drawn to the cashier folding a box, then angrily punching the register keys, and, not until the customer turns, mouthing, *I'm sorry,* does he recognize Paula Carrothers.

A surge of panic, a rush of fear, a punch in the gut. Andre supposes this moment was inevitable. Carthage isn't large. Yet now that the moment's here, he's unprepared, stunned and sheepish, the feeling of his youth when after a lift, he'd pass a patrol. Then, like now, his instincts kick in. *Play it cool, like nothing's happened, it's just a coincidence.*

Paula Carrothers, who at six feet seems taller in person, doesn't seem to recognize him—or perhaps she too plays it cool. The cashier shoves the box toward her, mumbles hard syllables, and Andre wonders what's inside the box. He doubts Paula Carrothers is a regular here, and part of him wonders whether the box contains something nefarious, perhaps contraband, perhaps a secret that, if discovered, would represent the final blow to her career.

She opens her purse, pays with two fifties, and the cashier groans as though cash is inconvenient. He takes the bills, drops a couple coins onto the counter, folds his infected arms as though to emphasize that he's not driven by a desire to receive an online review that praises his exceptional customer service. Paula doesn't seem fazed. Perhaps by now she's grown accustomed to assholes. She peels the coins from the glass counter, thanking the cashier, and, as she makes her way toward the door, again mouths, *I'm sorry.* Then she's gone, sleigh bells ringing. The cashier signals Andre to approach, but not before mumbling, "Bitch."

"You have cell phones?"

The man doesn't make eye contact, shakes his head, saying, "You need to make a call, you use ours. Five dollars first minute. One dollar each minute more. Local calls only. Pay first."

"Was that . . . ? That's what's-her-name?" Andre, playing it smooth, leans in—the cashier smells like boiled sausage—and says, "Politicians, I tell ya."

The cashier brings his oxygen mask to his face and, peering over the mask, gives Andre a glance whose message is clear: *Mind your own fucking business.* Andre respects the cashier's fidelity to protecting the sanctity of the customer–sketchy pharmacist relationship. A man has to have a code. To atone for his faux pas, Andre asks for a box of cigars, which are expensive and on a high shelf behind the counter.

"Make that two boxes," Andre says.

The cashier groans, takes great pains to rise from his stool, grunting, straining, and Andre wonders whether open sores cover the cashier's entire body.

"Excuse me. Excuse me! I'm sorry." Paula Carrothers flies through the door, face blanched, sweaty and breathless. "I need your phone. Please. It's an emergency."

The cashier sits, without the cigars, says, "No phone for public use."

She's near tears. "They slashed my tires."

"Not my problem. You." The cashier points his thumb at Andre. "You want cigars or not?"

"I can pay," she says. "I'll be quick. A local call."

"If you want a phone," the cashier says, "go to Geraldine's."

"That's a mile away," she says, and Andre thinks: A mile down an unlit haunted road with no sidewalks. If those boys don't come back and get her, a coyote or drunk driver or slave ghost will. She says, "Please. My phone isn't getting any reception."

"No cell towers out here. They let the *government* spy on you," the cashier says with accusation, as though Paula Carrothers runs an intelligence agency. "They tried to put one up last year. We had a little talk. Now they don't bother."

"Sir, would you mind checking your phone, please?" She tries Andre, opens her purse, retrieves a fistful of cash that she splays and counts. "I have fifty. One. Two. Three. Fifty-three dollars. One phone call. It's yours."

He pats his jacket, not really thinking. Of course, she can

use his phone. Of course, she doesn't have to pay. But then he remembers: Fucking Gypsy stole my phone. "I'm sorry, I don't . . ."

She doesn't believe him.

"Here." She removes her ring, a gold band with a modest sapphire, jewelry for which a pawnshop might pay. "You can have it. Here. It's yours. It's worth a lot."

He thinks she's overreacting. Now is not 1950, and she is not a black college student registering colored voters. Worst-case scenario, she'll wait an hour. Maybe two. This bargaining for your life, Paula Carrothers, it's unseemly. But he considers her week. A rock through her window, slashed tires, the psychotic pornographic e-mails. And those are the crimes that he knows about.

"Please," Paula says. "Tell me what I have to do."

A pause. A long, awkward pause. An impasse? A stalemate? No. The cashier's won. Paula rushes out the door, sleigh bells ringing.

"Horse-throwed." The cashier scoffs. "Those cigars. They're expensive. Show me the money before I get up."

Andre buys the Dutch gin, rejects the cigars, hurries outside, where the pickup, boys, pit bull are gone. They've slashed all four tires of her sporty premium sedan, a car that, at rallies, Tyler loves to mock. To his surprise, his tires are fine, and inside his Jeep, he fidgets with the radio, sneaks a glance at Paula, who's clearly panicking in her car, gripping her phone with both hands, shaking and waving the phone, as though hopeful that if she holds it at the right angle, in the right spot, at the right moment, then, perhaps, she'll receive reception.

Paula slams her phone against her dash, screaming, shaking, an eruption of frustration that surprises Andre. He sets aside that she's his political opponent, sets aside that, perhaps, her peril is his fault. If she were a stranded stranger on the streets, he'd offer help. It is, he supposes, the right thing to do. He could offer her a ride, but she won't accept. Not that he can blame her. Juvie was full of young men who helped a desperate woman. That's the tough part about being a damsel in distress: no way to tell who's the hero and who's the villain.

Maybe he'll offer help and let her decide. If she refuses, he'll have done his duty and can end the day conscience clear. First, though, he hides all the campaign materials that clutter the back seat, propaganda that includes a new Wanted poster that accuses her of treason. He ignores his instinct to mind his own business, leaves the engine running, passes her back seat, where sits a stack of sample ballots and voter guides, the typical and unsurprising materials that officials prepare before an election. Tyler insists that Paula has a conflict of interest, that a woman whose fate depends upon an election shouldn't control the ballot. He's certain that Paula will cheat, voiding registrations, stuffing ballot boxes, *Dre, I'm not being ridiculous, Lazarus will rise from the dead and vote against liberty. Brother, don't you watch the news?* Andre guesses that she's only now leaving work. She has a reputation for working late, a reputation more insult than compliment. Paula Carrothers is married to her work, not to a man.

He taps her window—knocking, he fears, is aggressive—startles her nonetheless. She drops her phone, grabs her purse, presses it against her breasts. Her eyes are wide, face pale, jaw dropped. Does he really look that terrifying or has he merely surprised her? She slips one hand inside her purse, and he suspects—no, he knows, through intuition, through experience, through common sense—that Paula Carrothers has her finger on the trigger of a loaded gun.

Good for you, Paula Carrothers.

"You okay?" He keeps his distance, shows open palms, softens his tone and stare. "Listen, you don't know me, but . . ."

She can't hear. The sedan must be soundproof. She sets her purse in her lap, keeps one hand inside, uses the other to crack the window.

He says, "Need a lift to Geraldine's?"

"Thank you." She doesn't pause to consider. "But someone will be along."

"I'm heading that way. I can—"

"No." She's quick. "I mean, no thank you."

"Do you want someone to wait with you? I can wait in my car."

She shakes her head no, and he tries not to resent the ease with which she dismisses his help. Sure, he may look like a panhandler, but he can't help but wonder, if he were a white panhandler, a blue-eyed, blond-haired, could-be-in-a-grunge-band panhandler, then would she so quickly reject his help?

"Maybe," she says, "you could call for me. He has a phone inside. He lets other people use it. I'll give you money. Call 911 and the sheriff will send a patrol."

Hell no. Call the cops and the cops ask questions. At the very least, they'll ask his name and why he's here this late. He could call, request help, hang up, but that too comes with risk. Juvie's full of boys who tried to do the right thing. Good boys who gave fake names or no name at all. Didn't matter. Cops always find a way to fuck you. God forbid they search his Jeep, with its after-hours booze and its campaign propaganda and its laptop memorializing the campaign's every bad deed. Cops might get the wrong idea. Might think he's the asshole who slashed her tires, smashed her window, sent those fucked-up pornographic e-mails. He don't have no alibi. Don't have no friends. All he's got is means, motive, and opportunity. A brother in Carthage won't get no fair trial. Hell, a brother terrorizing a single white female, a county manager at that, that's a crime for which a judge, in an election year, would sentence a brother to death.

Now he's got a fresh dilemma. If he refuses to make the call, Paula Carrothers is gonna freak. A stranger offers a ride but won't make a call. That's got serial killer written all over it. She'll ask questions; she'll report him to the police. The last thing he needs is an APB out on his black ass. He should've never offered to help. No good deed . . .

He has one choice, says, "Sure. Call the sheriff?"

"Thank you. Thank you. Tell them that Paula Carrothers is stranded. Here." Both hands are inside her purse, one digging for cash, the other clutching the gun. Through the cracked window, with a trembling hand, she slips fifty-three dollars as though she's feeding a crocodile: nervous, cautious, a quick recoil, fearing she might lose her fingers. She flinches, withdraws her hand too soon, and the cash falls. He kneels, collecting the bills, as she apologizes. The change, she adds, is his.

He says, "Be right back."

The cashier eats a meatloaf sandwich, chews like a grazing cow, a lettuce leaf pulled, chomp by chomp, into his mouth. Andre checks his watch. Ninety seconds should do. He notices, on sale beside the door, Confederate garden gnomes. Pudgy white-bearded gnomes in rebel gray. A button-nosed artillery officer with sash and saber. A pink-cheeked private thrusting a bayonet. Andre picks up one—a gnome Scarlett O'Hara—doesn't see a price.

"You can't afford it," the cashier says with mouth full. "Put it down."

"I'm looking for a price."

"Put it down."

"What did the county manager have in that box?"

"Get the fuck out of my shop."

"And why don't you let her use your shitty phone?"

"Get out of my shop." The cashier gasps for breath. "And don't ever come back, you black monkey piece of shit."

Black monkey piece of shit. Andre supposes, on the spectrum of racial slurs, he's heard worse. Andre has what he needs, leaves the store to find Paula's eyes fixed on the door. He checks his watch; ninety seconds on the mark.

"Well?" she says. "Did he let you call?"

"He told me to fuck off," Andre says. "Told me I wasn't welcome back. Called me a black monkey piece of shit."

"Oh." She deflates. "I'm sorry. He shouldn't've. Thank you. Really. You're kind to try."

"You sure you don't want that ride?" He considers offering to wait with her, or maybe he could call from Geraldine's. But he's tired, irritated, realizes he's hanging around a crime scene. He's already more involved than he wants to be. He says, "Geraldine's is a mile up the road?"

This time, she considers his offer, thinking harder than before, and, for a moment, he believes she might accept. He wonders about her decision-making mechanism, the arithmetic passing through her mind. On the one hand this stranger might harm her, but she's got to weigh that against the probability of alternatives: walk the mile, drive on rims, stay here and live, stay here and die, the unconscious calculus that women make every day. Paula Carrothers politely declines, repeats that someone will come along, but, in her voice, Andre senses that she's not quite sure.

"You be safe," he says. "Sorry those boys slashed your tires."

"It's not your fault," she says. "You tried your best."

He wishes either statement was true.

In his Jeep, he realizes he's kept her cash. Good thing the kid isn't here. The kid would never have left her stranded, but, then again, if Brendan were here, Paula would've accepted a ride. He's steering through the parking lot, hoping that she'll remain safe, when he hears a sudden crash. At first, he thinks Paula's fired her gun. But another explosion, and the night sky, for an instant, brightens like a summer day. Last night of the fair. A fireworks bonanza. A star. A heart. A smiley face and four-leaf clover. A spectacular celebration of Carthage in red, white, and blue.

PART VI

ELECTION DAY

CHAPTER TWENTY-THREE

Four thirty A.M.

The clock radio comes alive, plays a forecast that threatens thunderstorms. He grabs the radio, pitches it across the room, where pieces break against the wall, but the clock radio remains intact, at least enough to broadcast static as loud as a police siren. He buries his head beneath two pillows, tries to block out the noise, but the clock radio is relentless. He rises, cursing the clock; in this moment, he hates everyone and everything: hates Carthage and Election Day and American democracy, but, above all else, right now, he hates that he's allowed his life to come to this. In twenty-four hours, these people . . . these fucking people . . . will decide whether he will keep a job that, if he's being honest, he may no longer want.

He rips the nine-volt from the clock with a short, satisfying jerk, drops the damn thing and kicks it to the corner. He's exhausted, a little drowsy, needs ten more minutes' sleep. But he worries now, since he's awake, that he may not fall back asleep, and worries that if he does fall asleep, then he doesn't have an alarm to tell him to wake. A conundrum that, to him, feels like a metaphor for his entire life.

On the attic landline, sitting in his boxer briefs, Andre starts a conference call. Everyone goes around, says their name. Mr. DeVille. Two PISA vice presidents and their team of in-house counsel. PISA's CEO is also on the line, but he is not in the same room as his staff. He's off somewhere, he says, maybe Monterrey or Montreal; his connection's poor. No one can quite make out what he says. His staff urges moving the microphone closer or maybe speaking louder—*Sir, can you hang up and call from a landline?* The meeting begins ten minutes later, and now his connection's worse, his voice booming in and out, skipping sentences, with an echo like he's whispering into a vast, cavernous void. One PISA staffer says in frustration: "Why does he always do this?" Mr. DeVille loses patience, pitches an easy question that signals for Andre to begin.

The trick to a successful Election Day briefing, Mrs. Fitz always said, is to be optimistically noncommittal. The briefing should manage expectations, should ensure that no one takes Election Day for granted, should prepare the client for the possibility of a win or a loss. Ask any veteran consultant who will prevail on Election Day, and if she's any good, she'll answer that the election will be close. Andre's delivered this assessment to scores of clients, but this time the line is true. The latest poll, now three days old, has the initiatives ahead by two, within the poll's three-point margin of error. The poll also confirms a trend: the undecideds have made up their minds.

Andre explains all that could go wrong. Better-educated voters could show up in droves. The chronically unemployed could stay at home. Young white men, God bless 'em, remain reliably loyal to the campaign, but middle-aged white women? Well, Carthage brims with middle-aged white women, and they remain, what's the word? *Unreliable, unpredictable, fickle*? They know for which side they will vote, but these past three weeks, as the campaign turned nasty, the uncivil tone may have deterred white women from visiting the polls.

Turnout is key. Has Andre already said this? He's still a little stoned, fears he's repeating himself. But this fact is essential. He runs down the hard numbers. Corporate clients love hard numbers, which affirm their faith that elections are more science than art. Carthage has a total population of about 28,500. A voting-age population of roughly 20,200. The liberty campaign launched an aggressive voter-registration effort, which increased the total number of registered voters to about 17,900. Historically, turnout during a municipal spring election, well, it's embarrassingly low. An average of between 8 and 12 percent.

"In order to win, what turnout do we need?" someone asks, to which Andre says, "I'll feel more confident if turnout tops eighteen percent. Anything less than fifteen, and we're in trouble."

"And a turnout between fifteen and eighteen?"

"That's anyone's guess." Mr. DeVille is upbeat. "Dre, you've done a fine job. All my years in politics, I've never seen a race this close."

Mr. DeVille's praise worries Andre. Say what one will about Ricardo DeVille, but the old man's chaired brutal campaigns that involved recounts and lawsuits and hanging chads. Andre guesses that Mr. DeVille wears a brave face for the client, that his boss believes that, after spending $350,000, this triflin' race in a triflin' town shouldn't be this close. Truth is, the old man's right.

Andre offers more concrete numbers. Encouraging signs. Thus far, the county has received forty-five overseas military ballots, which the campaign expects to trend their way. The campaign has also completed its senior-citizen outreach, nine hundred older residents shuttled to the polls. In total, about one thousand people have voted early, a Carthaginian record.

Turnout is key.

The PISA chief asks a question, which someone, perhaps a lawyer, translates. The boss wants to know how much cash remains. The campaign coffers are empty, Andre explains, a bank account with less than fifty dollars, the final cashier's check cut to produce Sunday-morning ads on Christian talk radio.

The campaign, however, has six thousand in petty cash, though Andre reports that the campaign has three. This three grand, he explains, is walking-around cash: Lunch for supporters. Rental cars. Change for parking meters.

"I once set up a daycare for campaign volunteers," Mr. DeVille says. "Keeping feet on the streets is expensive."

As for the unreported three grand, Andre plans to keep it for himself. The past few weeks, he's fixed the books. Created small expenses that no one will question. He doesn't take pride in his theft, but he'd feel different if he were stealing from Mrs. Fitz. Instead he's stealing from Mr. DeVille, the firm, and PISA. Andre doesn't rationalize the theft. He knows what he is, and he knows what he's done. But he might be unemployed in twelve hours, and a safety net seems like good common sense.

The conference call is nearing its end when, to his surprise, Duke Boshears weighs in. Did Duke say his name at the beginning, during the participant roll call? No, of course the asshole did not.

Duke Boshears compares the campaign to the Battle of Waterloo, compares Andre to Jefferson Davis, a pair of twisted historical analogies that confuses everyone. Duke complains that he asked for regular updates and that Andre refused. Complains that he recommended the campaign launch robocalls and that Andre refused. Complains that he recommended Andre spread darker dirt about Paula Carrothers and that Andre refused. He complains about the lack of campaign signs, the lack of transparency, the lack of good straw men.

"I like Chalene and Tyler. God bless 'em. They are good Christian people. But they were wrong for this campaign," he says. "If Andre would've asked, I would have told him. Run a campaign with class. Don't pin your hopes on folks like the Lees. But no one asked me."

Andre thinks of the fickle middle-aged white women, wonders how Victoria Boshears will vote. She, perhaps more than any other voter, is a bellwether for the campaign's success. He doesn't regret her unauthorized endorsement, but he acknowledges the endorsement may have been an overreaction to the slap.

"I've lived in Carthage my whole life," Duke yells. "I've run for office multiple times. Andre and that Scottish boy, we had one short superficial meeting."

Andre misses the kid, wishes he were here.

"I'm sorry," the CEO says. "My line went silent there. Couldn't hear a thing. Last thing I heard, we were keeping feet on the street. Did I miss anything important?"

A choir of PISA lawyers says, "No."

Mr. DeVille wraps up the call, promises that Andre will e-mail updates throughout the day. Duke interrupts. "I hope, for once, that Mr. Ross will include me on these e-mails."

"Certainly," Andre says, but knows he won't. The call ends, and Andre leans deep into his chair. If there's one upside to losing, it's that a defeat will ruin Duke Boshears. The attic light flickers, then goes out. At first, he assumes the lightbulb has burned out, but he realizes that all the machines have fallen silent. Through a window, the light of the stars and the moon casts his shadow across the conference table. The silhouette makes him wonder whether this is an omen: a presentiment of trouble to come.

He finds the burner he bought online, sends a text to Brendan: *Miss you, my friend, on Judgment Day!*

A bronzed cannon guards the front of the Old Confederate Armory, and behind the one-story stone structure, just beyond a grove of plum trees, is a field of tall grass, a wooden cross standing in its center. Andre holds no illusions about this site. The Old Confederate Armory was once the clubhouse of secret societies and fraternities of terror. Folks around Carthage admit as much, claim that the armory's rich cultural history is a part of the building's charm. The Anabaptists now own the armory, rent out the space for cotillions and deb balls, and, before he knew what he knows now, Andre agreed to let the armory serve as Election Day headquarters.

The irony is not lost upon him. Here a black man ends his leadership of a secret dark-money grassroots campaign, an act of demagoguery cloaked in patriotism, rebellion, and Southern pride. He never intended to run this kind of campaign, but the past three days, even by his own standards, this campaign has turned ugly. Last night, a robocall went out to every home in Carthage, the caller claiming to be Esther Silverstein from Brooklyn, New York. Esther claimed that Paula Carrothers was a friend. *Paula is a strong progressive feminist, with strong progressive views.* Esther praised Paula as the champion of gun control and abortion-on-demand. *Educated secular thinkers support Paula Carrothers.* Andre recognized the meddling of Duke Boshears, who twice proposed such a call, and who, two years ago, authorized a similar robocall from Señor Jose Iglesias of Brownsville, Texas, which featured Iglesias praising Boshears's opponent.

Inside the armory is a large open space with brick walls and Wi-Fi. A junior pastor, a fourteen-year-old prodigy, leads the campaign in prayer. The boy has slicked-back hair and a chalk-striped suit, a wardrobe less like a preacher's and more like an investment banker's. The boy prays with a light, smoky tone, infused with passion and sincerity, quotes the scripture from memory with the confidence of a man who's heard the Word directly from God. If he grew up in a different part of the country, perhaps New York or L.A., his parents would've enrolled him in an after-school drama program. Instead of skipping school to preach the gospel in a former Klan clubhouse, he'd probably play the stage manager in a community center production of *Our Town*.

Amen.

The prayer ends, and everyone turns toward the dais, onto which two flag-toting teens march in unison. The national anthem blasts from a portable CD player, and everyone brings their hand to their heart. Andre doesn't remember approving all this pageantry, suspects that Chalene and Tyler didn't either. The past few days, the robocalls, the misogynist graffiti, the whisper campaign that Paula Carrothers had a secret, illegitimate Negro child with her lesbian lover—he wonders at what point he lost control. He thinks of a months-old conversation about Nathan Bedford Forrest, the Confederate general and Southern folk hero who later founded the Klan. Tyler swears that Forrest, for whom the local high school is named, wasn't all that bad. That Forrest was a military genius, the best strategist of the war, who, yes, also happened to found the Klan. But Forrest, Tyler argued, renounced the organization once members pursued violence.

He can't be blamed for the radical acts of others. Brendan thought the argument bullshit. *So it's okay to pursue an agenda of white supremacy, but God forbid someone gets hurt?* Andre agreed that Tyler's argument was bullshit. But this morning, Andre finds himself gaining sympathy for the Klan's first grand wizard.

The national anthem ends, and the teens plant the flags into brass stands.

Tyler Lee, climbing the dais, looks tired, almost seasick.

"My Chalene wrote a few lines." He unfolds a sheet of sweat-soaked paper. "But I can't read her writing."

He gets a supportive laugh.

"But I think—" He clears his throat. "She wants y'all to know how much she loves ya. And she wishes she were here. She asks for your prayers."

His face goes blank, and the crowd shouts encouragements.

"Okay, y'all," he says. "The band's already playing. All we have to do is dance."

The room explodes in activity. Most volunteers are Election Day veterans, have worked past presidential or statewide campaigns. They understand the logistics of mobilizing supporters. A team to work the phones, a team to knock on doors, a team to drive voters to the polls. Six homeschooled teens and the teenage pastor open their laptops, send reminders to supporters to vote.

First these volunteers, some twenty strong, must cast their own ballots. They will travel together the four blocks to the county hall. An act of solidarity. An affirmation of community. A show of strength.

"Brother." Tyler takes Andre aside, waits for everyone to leave. "Brother, I'm sorry. I should've done better. I should've—"

"You did fine." What good is the truth now? "Everyone understands."

In the parking lot, supporters cram into trucks and passenger vans. Tyler's phone buzzes, and he wanders toward a semi-private space, abandoning Andre near six middle-aged white men wearing paramilitary attire. One guy, face smeared with paint, wears a bulletproof vest. These men are not observers permitted inside the polling places—Andre has trusted that task to others—these six are, as Tyler has explained, insurance. There just in case something goes wrong.

These assholes clearly don't know that Andre is on their side. If they did, they probably wouldn't concentrate, upon Andre, their most lethal stares. He's pretty used to the hostile glower of white men. All black men, he supposes, are. On the bus. At work. In line at the post office. Black men experience this stare every day. But this lifetime of experience doesn't make him feel any less hunted, any less like a hare that's fallen beneath a coyote's glare. Tyler waves to the men. "Dre. Let's roll."

The trucks and vans leave the lot slowly, as if on parade, a procession that ignores stop signs, in which drivers honk their horns and flag-toting teens surf inside truck beds. A hundred years ago, Andre thinks, a lynch mob probably left the armory with equal enthusiasm. And, as quick as it began, the parade ends. Four blocks, over and done.

In the county hall parking lot, Tyler drives past VOTE HERE signs and an empty spot reserved for Paula Carrothers. Andre hasn't heard any rumors about someone slashing her tires, has no idea how she got home. But he's impressed that she's managed to keep that night secret, and he wonders what fresh indignities she's quietly suffered since.

"Mind if we just sit here?" Tyler puts the truck in park, watches their supporters spill out of the vans, some standing in line, some setting up camp on the sidewalk forty-five feet from the hall's front door. "Just for a second while we catch our breath."

Paula Carrothers unlocks the county hall doors, and folks in line jeer. Someone calls her a Nazi. But Paula's a pro, ignores the heckles to declare the polls open.

CHAPTER TWENTY-FOUR

Andre explains that Election Days are inherently dull.

Spent in hotel conference rooms or candidate garages or strip-mall storefronts that serve as campaign headquarters, Election Days are all about numbers, mostly accounting and scheduling: keeping tallies of turnout, keeping track of turn-aways, keeping field teams focused and on schedule. Most campaign consultants could spend their entire day on their cell, probably surrounded by cheap-ass snacks, the same empty-calorie, self-loathing-inducing junk food that the high school intern picked up at a corner gas station.

Therefore, on Election Day, campaign staffs often produce unnecessary drama, and campaign consultants, who must show that they have fought until the bitter end, are world-class divas. Often, the campaign will harass the local election administrator, the municipal official who actually runs the election. Maybe call once an hour in the morning, twice an hour in the afternoon, and, if the campaign is gonna lose, call nonstop minutes before the polls close. In each call, which should be held on speaker-phone, the campaign will memorialize each complaint, both rumored and confirmed. Lines are too long. Poll workers too rude. Report the problem no matter the size. Always threaten to sue, or at least to cause a public stink. The local news is hungry for any Election Day trouble; reporters have little to do until the embargo on exit polls ends.

Sometimes the campaign gets lucky. A problem at a polling place that serves a historically screwed-over demographic. Shenanigans at a majority-black precinct are a pot of gold at the end of the rainbow. God bless you if there are photos. Old black women in funny church hats stacked twenty-five deep. In most cases, the problem will have little impact on the outcome, but it's the principle. Every campaign consultant dreams about the opportunity to compare a local election administrator to George Wallace standing in the schoolhouse door.

And, who knows, maybe the Department of Justice is watching. Maybe the campaign will identify some fuckup that the feds can later use to bring a high-profile case. The United States vs. the asshole local election administrator. But don't count on the feds: they're slow and cautious, and worst of all, they hate to invalidate election returns. A do-over is out of the question. Americans didn't want to vote the first time; they'll be damned if they'll be made to do so twice. No. Do-overs aren't our national tradition. Sure, every once in a while it will happen, but do-overs are expensive and as rare as a citizen who knows the name of their lieutenant governor. So, the candidate is out of luck, but, hopefully, the problem will be fixed and won't repeat next time around. Maybe. Hopefully. Probably not.

The reality is elections are imperfect, the same as any other of man's creations. Pacemakers. Plane engines. Prophylactics. Everything has a failure rate, errors are bound to happen, and sometimes those mistakes break our hearts. Why should elections be any different?

Andre explains all this to Tyler as the two share half a Dutch apple pie at a diner across the street from the county hall. From here, the two can watch their supporters hassle voters entering the polls. The supporters are six, including three beautiful brunettes from the Gray Wolf, now in patriotic bikinis, who spin pastel signs that say VOTE HERE and I KISS FOR LIBERTY. The law requires the team to stay two hundred feet from the county hall's entrance, but Andre guesses that these six are probably fifty feet at best. No one cares.

"It's all bullshit," Tyler says with a mouth full of apple pie. "I knew it."

"Knew what?"

"'Every vote counts,'" Tyler says. "That's a lie we tell our children."

"That wasn't my point," Andre says. "I'm just saying—"

The phone rings on Tyler's hip. It's the armory checking in. Word for word, Tyler repeats their report. The campaign's observers, stationed inside the county hall, have provided a tally of the people who visited the polls. The campaign has failed to meet yet another hourly goal, but these shortcomings are manageable, significant enough to cause trouble if the trend continues, but small enough that they can be cured by a strong showing of after-work voters. The observers also share the names of those turned away. Thus far, poll workers have refused to provide ballots to twenty-five voters, ten of whom were black, they note, and didn't have a photo ID.

"Do we need to go over there?" Andre asks once the call ends.

"We'd only get in the way." Tyler sends Chalene a text with an update. She thinks Tyler is managing the team at the armory, because this is what Tyler has chosen to share. To Andre the whole situation is comical. Five hours since the polls opened, and they have yet to return to the armory. Tyler is like a truant on his way to school, easily distracted, willfully lost, eager to corrupt classmates along the way.

Andre can't complain. He's spent Election Day in worse dives than this. Indeed, this diner is a nice hangout: clean, nearly empty, smells like French toast. A handwritten sign promises free Danish for anyone who wears an *I Voted* sticker, and on the radio plays Christian talk. Andre and Tyler sit in a red-leatherette corner booth, where, Tyler says, he and Chalene had their first date, and where, each year, they celebrate their anniversary. They know Tyler here. They like Tyler here. Tyler's Dutch apple pie is on the house.

"What's the point if Election Day is rigged?" Tyler says.

"The fix isn't in on Election Day," Andre says. "If you learned anything from our time together, I hope you learned that the fix was in thirteen weeks ago."

"Well, tell me this—"

Now the phone on Andre's hip rings. Andre knows he's a fool to get his hopes up that it might be Brendan, but part of him is certain that the kid will call today. But it isn't Brendan. Indeed, it's the opposite of Brendan: Duke Boshears, calling for an update, the tenth time he's called this morning. Andre presses ignore, the same as each time before, starts to tell the tale of the Philly poll workers who closed the polls early because they won a radio contest for Boyz II Men tickets. He's nearly through when the waitress comes to refill their mugs. She is not the waitress who seated them. Must have just started her shift. She's maybe thirty, clearly exhausted; her apron is pristine, and she wears an *I Voted* sticker.

"You know I'd vote twice for liberty if I could," she says.

The waitress makes small talk, tells Tyler that this morning, she set two bowls on opposite sides of her barn, and beside one bowl she placed an index card that said *yes*, and beside the other bowl an index card that said *no*. Then she asked her favorite goat—the one with the duplicitous personality—whether the liberty campaign would succeed, and the goat chose yes.

"My goats are never wrong," the waitress says.

"That's what I hear, Annette," Tyler says.

"And how's Chalene?" she says. "I hear she's taken ill."

"They have her on bed rest. Gave her something to sleep. She should be sawing wood now. Doctor said to come back if the headaches return."

Tyler's shared this line with everyone who's asked, and almost everyone to pass through the diner has asked. Everyone worries about Chalene; everyone knows her past. Tyler has become superstitious, dares not utter the word *preeclampsia*, as though certain that speaking it aloud might bring it into being. He omits important details: test for protein in her urine, monitoring her liver enzymes, a prescription to treat her hypertension. She's fine now, the physician assistant said, but if things change, the doctors will have to perform a C-section. Tyler wears a brave face, but he's clearly terrified. This time, the doctors said, there might be risk to both Chalene and their child. *She must take it easy.* Tyler wants to be at home with his wife, but Chalene insists he work the campaign. And because he will not cause her stress, he's camped out here, eating pie, surrounded by friends and fond memories, waiting for any excuse to return home.

When the waitress leaves, Tyler says, "That's Annette Blackett. She treats her goats better than she treats her children. She's a sweetheart, but she's a little touched. Thinks goats have powers, can predict the future. Last year, she asked her goat whether she and her husband would get a divorce. Goat said yes."

"A rough way to end your marriage."

"Rougher for the goat. Husband shot the little sucker, butchered it, ground it, mixed it in with beef. Did the whole thing in secret, one afternoon, and then fed it to Annette for dinner on Taco Tuesday."

"Jesus."

"Quite the scandal. Everyone was talkin'. But you know what? Goat was right. They ain't married no more."

"What happened to the husband?"

"Oh, nothing. He's still sheriff. It's not illegal to kill a goat or nothing. That would be silly."

Across the street, a black van parks outside the county hall. The van is windowless, something that television spies might use on a stakeout. The door slides open, and out pour a dozen women. Andre assumes the van is one of three that the campaign has rented to ferry supporters to the polls, but he wishes the campaign had rented something less nefarious, a vehicle less preferred by human traffickers.

"You know Chalene, she's gonna miss you something bad. You've become one of her best friends, and you know she worries about you. You're at the top of her prayer list."

"Your wife just likes to worry."

"She thinks you should stay here," Tyler says. "She's even got a gal picked out for you."

"Let me guess. It's the only other black person Chalene knows."

"Yeah. Reckon so." Tyler laughs. "'Tween you and me, my wife's trash at matchmaking. She's the one that hooked up Annette Blackett and the sheriff."

The diner goes quiet, and Andre feels a sudden alarm in the air. All eyes are on Tyler, who is a step behind in recognizing that the atmosphere has changed. Then Tyler and Andre both hear it, Chalene's voice on the radio, and Tyler slams his fist against the tabletop.

Playing hooky is now over.

Chalene scowls, arms crossed, atop the parlor's folded-out couch, which is messy with campaign flyers and county maps. She wears makeup and her best string of replica pearls. Her maternity dress is also her best, a floral pattern with a pussy bow, though the dress rides up to reveal her lower legs, which are so swollen that her ankles have disappeared, replaced by a seamless merger of calf and heel.

"Of course I dressed up," she shouts at Tyler. "It was *Teach and Talk* with Pastor Paul."

"It was a radio interview."

"Listeners can tell what you're wearing," she yells as Tyler storms into the backyard. "I don't understand what the big deal is. Was just a phone call."

Andre sits at the kitchen table eating butter cookies from a tin. He would have preferred to miss the past half hour, but he had to use the bathroom and, afterward, was held against his will, made a party to this silly squabble: a witness to give evidence, a juror to decide fault. His thoughts he keeps to himself, though he agrees with Tyler. The doctor has prescribed total bed rest, and Chalene has neither remained in bed nor tried to rest. In fact, here, she's set up a satellite headquarters. A dry-erase board by her side. The campaign's loaner tablet on her lap. Two cell phones within her reach. When Andre and Tyler arrived here, they caught her vacuuming.

"I know you two weren't at the armory," she says with

accusation. "I expect such bad behavior from my Tyler, but you, Dre? You're a professional. It's like you don't even care if we win. I'm disappointed."

He crosses the room, sits at the foot of her bed, offers her a butter cookie. "I'll try to find a way to live with your disappointment."

"You're gonna be a smart Samson now?" She takes two cookies. "My Tyler can be such a child."

Her tablet pings, and Andre checks his watch. The polls close in four hours. Right about now, a team back in Washington should be sending, via social media and e-mail, a short video to supporters. The video, twice focus-grouped, is a reminder to vote, mixing clips of enthusiastic Carthage residents with stock footage of attractive millennials casting their ballot, the whole sixty seconds set to a booming inspirational symphony.

"Look at the latest numbers." Chalene swipes at her tablet. "We got an uptick. If the weather holds, Dre, we might just pull this out."

"It'll come down to after-work voters," Dre says. "The close ones always do."

Chalene starts to read the latest list of turn-aways, which she's received from the armory, shares that she has a spy at the county hall, someone who works directly for Paula Carrothers and who texts inside information. Andre, though, has focused his attention outside, where Tyler has an axe and is chopping down a tree. Andre watches in awe, thinks that felling a tree should be a rite of passage. A tree becomes a log. A boy becomes a man. Andre wants to get in on the action, wants to know whether Tyler has a second axe.

"Dre," Chalene says. "Dre, are you paying attention?"

"No."

"What is wrong with you? Do you care if we win?"

Andre searches his feelings and, to his surprise, realizes that he doesn't know the answer. He thinks, Of course I want to win: I need to win. But thirteen weeks ago, he imagined that an Election Day win would reinvigorate his life. A victory would restore his reputation at the firm, would restore Mrs. Fitz's faith in him—quite possibly restore his faith in himself. And if he was lucky, these thirteen weeks would permit him the time and space to get over Cassie. But look at him now: none of that has come to pass, and, deep down, he fears that none of it ever will. A world without Mrs. Fitz at work; a world without Cassie at home. It is an empty, hopeless world for which he has no enthusiasm. So what's he got to gain with a win today? Perhaps he'll keep his job, which is no small reward; a paycheck is a paycheck is a paycheck, especially for a once-poor black kid whose family often teetered on the brink of homelessness.

"Really, Dre, this is important," she lectures in the grating, exasperated tone that she reserves for her sons. "You're being unprofessional. Irrational. If you don't start paying attention—"

"Oh, fuck you." His patience is exhausted.

She sits back, surprised.

"I'm being irrational? You're the one who's ignoring the doctor's advice. Where's the rationality in that?"

"That is none of your business."

"You're driving your husband crazy."

"Oh, you're concerned about my Tyler," she says. "When did you two become buddies?"

They sit in silence, watch Tyler take a final chop at a small tree that has begun to bend. Tyler kicks the tree, a full-on fireman's stomp-down-the-door kick, and after the tree falls, crashing noisily against the sunburned grass, he chops at another. Chalene takes a face towel, wipes the makeup her tears have begun to smear.

"I don't like just sitting here, peeing in a jug, afraid of a headache. All I can do is think about all that can go wrong, while staring at the wallpaper that my Tyler said he'd replace two years ago. I'm six weeks from my delivery date. I'm supposed to do that the entire time?"

"I'm sorry, I shouldn't have—"

"Last time, the doctors kept me in the hospital. Flat on my back. Three counties away. All because I had a little headache. I lost my job. I couldn't see my boys every day. I couldn't go to service. And still, in the end . . ." Her voice breaks. "I swore if I had to do bed rest again, I was going to do it here."

She takes another cookie, crushes it in her fist.

"Bed rest doesn't work anyway," she says. "I read that on a pregnancy website. Doctors don't know the answers, so they just tell women bed rest because they can't think of anything else. Bed rest and squeeze this tiny little ball."

She produces a red stress ball, pitches it across the room.

Outside, another tree falls, this time a taller, thicker one. Tyler hops atop the fallen tree, legs spread, knees bent, balances as he swings the axe furiously at a spot between his feet. Chunks of tree fly in every direction, and Andre worries that Tyler may hurt himself.

"So since we're asking each other personal questions . . . ," she says.

"Oh God. What are you about to say?"

"Aren't you lonely?"

"Where did that come from?"

"You never talk about a wife or girlfriend. I know you have a brother, but I don't know anything about him. And after Brendan left . . ."

"Really? You want to have this conversation now?"

"If not now, then when?"

"So this is where you say that I need Jesus in my life."

"No, Dre, this is where I say that you need someone who loves you in your life."

She has caught him off guard. He purposely avoids asking himself this question—something he learned in juvie, the loneliest place on earth and yet one place you're never alone. Truth is: tomorrow he'll set down in Washington and no one will greet him at the gate. Or at baggage claim. Or at his condo. He says, "I have lots of friends back in Washington."

"I don't believe you."

"Some people are just built to be alone."

"I don't believe that either."

What does she want him to say? That his loneliness was entirely preventable? At twenty, he made the choice to prioritize his career. He was seduced by a future full of glamour and power and money. How can he explain that his career gave him purpose, permission to be ambitious, and a famous mentor who watched over him? But, true, it did not produce friends. For some reason, he took it for granted, thought friends would come naturally. After all, how hard could it be to make friends? Fucking six-year-olds on a playground do it. Harder than he thought, he's learned. The past few years, the closest thing he's had to a friend was Brendan, whom he misses more than he wants to admit. Sometimes, in that empty house, he finds himself having imaginary conversations with the kid. Perhaps the kid will call today. God, he feels pathetic that he hopes so.

"Tyler and I should get going to the armory." He stares down at his feet, embarrassed. "If the bed rest gets unbearable, call me. I'll bring you something to drink."

"Dre, baby . . ."

"Seriously. A good whiskey will help pass the time and it takes care of those pesky thoughts. A bad whiskey will do that too."

"Dre, baby, I need you to listen." She takes his hand, gives it a strong squeeze. He raises his face to see a thick run of blood from her nose. "Dre, baby, get my Tyler. I have a headache."

CHAPTER TWENTY-FIVE

Carthage County Medical Clinic is a flat brick building that was once a whites-only YMCA. Andre sits in the waiting room, a small space with an empty coffeepot and uncomfortable lime chairs. The rest of the clinic lies behind a magnetically sealed door, which, to enter, requires a pass card or the permission of the sloe-eyed nurse, who dozes off behind a window six inches thick.

The waiting room is empty except for Dre and two middle-aged women who he guesses are twins, and who will soon lose their stepmother. The twins bicker; one clearly adores the dying woman, the other clearly doesn't. Andre doesn't mean to eavesdrop, but the sisters are having this disagreement, loudly, right here before him. He tries hard to demonstrate that he's minding his own business: leafing through a hunting magazine, playing solitaire on his phone, studying the fake upside-down fish that bob in a hundred-gallon tank, but their disagreement grows more intense—now they're shouting—and he starts to wonder whether he should intervene.

He does, after all, have wisdom to share. For nearly a

decade after his release, he didn't speak to Hector, but seven years ago, one day, out of the blue, Hector called the firm, threatened to cause a scene at his fancy-ass office unless Andre agreed to meet. Andre assumed that Hector had a scheme, some petty hood bullshit Andre had long ago outgrown. Instead, when the two met at Union Station, sitting beside a mobile kiosk where Hector sold Swiss sunglasses, Big Brother announced that he was six months sober, that he'd found a woman whom he planned to marry, that his recovery demanded that he try to make amends for all the pain he caused. For the next half hour, Andre listened to Hector confess his sins. The time he threw salt in Andre's eyes; the time he busted Andre's nose. Each and every time he called their mother a bitch or a selfish ho. *Yo, Dre. I know that bothered you, man. I mean, she was a selfish ho. But I shouldn't have called her that in front of you. I apologize.* Andre listened to each offense, trivial annoyances long forgotten, only to realize this asshole had no plan to seek forgiveness for the lone sin about which Andre cared.

"Nigga, you made me take the fall for a crime you committed." Andre could not govern his rage. "Don't you owe me an apology for that?"

"Well. If you feel I need to apologize for that, then I apologize."

"If? Motherfucker, did you say *if*?" Andre shouted. People were looking. "I spent two years inside for you."

"Two years. Please. That what you crying about? It was clearly the best thing for you. Told you it would be." Hector spoke with a reasoned tone. "Look at you. Just look at you. Wearing a suit. Working downtown. I bet you make all kinds of money. Meet all kinds of girls."

Andre rose. "Don't ever call me again."

"How am I wrong?" Hector grabbed his wrist. "Look at you and look at me."

"You expect me to thank you?"

"Dre, what do you want from me?"

"An apology, asshole. Isn't that the entire fucking point?" A small, intense explosion detonated inside him, and he tried to push over the mobile kiosk, gave it everything he had, but the kiosk was heavy and sturdy, well balanced and well made. It wasn't going anywhere. So Andre grabbed the most expensive pair of sunglasses, clutched the overpriced shades between his fists, trying to snap the frame in two, but the sunglasses, too, were sturdy and well made. Fucking Swiss know how to make a good pair of shades. Andre smashed the glasses against the ground, stomping on them with all his weight, bending the frames, scraping the lenses, the two-hundred-dollar price tag torn beneath his heel.

"You feel better?" Hector said.

"No." Andre's anger morphed into exhaustion, and he wept on the bench. "You didn't even come see me inside."

"I didn't think you'd accept my visit."

"You should've at least tried."

"Dre, making amends isn't just about apologizing. It's about making things right. I know I fucked up. I know you got a good life now that don't include me. But there ain't a day where I don't think about you."

"I'm still mad at you."

"We don't have to fix everything right now. Today's just the first day. If it takes years for you and me to get right, shit, Dre, I got nothing but time."

In the waiting room, the twins are screaming—is this some hidden-camera show?—and Andre steps outside, finds a quiet space beside the waist-high chain-link fence that surrounds a filled-in swimming pool. Polls close in fifteen minutes, and he realizes he's wasted his entire day. Mrs. Fitz would be ashamed. And his grief springs anew, as fresh and as raw as the day she died. Tonight will be his first professional election night without her. On nights he'd win, he'd call like a son phoning his parents, not to boast, not to solicit praise, but to receive a form of validation, as though to say, *Look at what you taught me to do.* On nights he'd lose, he'd find comfort in their conversations, asking what he might learn from failure, hearing in her voice that she was neither disappointed nor ashamed. This same woman would not simply abandon him. Of this he's nearly convinced himself, at least enough to get through another day.

He phones the armory, starts to ask for an hourly update, for Tyler he says, when an ambulance bolts into the parking lot, sirens wailing. Andre finds himself gawking, curious about what horror might be inside. An overdose. A heart attack. A hunting accident. In Carthage you never know. The paramedics, tall, lean black men, jump out, open the back doors to reveal no one inside. They slide out a gurney and disappear into the hospital.

Maybe four minutes pass before the paramedics are back, slamming open the hospital doors. They are a tornado, a concentrated swirl of chaos, pushing hard and fast through the hospital doors, with Chalene flat on her back on the gurney. The paramedics are shouting. She's shouting. Tyler Lee, holding her purse, is shouting. *Baby, hold on.* Chalene sweaty, pale, weak, and more swollen than before. Maybe she's in labor, maybe not. What does he know? Only that she's got an IV in her arm and she's breathing hard, trying to fight off a level of pain to which Andre will never be able to relate.

"Dre. Dre. There you are," she says, frantic. "We didn't finish our talk."

"They can't perform her procedure here," Tyler says. "We're going to a better hospital."

"Wait. I got things I need to say to Dre." She takes hold of Andre's hand, panting. "I never thanked you."

"Baby, let's do this later," Tyler says.

"We prayed for change in our lives. Then you came." She takes a deep breath to bear another rush of pain. "It might mean nothing to you, and you might think we're just a bunch of backwoods hicks, but these past thirteen weeks, you've changed our lives. You have shown us what is possible. You've—"

She curls in pain, and Andre feels the urgency of the moment. He doesn't need anyone to explain that Chalene and her child are both in danger. Every minute counts. Why is she bothering with him?

"Come to the hospital with us, please. Please. I need you there," she begs. "Get in your car. Go to Children's Mercy. It's thirty miles north on Highway 74. Big concrete eyesore, you can't miss it."

"Ma'am," the paramedic says, "we gotta go."

"Not until Dre promises." She screams. Sobs. Grips his wrist with both hands. "Promise me! Please, Dre. Promise. Children's Mercy Hospital. Thirty miles. North."

"I promise."

"Dre, be serious."

"I promise." He kisses her forehead. "Ugly concrete building. Thirty miles north. I'll be right behind you. I promise."

Tyler gives Andre a big bear hug as the paramedics load Chalene into the ambulance. Tyler jumps in as Chalene blows Andre a kiss, her eyeline unbroken until the ambulance doors shut. The ambulance flees the parking lot, siren blaring, makes the turn north before vanishing into the twilight.

Andre checks his watch. The polls just closed. Maybe, if anyone's in line, they'll get to vote, but his campaign has come to an end. So he gets in his Jeep, turns over the engine, and, as he pulls out of the parking lot, turns south toward home.

On public radio, the only station that will dedicate the entire night to local contests, a warm voice says, "Welcome to election night, South Carolina. Polls around the Palmetto State are now closed."

Andre doesn't need public radio to know that the turnout in Carthage was good. Around six this evening, the polls saw a surge of after-work voters. Overall turnout didn't reach 20 percent, but his instincts say he achieved the win. Best thing about modern elections is that they lack suspense. No hand counts. No human error. No ambiguous marking of ballots. Paula Carrothers had six machines at one polling place. She'll download the data onto a thumb drive and instantly tally the results. Democracy, as easy as ordering pizza online.

He drives past the armory, sees men and women and children celebrating in the parking lot. Word must have come straight from county hall, and he feels good, better than he's felt in a long time, and considers stopping, maybe celebrating with the team, but what's the point? Truth is, sixty seconds ago, the people of Carthage outlived their use.

He turns the radio to jazz, one of those sixties-era ensembles improvising a pithy five beats to the measure, with a wild, talented percussionist beating the shit out of a drum. Andre taps his fingers against the wheel, mimicking the fast beat, as Carthage whips past, swaths of open land freckled by foreclosed homes and a trailer-park billboard that reads, IF YOU LIVED HERE, YOU'D BE HOME NOW. He doesn't want to learn the details of the election results, doesn't want to learn the turnout or margin of victory, because as soon as he learns, he'll know whether Mr. DeVille will fire him. For now, Andre wants to chase this feeling of victory, wants, for the first time in a long time, to feel like a winner. Please. Just for a little while longer. I need to feel good.

On the back road that heads home, he speeds past a pond

on which the moon smiles. His cell rings in his pocket, and as he digs in his pants, the phone slips onto the heavy-duty rubber floor mat. He starts a blind search, eyes fixed on the road, one hand on the wheel, the other hand patting random patches of floor mat. Mr. DeVille? Vera? Probably Duke Boshears. His gut says this call is important, so he takes a gamble, drops his eyes for a moment to retrieve the glowing phone, raises his gaze in time to see a coyote crossing the road. Andre brakes hard, dropping his phone again, the Jeep screaming to a halt but not before smashing into the coyote, which takes a tumble down the dirt road. In the beam of the Jeep's headlights, the coyote rises, stumbles, falls, rises, stumbles, falls, a spastic dance, repeated until the coyote collapses onto the road.

Andre unbuckles his seat belt, rushes toward the coyote, which lies on the ground, face twitching, chest rising and falling, each breath shallower than the last. The coyote freezes in time, chest still, eyes open, long tongue dangling across thin white lips. Andre brushes the bloody, matted fur, and for a moment he feels as though he's watching himself from afar, sees himself, small and vulnerable, a man beat down and alone, standing in the headlights of his rented Jeep, weeping, hands bloodied, pants caked in mud, and Andre feels nothing but pity for the man he sees.

In the distance a locomotive blows its whistle, and he wonders where the train will go. He drags himself back inside the Jeep, starts the engine. Maybe he should drive until the sun comes up. Wherever he runs out of gas, that will be where he starts anew. Maybe he'll end up someplace where he can meet someone and fall in love. Someplace special, someplace with palm trees, someplace where no one bothers to vote.

ACKNOWLEDGMENTS

Oh my goodness, I wrote a novel and, oh my goodness, you just read it. Please bear with me. Just one more thing before you go. I need to thank some people.

For their thoughtful review of earlier drafts, I'm grateful to Lorrie Moore, Lynda Barry, Ron Kuka, Judith Mitchell, and Brandi Wright. I feel duty-bound to express my gratitude to those who read other projects, novels, and parts of novels that didn't make it across the finish line. That's Laura Coates, Ravi Sinha, Isaac Means, and Liz. I love you, I miss you. I think of each of you every day.

I received the warm encouragement and unflinching support of my colleagues: Chelsea Gill, Renagh O'Leary, Michele LaVigne, Margaret Raymond, Adam Stevenson, Jini Jasti, and Peggy Hacker, who has the power to make cake magically appear. This book would not have been possible without the friendship and support of Carrie Sperling, who never—ever—lost faith. I'm also grateful to my parents, Aunt Bert, Harvey Grossinger, Elly Williams, Molly Jacobs, Jesse Lee Kercheval,

Bailey Flannigan, David Haynes, and the folks of Kimbilio, without whom characters like Dre would not exist.

A special shout-out to the team at the Friedrich Agency: Lucy Carson, Kent Wolf, and Heather Carr. I'm grateful to Eric Reid at WME. Lastly, a special thanks to the wonderful and encouraging Zack Wagman, Dominique Lear, Laura Cherkas, Aja Pollock, and the whole team at Ecco. You're all amazing.

Okay. Thank you. Until next time.